T0274332

THE LOST SOULS OF BENZAITEN

THE LOST SOULS OF BENZAITEN

Kelly Murashige

Published in the United States by Soho Teen
an imprint of Soho Press, Inc.
227 W 17th Street
New York, NY 10011

Library of Congress Cataloging-in-Publication Data
Names: Murashige, Kelly, author.
Title: The lost souls of Benzaiten / Kelly Murashige.
Description: New York, NY : Soho Teen, 2024. | Audience: Ages 14 and up.
Audience: Grades 10-12. | Identifiers: LCCN 2023056190

ISBN 978-1-64129-574-1
eISBN 978-1-64129-575-8

Subjects: CYAC: Psychic trauma—Fiction. | Self-actualization—
Fiction. | Goddesses—Fiction. | Mythology, Japanese—Fiction. |
Dead—Fiction. | Fantasy. | LCGFT: Fantasy fiction. | Novels.
Classification: LCC PZ7.1.M8385 Lo 2024 | DDC [Fic]—dc23
LC record available at https://lccn.loc.gov/2023056190

Interior design: Janine Agro, Soho Press, Inc.

Printed in the United States of America

10 9 8 7 6 5 4 3 2 1

To my mother, who has read essentially everything I've ever written and believed in me even when I didn't believe in myself;

my father, who only wanted to read my work once it was published because he was sure it would be someday;

and everyone who has ever lost their voice. I hear you. I'm listening. Keep holding on.

A NOTE FROM THE AUTHOR

Please be warned that this book contains depictions of struggles with mental health, including feelings of hopelessness; death, grief, and loss, including those of teenagers, children, and infants; and details of a car accident. Though this is, ultimately, a hopeful book, if reading about these subjects may be harmful to you, please take a moment, ensure you have a healthy support system, and, if necessary, set this book aside for now. I wish you all the best.

I also wanted to take a moment to discuss Japanese/Shinto culture. Benzaiten and Daikokuten are indeed part of the Shichifukujin, or Seven Gods of Fortune, but I took many, many creative liberties. Thank you to Atsuka for enduring my strange questions and Jill for battling the ever-evolving topic of romanization with me.

On a more personal note: I can't say Machi's story is my own. But I also can't say it isn't. In some ways, both big and small, I *have* experienced what Machi has—and I don't think I'm the only one.

As far as I know, nobody in real life has gone on magical adventures with a Japanese deity after praying to become a robot vacuum cleaner. I imagine, though, almost everyone has experienced at least some of what Machi is dealing with: going through a friendship breakup, losing loved ones, and feeling silenced in a world that's only ever getting louder. Though

Machi's inability to speak is, as she acknowledges from the beginning, purely psychological, there are many reasons why a person might not be able to voice their thoughts aloud. And there are many reasons why it's still important to listen.

I don't know if *The Lost Souls of Benzaiten* will change anyone's life. I don't know if it will make someone still stinging from a friendship breakup believe it's possible to change and grow and heal. I don't know if it will make the quiet kids feel seen or the quirky kids realize being different isn't a bad thing. I don't know if it will give someone enough hope to push on to tomorrow.

But I pray it does.

Thank you for reading. I'm so glad you're here.

Thank you,
Kelly Murashige

THE LOST SOULS OF BENZAITEN

CHAPTER ONE

I IMAGINE A first appointment with a new therapist is never easy. However, it is about eight million times more difficult when you don't talk.

In my defense, this doctor has been forewarned. My parents called ahead of time. They told the others beforehand too, but I'm hoping this therapist will be smart enough to know when he asks me, *And what brings you here today?* my only response will be to slowly lift my eyes to his face and stare at him like I'm trying to suck out his soul.

That being said (or, well, unsaid), as soon as the door to his office opens, I shoot to my feet, then start to sit, then change my mind and hover in an awkward squatting position like I'm about to lay an egg in his waiting room.

He blinks, his expression unreadable. After a few excruciating seconds of silence, he says, "You must be Machi."

I chew my lip. It's good to know I'm as socially incompetent as ever.

"It's a pleasure to meet you," he says. "I'm Dr. Tsui. Would you like to come in?"

Not really, but I don't have a choice.

I follow him into his office, casting one last backward look at the exit like I'm about to be imprisoned for a crime I never meant to commit. I mean, it's not *illegal* to stop talking, is it? Why *can't* I plead the Fifth for the rest of my life?

"Welcome to my office," Dr. Tsui says, closing the door behind me.

I can practically hear Angel's scoff.

What a dork, she would say.

I think Sunny would like him. *He seems nice. Compassionate. You need someone who understands you without making you explain everything that brought you here.*

But I can easily explain what brought me here.

They did.

The walls of Dr. Tsui's office are purple. Not a deep, claustrophobic mauve but a calming shade of lavender. To the left, light filters in through the window blinds. A trio of figurines sits on his desk in the corner. Made of porcelain and painted with muted colors, they look like triplets. They wear their hair in flowery buns, the blossoms light pink and purple. Each woman holds a musical instrument, her expression placid as she plays a song no one but her sisters can hear.

I stop in front of the two identical plush chairs placed in the center of the room, then lift my eyes to Dr. Tsui, waiting for him to take a seat.

His smile is kind. "Choose whichever one is calling your name."

I try not to frown. So he just lets his clients pick whichever chair they want? He's constantly switching from one seat to the next, as if doctor and patient are interchangeable?

I bite the inside of my cheek, my temples throbbing with the beginnings of an overthinking headache. If I sit in the chair he usually takes, whichever one that is, he'll think I'm trying to undermine him. But if I take the one all his patients choose, I'll be just like the other wrecks who come to his office, weeping over breakups and narcissistic mothers and the universal yet crushing burden of being alive. And God forbid I switch seats from session to session. That would tell him I'm the kind of person who bounces between two chairs, two roles, two identities, never knowing who I really am.

Maybe I just need to sit down.

I perch on the edge of the closest seat, careful not to let my shoulders brush the back. I don't like being touched. Not by people. Not by things. Not ever again.

Taking the other seat and picking up a clipboard from the table, Dr. Tsui regards me through his thin, rectangular glasses.

I scrutinize his expression. If my seating decision has displeased him, he doesn't let it show.

"I've heard you are, at the moment, not willing to communicate verbally."

I nod, a bobblehead in a tacky gift shop bought on a whim and forgotten in the car.

"You have a whiteboard, though," he says. "Is that right?"

Another nod. I carry it everywhere I go. By now, a year into my silence, it's a part of me. Every time I step outside, it's tucked away in my bag, bumping against my side like the world's most pathetic metronome.

"I also asked if you could fill out the intake form," he continues. "Did you happen to bring that today?"

I nod again. At this rate, I'm going to give myself a neck ache.

I guess I should be used to it by now. When I first went silent, I didn't even have a whiteboard. I just nodded and shook my head. But the only people who ever interacted with me, aside from my long string of therapists, were my parents. Eventually, they stopped asking questions.

Reaching into my bag, I pull out the thin, cerulean folder I bought before my freshman year. I thought I was going to fill it with my chemistry notes and study guides and graded essays with the words *GREAT JOB* written at the top. But I'm not in school anymore.

"That's a nice folder," he says. "Very blue."

I don't say anything. I mean, yeah, no kidding, but even if I hadn't stopped talking, I still wouldn't have responded. What could I have said? *Thanks, I bought it myself?*

I give him a tight-lipped smile and hand him the intake form. "Thank you," he says. "Would it be okay if I read this now?" I nod, and his eyes fall to the papers.

INTAKE FORM: Dr. Tsui
Patient Name: Machi
Date of First Appointment: June 3
Narrative (What brings you to my office?):

Hi. My name is Machi. I'm seventeen years old. I have listed my address and phone number on the bottom of the sheet, as requested. I found you through online searches. Or my parents did. Sheryl, my previous therapist, gave me some referrals, but every time I tried to look up the names, I started to spiral. I don't take change well. Every time something has changed, it's been for the worse.

That's probably not a good thing to say—write—to a new doctor. It doesn't sound very hopeful, does it? But then again, if I were hopeful, I wouldn't be here.

I'm a student, but I don't go to a regular high school anymore. I do my classes online. It's frustrating when the online programs tell me I'm wrong for putting $(f(a + h) - f(a))/h$ instead of $[f(a + h) - f(a)]/h$, but that's a price I'm willing to pay.

You asked me to state, in my own words, what brought me here. When I used to write to Sheryl, she said she felt like I was holding back.

I mean, she didn't say it like *that*; she said something like *You know I'm always here for you, Machi, no matter what you tell me*, which was so sweet and comforting, it made me want to blurt out all my secrets, from the little things, like the time I spit out a piece of stew meat in a napkin and threw it away because my mother went through a *Cooking Mama* phase and burned everything she touched, to the one big thing: what really happened to make me stop talking.

I didn't get to tell her, though. Not everything. She left before I could.

So instead of giving you the diplomatic answer as to why I'm here, which is that I'm dedicated to bettering myself and becoming a functioning being in society, I'm going to be honest: I'm here because I have to be.

I go to doctors because it's what my parents want. I've always caused them so much stress. Losing the will to speak didn't help. And going to doctors also means *paying* for doctors, which puts more stress on them. According to them, the money is less important than my mental health, but that only makes it worse.

Sheryl said it's best not to think about it that way. *What we put out into the world, whether it's voiced or written or simply thought, has power.*

Her words, not mine.

That was the one thing I didn't like about her: her optimism. Visible in everything from the cross-stiches—JUST BREATHE and HAVE YOU SMILED TODAY?—hanging on her walls to the bouquet of cake pops set in a mug on the table between us. Her cheeriness was downright grating in our early sessions, but I grew to tolerate it. I never did take a cake pop, though. That would have felt like a step too far. Like I was just taking and taking and taking.

Now she's gone, and there's nothing left for me to take.

Anyway, going back to your prompts: Yes, I have been to doctors before. There was Sheryl, obviously, but I saw some others before. They didn't help.

The second doctor I saw, for example, displayed all his diplomas in his waiting room, a nonverbal way of saying *I AM VERY IMPORTANT*. Clearly. The man had gone to Harvard. But all he did was observe me with startlingly light eyes. When he finally spoke, he said, *Tell me about all the things that made you hurt so much, you stopped talking.*

I didn't know how to answer. How could I? Every time I tried to write, he would shake his head like I was disappointing him, and I would sink just a little lower, shame burning at the corners of my eyes. So instead of responding, I used our session time to examine his room. Everything was beige, from the chairs to the walls to the desk and the little inbox perfectly aligned with the left corner. An emergency kit hung on a hook above his head. It was the old-fashioned type, a white metal box with a red plus sign. I imagined if it ever fell from the hook, it would conk him on the head, which, granted, *would* be quite the emergency. We lasted two sessions, which is, coincidentally, how many weeks' worth of food and water you should store in case of a *real* emergency.

All the therapists I've seen tried to get me to recall the worst parts of my life. But the problem isn't that I've forgotten; it's that I remember.

I'm an only child. My parents have no history of mental health diagnoses. They're still married. Happily, I hope. They're also, as you know, not here because they're back in my mother's home state, where they lived before they had me. My maternal grandparents recently passed away, so my parents are getting things settled.

I don't have friends.

I don't have any problems with crime, drugs, or alcohol. I somehow doubt people admit they do, especially to doctors like you. For whatever it's worth, though, I'm being honest here.

The rest of your questions are optional, so I hope it's okay if I don't answer them. I think this was enough for you to read. Am I sitting silently while you're skimming through these notes? Probably. What else would I be doing?

As my appointment with Dr. Tsui nears its end, the clock ticking toward the hour, Dr. Tsui says, "I've enjoyed getting to learn more about you."

Doubtful.

"I know it's our first meeting," he says, "and I understand this has been difficult for you."

I stare at the wall. He already knows how I feel about Sheryl's abrupt departure. How I felt like I was so, *so* close to telling her everything that had happened with Angel and Sunny. How I even occasionally let myself think about the good times, if only because Sheryl was so focused on the positive, it made me want to be more like her.

How her leaving made me feel like every bad thing was happening all over again.

"Coming here today was a major step forward," Dr. Tsui says. "Would you be okay if I issued you a challenge?"

What are you, five? I can almost hear Angel saying.

"Well, it isn't *just* a challenge," he says. "It's also a gift."

Great. I just met him, and I'm already taking from him, just as I did with Sheryl.

Reaching into a shoulder bag slumped against the table—I bet he set it there so I couldn't discern which seat is actually his—he pulls out a notebook. I try not to look too interested as he holds it out.

"This is for you," he says. "You aren't obligated to write in it, but if you ever want to share some of your thoughts with me, on your own time, without having to scribble on your white-board, you can use this."

I take the journal, feeling its weight in my hands. A yin-yang symbol the size of my palm adorns the front cover.

"Oh, and one more thing."

Of course.

"Before our next session," Dr. Tsui says, "would you be willing to go on a little adventure? Visit someplace you've never been before? I would recommend someplace relaxing. A place where you could spend some time around people, even if you don't speak to them."

I pick at my nails. I'm not exactly the adventurous type. The most daring thing I've done recently is eat yogurt with yesterday's date printed beneath the BEST BY sticker.

"I prepared a list of places you could explore. You can find that on the front page of the notebook. Forgive my handwriting."

See? imaginary-Angel says. *A dork.*

I don't know, imaginary-Sunny says. *I think he's just being nice.*

Okay, great. I've started hearing my former friends' voices in my head. But I'm sure a little trip to—I open to the notebook and glance at the first line—a *small, hole-in-the-wall coffee shop* will fix me right up. Because a good espresso will make me all better. Espresso to heal the depresso, as they say.

"Would that be okay?" Dr. Tsui asks. "Again, you don't have to write in the journal, but would you be willing to visit one of those places?"

I bite down. My teeth clink like ice cubes in a glass. I don't want to go anywhere. But I promised my parents I would *try* to get better. Compared to what my mother's going through now, stopping by one animal shelter or coffee shop is nothing.

I don't want to go anywhere, though. Not as myself.

I imagine waking up as someone different. Waltzing into a bookstore, leaning on the display, and asking the workers for all their recommendations, a grin on my face and a sparkle in my eye. Maybe if it were that easy, things would be different. Maybe I would be happy.

I let out a breath, still staring at the page, painfully aware of the silence. I wonder what Dr. Tsui is looking at. Me, I guess, but he's bound to get bored after a second or two. I'm not particularly interesting. Not the kind of girl people write songs and poems about, or the one people take photos of on the street because there's just something so intriguing about her.

Angel was that kind of girl. Sunny too. While Angel was visually striking, her confidence palpable and impossible to ignore, Sunny had a beautiful quietness to her. A captivating sort of poise. I would find myself looking at them sometimes, thinking I was lucky to have them.

Until I wasn't.

I look up at Dr. Tsui. Balancing the notebook on my knee, I nod.

HOME, I TEXT my parents as I unlock the front door. The off-white paint slapped across the doorframe has begun to crack, peeling off like drooping petals from a pistil. My father keeps saying he'll deal with it soon, but considering he's in a completely different state for his in-laws' dual funeral and his daughter is at home eating expired yogurt and having her first appointment with her seventh therapist, I think the door is pretty low on his list of priorities.

I've just stepped into the apartment when my mother sends back a thumbs-up. She's usually much more verbose, the type to send huge, blocky messages that take up my entire phone screen, but I know she's busy—and possibly still upset with me.

In a lengthy email I wrote and deleted at two in the morning the day before my parents left, I tried to explain I had decided to stay home not because I don't love them, or because I want to spite my grandparents, or even because death and packing are two of my greatest fears.

I just couldn't stop thinking about how my first time visiting my grandparents' town would be for the funeral, because my grandparents had died and I hadn't even been there, and even once I arrived, I wouldn't be able to talk. If we ran into one of my grandparents' friends, what would I say?

Well, nothing. I would say nothing.

How would I act? Would I have to hold up my whiteboard? Would my parents do the explaining for me, their heads bowed like they were taking on the weight of my sins? At the funeral, people would whisper about me. *There was always something "off" about her. Those poor parents. Their family is such a trainwreck.*

Then there's the racism.

My phone buzzes. My father has sent a heart, likely to offset the curtness of my mother's thumbs-up.

When I first went quiet last year, my parents would cry and hold me too close, saying, *We love you, Machi. Please tell us what's wrong.* It made me sick to see them upset, so I closed my door and tuned them out, my head full of so much noise.

If they knew why I stopped talking, I don't think they would love me anymore.

I perch on my bed, open the notebook from Dr. Tsui, and spend about ten minutes trying to convince myself to visit one of the places he suggested. But I just can't stop thinking. Of my grandparents and my parents and that toxic town where my mother grew up, a cesspool of crooked convictions and backward beliefs. Of the funeral I will not be attending because I am a bad daughter. Of Sunny. Of Angel. Of what we once were and what we could still be. Of how meaningless everything is because we aren't.

I don't know where to go. Just looking at Dr. Tsui's list makes me sick. I mean, really? A fabric store? What am I going to do? Bundle myself in layers of cotton and polyester to sweat out all my sorrows? Or I could go to the animal shelter, watch a bunch of sad animals wait and wait to get chosen, only to find them there again the next week, and the week after that, and the week after that because some of us just aren't wanted.

I've never had a pet. My parents said our apartment was messy enough without an animal shedding all over the place. One of the neighbors has a cat, though, and I swear I hear her robot vacuum cleaner beeping, humming, and singing at least four times a day. A few months ago, I fell asleep in the living room with my head set against the wall separating our unit from hers. My dream-self stumbled through my old school, cramming for an exam I hadn't studied for, and the robot warbled beside me, letting out an apologetic chirp every time it got underfoot.

As afternoon bleeds into evening, then into night, I abandon all hope of finishing my homework. The assignment from Dr. Tsui and my various essays and responses for my online classes will just have to wait until tomorrow, when I'm *not* tumbling down a Yelp rabbit hole.

Yelp. How pathetic. Of all the sites I could have gotten addicted to, I had to choose the one where people can leave scathing reviews of all the things they hate. It's a good thing *I* don't have a Yelp page.

But if I had one, no one would care enough to say anything about me, good or bad.

Silence hurts. Indifference hurts. It all hurts. And running around town, hopping from cafés and bookstores to animal shelters and cultural centers and checking off each item on Dr. Tsui's list isn't going to change that. *Nothing* will change that. Nothing will change ever.

I tighten my grip on Dr. Tsui's list and rip the page from the notebook. I could tear it in half right now. Tear it once, then again, then again until nothing is left.

Vvvrrrrr. Zziiip.

My eyes flick to the wall. On the other side, the neighbor's robot vacuum cleaner comes back to life, summoned to serve its one and only purpose.

Breathing out, I set the list on the old, tattered loveseat, grab my canvas bag and whiteboard, and head out with three words echoing in my mind: One. Last. Try.

CHAPTER TWO

THIS ISN'T THE first time I've turned to divine intervention. Since my life fell apart, I've made the trek to two churches and two Buddhist temples.

I've yet to say a single prayer.

There was nothing wrong with those places of worship. Each was beautiful, painted white or red or a rich brown. The colors of home. But every time I stepped off the bus, my knees shaking, I would only see the people. All the people. At the churches, they were standing with their hands raised and their voices lifting like doves to the skies. The temples were less crowded, but that only made things worse. Everyone there knew what they were doing. I just stood on the sidewalk, a pale, five-foot-three aberration.

At the second temple, which I visited after my first and last session with the third therapist my parents forced me to talk to, I spotted a little boy with his parents, their heads bowed. Twenty feet separated us, but I could see his hands balling into tiny fists as he squished his eyes closed to boost the strength of his prayer. I imagined he was praying for his sick grandmother, his precious Nana, who went to every single one of his soccer games—until the day she started coughing. She was his first loved one to fall seriously ill. There he was, battling all these new, turbulent emotions, and there *I* was, some interloper wearing a backpack with a small bell key chain hanging from the zipper. If I got any closer, the bell would ring, and from that day forward, he would hate the sound of jingling because it would remind him of the time that strange girl invaded a sacred space in his time of need. If his grandmother were to pass away, Christmas would become a total nightmare for him, and upon moving into a new home as an adult, he would rip the doorbell out of the front door with his bare hands just to avoid the sound. His partner would ask, *What's gotten into you?* and he wouldn't know how to explain his hatred of bells and how it all started because of me, that weird, quiet girl who could never figure out what to do with her hands.

But I'm sure the fifth time's the charm.

I look up at the shrine I've chosen. It isn't in such disrepair that it attracts urban legends and those who chase them, but it's not pretty enough to catch people's eyes and leave them breathless. The torii is at least fifty feet tall, but it's faded, the usual bright red-orange peeling to reveal a pale salmon under-coat. The gate hasn't been maintained for what looks like years.

Good.

I mean, not *good*. I'm not *glad* a place of worship has fallen to ruin.

My grandparents used to love visiting shrines when they stayed with us. That was the sole thing they admitted they didn't like about their own town: it didn't have any shrines or temples. Why would it when my grandparents were essentially the only Japanese family around?

They never visited this particular shrine, though. I don't think anyone has. It isn't listed on most shrine directories. It doesn't have a marker in Google Maps. It doesn't even have its own Yelp page. That's the whole reason I tumbled down the Yelp rabbit hole in the first place: I was looking for a place of worship no one would ever think to visit. Which means I might just be able to make this prayer alone.

On tiptoes, I peer around the edge of the gate. It's eight at night and deathly quiet. There are no families. No children. No individuals with hands clasped and heads lowered.

After placing my boots just off the stone path, I bow and enter. I picture myself sinking into the center of the Earth with every step, but the pavement holds me, unforgiving beneath my socks. They're my favorite pair, a cartoon penguin face printed on each heel. My parents got them for me for Christmas a few years ago. I never wore them around Angel. I was afraid she would hate them. Or worse, she would love them, and I would wear them down to bare threads.

I stop at the large wooden box beside the altar and bow. My heart knocks against my chest, a prisoner dragging a chipped mug along the bars of my ribs.

My parents and I are almost entirely unfamiliar with Shinto beliefs, so I had to look up how to pray at a shrine, sitting in my darkened room with one leg hanging off the edge of my bed, my laptop balanced on one knee.

It feels like a small betrayal, doing all this research only after my grandparents' deaths. If I had really cared about the racism they faced, I would have embraced my culture while they were still alive to appreciate it. I wish they could have lived with us instead of spending so much time trying to convince us to move back. Maybe then, I wouldn't have to rely on internet strangers to educate me.

Maybe then, they wouldn't have died alone.

I press the pad of my thumb into my coin. According to tradition, I'm supposed to offer a five-yen coin. A nickel's the closest thing I've got. It isn't even a *good* nickel, corrosion leaving the edges white and light-green. This was all I could find, though, and I don't know if anyone's listening anyway.

The shrine's hanging bell has begun to deteriorate, rust

running along the insides. But when I ring it, the chimes are sweet and clear: *clang, clang, clang.*

I bow my head to make my prayer: *I wish—*

There are a lot of ends to that sentence: I wish I had just sucked it up and gone to the funeral with my parents because at least then one aspect of my life wouldn't be a trash fire; I wish I hadn't ruined things with Angel and Sunny; I wish . . .

My eyelids drop. I listen to the stillness. I'm not expecting to hear a flourish of bells or the heavenly voices of angels as my prayer is lifted to the skies, but I keep my eyes closed anyway. It's not like there's anyone to see. Not here. Not at home. Not at Sheryl's office. There's no one anywhere.

"Did someone call for Lady Luck?"

I stiffen at the sound of an unfamiliar voice, my brain short-circuiting before I can even open my eyes.

I thought I was alone.

Breathe. I just have to breathe. If Sheryl were here, she would tell me to think of three happy facts to calm myself down.

One: Otters sometimes hold hands when floating down a river.
Two: Cows have best friends.
Three: I do not hold hands with anyone and do not have best friends.

Well, Sheryl would say, *at least you got TWO happy facts.*

I exhale, open my eyes, and turn.

There's no one behind me.

Rotating on my penguin sock, I make a complete circle. I see nothing but the wooden offering box, a smattering of thin trees, and, in the distance, the washed-out torii.

"Hora!" The voice sounds like it belongs to a young woman. "Up here."

I tilt my chin upward, the moon shining high above me.

A figure is perched on a tree branch like a snowy owl, her

long white skirt a ghost flowing in the breeze. I start to follow the swathe of white up to a face, but before I can inspect it closely, the silhouette leaps from the tree. When it lands—that was, like, a twenty-foot jump—there's a girl in front of me, her irises a mishmash of gold-leaf fragments.

She cocks her head to the side. "Are you going to answer my question?"

I watch her with a wary gaze and shake my head. She must be a shrine attendant. A miko, I remember they're called. I don't know why one would be here when it's late and nobody is praying. Well, nobody except me.

The girl doesn't look like a miko, though. Instead of a red hakama, she wears a plain white dress, almost like a nightgown. She's pretty, especially with the gold contacts, but her face is young. She could be my age.

"You're so quiet. You should be singing my praises." She lifts her chin and puts her hands on her hips. "I very much enjoy music, I'll have you know."

I hope she doesn't think that makes her special. Everyone likes music. Sunny did, naturally. It was her life. But Angel did too. At the peak of one of her experimental phases, Angel said, *God, I wish I could take this electropop and stab it into my veins.* Typical Angel, really.

"'Why, beautiful being,'" the girl says, pitching up her voice to, I assume, mimic what she thinks I sound like. Hint: I do *not* sound like Minnie Mouse. "'Where did you—a well-spoken, stunning, in*cre*dibly graceful individual—come from? And why should I be singing your praises?'

"Well," she continues, dropping her voice back to its usual clarion tone, "let me tell you. I have no idea why you would show up here, of all places. This shrine has been abandoned for years. Years and years. Like, probably longer than you've been alive. How old are you?"

Old enough to know the rules of stranger danger.

"I'm going to guess a teenager? So yeah, longer than you've been alive. I mean, people have stopped just to see what's here, maybe thrown in some money. Trash too, which is *very* rude. Once, I got a lollipop, still in the wrapper and everything, but it was blue raspberry. Yuck."

I just look at her. She can't seriously be saying people pray to *her*, as if she's the actual patron of this shrine.

"I heard you," she says. She takes a seat on the wooden offering box, her dress draping over the slats. I watch her arrange her skirt over her knees and realize her leap from the tree should have shattered every bone in her legs. "When you prayed to me."

A small chill rustles along my skin. There's no way she actually heard my prayer. If she had, she wouldn't be traipsing around the shrine grounds in a nightgown and poking fun at my voice, which she's never even heard.

I study her. Her long, dark hair has been pulled back into a ponytail, but a small section falls to frame her face. Her bangs part slightly in the middle and end just before dipping into her eyes. Her thin eyelashes curl upward. Her expression exudes confidence. There's nothing to indicate she's joking. No surreptitious smirk. No hint of malice. I'm sure she's kidding, though. She has to be.

"Nothing to say?" she asks.

I shake my head.

"What is *with* you?" She leans forward. Her eyes are such an unnatural color, flashing gold whenever she moves. "You can talk, can't you? From what *I* understand—which is a lot, as I am actually extremely intelligent, even among the gods—the problem isn't getting mortals to talk; it's getting them to shut up. I mean, you should hear the kinds of prayers I get. Sometimes, I just want to be like, 'For Hotei's sake, get to the *point*.'"

I stare at her. She has to see the irony in that statement, right?

"But," she continues, "I see nothing physically wrong with you."

My throat tightens around words I'll never voice.

I've heard that one before. There *isn't* anything physically wrong with me. That's what all the doctors said.

"You should consider taking up weight training, though," she adds. "Your arms are small."

I frown. Her arms seem just as slender as mine, though the flowiness of her sleeves makes it difficult to tell.

I shake my head again and start heading back down the stone path, walking along the edge. I don't know who this girl is, what makes her so intent on getting me to talk, or why she seems to be expecting something of me when I have nothing to give, but I don't care. I made my wish. I'm done.

"Where are you going?" she calls out.

I keep walking. My socks are going to be filthy after my trek down this dusty path. Poor penguins.

"Machi," she says.

I stop. My feet press into the edge of the stone path.

Her ballet flats make no sound as she moves along the center of the path, right where the gods are meant to walk.

How could she possibly know my name?

When she stops beside me, I turn, scanning her face for some recognizable feature. She must know me from somewhere, though I can't imagine where. It can't be from school. I haven't gone in over a year. Now I'm just another blurred face in the periphery of my former classmates' memories, some girl whose name they never learned.

"I am Benzaiten, one of the Seven Gods of Fortune," she says. "This is my shrine."

Okay, now it's definitely time to go.

I'm about to reach the torii, my socks crunching against the stones, when she says, "'I wish to become one of those round robot vacuum cleaners.'"

I freeze. The wind picks up, flirting with my hair. I wrap my arms around myself and pivot on my heels.

"'How do you know that?'" she asks, her voice high and mocking again. "I told you already, silly child. Your prayer went to me. I heard it, up in the spirit world."

This girl is delusional and in need of help. I would email Sheryl, but she's not around anymore. I guess I could contact Dr. Tsui, but considering I spent the entirety of our first session convincing him I'm *not* out of my mind, I'm not sure I should type out an email and go: *Hey, I wasted the entire afternoon trying to muster up the courage to go to one of those places you suggested but got so overwhelmed by the calamitous state of my life, I wound up going to an obscure deity's even-more-obscure shrine, where I made a desperate prayer, only to be confronted by a girl who keeps insisting she's a goddess. This is Machi, by the way. You know. Your new client. Please help. Also, thanks for the notebook.*

So yeah. Maybe 911 would be better. Or, like, 911@gmail.com. If I *called* 911, the dispatcher would only hear my Darth-Vader breathing and this girl's inane rambling.

I put my hand to my pocket and take out my phone. Does 911 have a text line?

A sharp pain like carpet burn runs beneath my fingers. As I suck in a breath, I do a double take at my now-empty hand.

"Is this what phones look like in this day and age?" The girl stands five feet away with my phone, too far to have snatched it from my grasp without my noticing. Her golden eyes flick to me and dance with amusement. "Do I have your attention now?"

I storm over to her and extend a hand. I don't understand what's happening here, and frankly, I don't care anymore. I shouldn't have come. This, like so many other things in my life, was a big mistake.

She shakes her head. "I'm not returning this until you talk to me."

I swallow my anger and swipe for the phone, but she switches it to her other hand. "Listen, I came all the way over here just to see what could have led you to make such an unconventional request." She waves her free hand, ignoring my attempt to take my phone. "Inspiration for fine arts? Sure. More harmonious family occasions? Yes. The meet-cute to out-cute all meet-cutes? Can do. But a wish to be a vacuuming automaton? I had to see you for myself."

I reach for my phone again.

"If I give this back to you, will you tell me what you're thinking?" She waits for my nod. "All right, but if you're lying, prepare for divine punishment."

She deposits my phone in my hands and monitors my movements as I unlock my phone, open my notes, and type out a message. She taps one foot and hums a song I don't know, her voice full and warm like honey.

The moment I hand her my phone, she reads the message aloud: "'I don't talk.'" She drops her hand to her side, her lips pursed. "I *know* that. Why not?"

I shake my head. She's not the first person to ask—but she *is* the first to think she's a goddess.

"Then tell me, on this weird tippy-tappy device, why you would ever want to be a robot vacuum cleaner."

I take my phone and type out my answer, trying to hide my annoyance. I came here to get away from people. Away from everything. So of course I wound up stuck in a shrine with a chatterbox who refuses to let me go. *I'm tired of being human.*

I stare straight ahead as she reads my message. I don't want to see her expression. Don't want her to see mine.

She raises her eyes to me. Speaking just a little slower, like she wants to be sure we're understanding each other—which we're not—she says, "And you think asking to become a robot vacuum cleaner is going to fix that?"

I mean, yeah? Everyone loves those little round things. They're treated like humans, given names and showered with praise when they finish cleaning, but no one expects them to be anything more than what they are. They weren't built to mingle or get along with fellow machinery. They do what is asked of them, and that's it.

I don't mind cleaning. I like it. I could do that for the rest of my existence. I would be a lot happier than I am now.

The girl lies down on the offering box. Now I hope she *is* the actual goddess Benzaiten. Otherwise, her blatant disrespect is most definitely invoking the wrath of the gods.

But what if she's telling the truth?

I know how that sounds. Goddesses don't just appear in the regular world. I'm not even sure they exist. When my grandparents made us take them to shrines, I stayed in the car, watching them from a distance, and wondered what they were asking for. If they had just moved here, they could've had everything.

But they stayed, and now they have nothing.

"What's so bad about being a human?" the girl asks. "It seems so amazing."

I shake my head. Being human is a lot of things, but *amazing* is not one of them.

Then I shake my head again, harder. I don't know what I'm thinking. This girl is human too.

"What about a do-over?" She swings her legs off the box. "I can't grant your wish. We don't work like that. I can, however, help you learn to appreciate the human world and find your voice again."

I cross my arms. I don't need to appreciate this world, and I don't plan on ever using my voice. Even if this is a hoax, I'm not jinxing anything by changing my prayer.

"Here," she says, holding up my corroded nickel.

I glance at the offering box. The slats are too narrow for her to have stuck her hand in there, and I didn't see her open the lid with a key.

She tosses the nickel my way. I manage to clap it between my palms, which, given my lack of coordination, is quite the accomplishment.

Shaking my head, I pocket the coin and take out my phone. Once I've typed out my message, I hand it to her.

"'I don't want that prayer.'" She rolls her eyes. "I'm not playing around here. Even if I *could* make you into a robot vacuum cleaner, I wouldn't. So I'll tell you what: Redo your prayer, the way I suggested. Give me until a certain day, and if you aren't happy . . . I'll see what I can do about your robot vacuum wish."

I shuffle my feet and swipe my finger along my phone, only to almost drop it as she rockets to her feet.

"Tanabata," she shouts.

God bless you, I think to myself.

"It's the Star Festival. It's celebrated on a lot of different days, but because I'm one of the Seven Gods of Fortune, I'm saying it's on the seventh day of the seventh month. Seven, seven. I'll remember that way. You can hold me to it. Okay?" She wiggles her eyebrows, her hair shining under the light of the moon. "Deal?"

No. No deal. I don't want her to edit my prayer. It's *my* prayer. And it doesn't even matter anyway because *this isn't real.*

I shake my head.

The girl frowns. "Machi."

I shake my head again, harder. Then, pushing the nickel

deep into my pocket, I pivot on my heel and start walking away.

"Machi," she calls out. "Come on. Give me a chance."

I don't slow down. As I leave her behind, I feel the most disgusting sense of satisfaction. For once in my life, I get to be the one to walk away.

Just as I reach the bus stop, I catch a flash of dark blue in the corner of my eye. I whip around, preparing to run from the girl.

But when I turn, no one is there.

And the nickel is still in my pocket.

CHAPTER THREE

ANGEL ONCE TOLD me about this phenomenon called the ironic process theory. It's also called the white bear problem or the pink elephant paradox. People, she said, like having fun names for complex things to make themselves feel better about how complicated the world can be.

The concept describes how, when we try not to think about something, we're actually much more likely to think about it. If, for example, someone says not to think about a polar bear or a pink elephant, you'll immediately start thinking about a polar bear or a pink elephant. The more you want to get them out of your head, the louder their stomping gets, a parade of psychological torture.

I stare at my open browser window. I opened Yelp to check the hours for some of the places on Dr. Tsui's list but found myself looking for Benzaiten's shrine again.

It's not like I'm ignoring Dr. Tsui's assignment. Unless I want my parents to go on a therapist hunt again, I need to wait at least a couple of sessions before outright disobeying him. I just had to see if anyone has ever said anything about that shrine or the girl claiming to be the great goddess herself. There's still no page for the shrine, though, and no mention of any girl, even when I just Google *weird girl at Benzaiten shrine near me.*

I switch tabs, my fruitless search replaced by a picture of

the nearest animal shelter. The Yip Yap Shelter is close to my building, about five minutes away. I wonder if my neighbor got her cat there.

I close my laptop and tell myself I'll stop by today. I'll march my way over to just *one* place, put on my best smile—or at least not look like I'm being held hostage—and act normal long enough to tell Dr. Tsui I completed his assignment and had a wonderful, marvelous, animal-induced-oxytocin adventure.

I realize, as I step out of the apartment, I don't have to force myself. Dr. Tsui can't *make* me go anywhere. I could stop by the corner store instead, or leave the residential area and head for the nearest mall, or keep walking until I don't recognize anything or anyone and become someone else. Someone better. Someone who doesn't get interrupted when making a wish to become a robot vacuum cleaner. Who doesn't wake up in the middle of the night with Angel and Sunny's names frozen on her tongue.

I've thought about it. What I could be if I slipped out of this life, untied from the people I loved, and started over.

You look lost, someone would say as I opened the door to a cozy little diner with a punny name like Keep Your Eyes on the Fries or Egging On My Knees or Everyone Makes Mis-Steaks. *Do you need help?*

I would look at the person, a stranger with a kind face, familiar in all the best ways. I would accept the glass of water set in front of me, the condensation already dripping down the outsides. And I would say, *Yes*.

But when I get off the bus, I'm not at the animal shelter; I'm at the shrine.

I blink. I don't remember making the conscious decision to come back. Maybe that girl really *does* have magical powers.

Or maybe I just spaced out, the way I did when I promised

my parents I would do the laundry, only to start the washing machine without adding detergent.

In my defense, that was right after my robot vacuum cleaner nightmare, so I was a little out of it.

I raise my head. The torii looks just as worn and abandoned as it did last night. I must have passed it before in all the years we've lived here, but like everyone else, I didn't really see it.

I haven't yet processed what happened yesterday. The girl was definitely weird, but who am I to judge? I don't talk.

Still, I did an online search for Benzaiten earlier, and though I could only find pictures of woodblock prints from the 1800s and the occasional anime character with eyes taking up half her face, no interpretation looked much like the girl I met. While the girl from the shrine was near-manic, her golden eyes wild, Benzaiten's smile in the woodblock prints is restrained, like the Mona Lisa. She's elegant. Regal. She doesn't wear white nightgowns and drape herself over offering boxes. And, needless to say, deities generally don't appear to mortals.

If she does show up, she might explain who she really is and what she wants with me. I'm guessing she's either bored or under the impression that she can squeeze some money out of me.

Joke's on her. I'm *also* bored and poor.

I kick off my shoes, sending one flying. Hopping across the pavement, I pick up my boot and place it outside the torii with its mate. I'm just about to step inside when a shadow appears in the far-right corner of my vision.

I turn, my heart pounding.

But there's nothing there.

I wait a few seconds longer. When no one appears, I approach the offering box, moving carefully along the path.

The box is empty.

I take out my wallet, extract my nickel, and stuff everything back in my bag. Maybe I can make my actual wish now. Or if not, maybe the girl will show up again, and I can finally get some answers.

After bowing once, I take the coin and toss it into the air. *Pak.*

I blink. The girl sits on the offering box, her hair gleaming in the light. She opens her hand, revealing the nickel. "Now, Machi, there's no need for that."

I take my canvas bag and pull out my whiteboard. She juts out her chin, standing and moving closer. Tilting her head to one side, she lets her ponytail brush the bodice of her dress. "Really? You're not going to speak? Even after I appeared literally right in front of you like an apparition, nickel in hand?"

I start writing on my whiteboard, but she keeps trying to see what I'm saying before I'm done. We do a strange dance, our feet skittering in a tight circle as I work to avoid her and she cranes her neck to read my unfinished sentence.

"What are you doing?" She halts and sets her delicate hands on her hips. "Deities aren't exactly known for their patience."

I ignore her, completing my question, and turn the board around.

"'Who are you?'" she reads aloud. She rolls her eyes. "I told you this. I'm the goddess Benzaiten. What do I have to do to get you to believe me?"

I wipe the board, working on my next words. I guess she isn't going to give up this goddess charade.

"I hope you realize," she says as I write, "most people would be de*light*ed to meet me. We're not supposed to appear to humans, especially ones who don't seem all that interested in devoting themselves to us, but here I am, revealing myself to you, and this is the thanks I get?" She glances at the whiteboard. "Though that *is* cute. It's like a little speech bubble."

If she isn't an actress, she should consider it. I could imagine her on the big screen, a real Hollywood starlet with her own IMDb page and online fan club with a ten-dollar fee and a barely-up-and-running HTML site written in Papyrus, because she's just that elegant. Known for her dramatic flair, she would shine as the comic relief.

I'm not finding her all that funny right now, though.

"'You don't have to read everything I write out loud,'" she reads out loud. "Hey, you're the one refusing to talk. I get to do what I want with your responses." She continues reading. "'What do you want with me?'"

She raises her chin. Her cheekbones are high, shaping her face into a heart. She's unquestionably pretty. Her eyes are more amber than gold today. She must like experimenting with color contacts.

"First of all, *you* came to *me*. Remember? And second, I don't have to prove *anything* to you, considering you didn't even accept my very kind and helpful edits to your prayer." She runs a finger along her neckline and pulls out a necklace. Scores of little pendants hang from a black cord. Each one resembles a wide house, rectangular all along the sides except the top, which meets in the center at a point.

What is that? I write.

This time, she doesn't read it back to me. "These are all my unanswered prayers. Every time someone makes a wish at one of my shrines, it shows up on this cord. Once I answer it, it disappears."

So if I made a prayer to you, it would ~magically~ appear.

She rolls her eyes. "Don't squiggle me. *Yes*, it would appear. In fact, I already have your wish right here."

She dangles the necklace from her fingers, the pendants jangling like loose change, but before I can take a good look, she snaps it back.

"Your original wish, that is," she says. "The one you were just about to fix. Riiight?"

I narrow my eyes. *I don't want to change my prayer.*

She huffs. "Well, I can't do much with the one *you* gave me, now can I? I mean, honestly, Machi. A robot vacuum cleaner? Is that really what you want? So while all your classmates are applying to college and getting their first paychecks, you're going to be . . . what, exactly? Sucking up a bunch of dust and hair?"

I grind my teeth. I should've just gone to the animal shelter. I could be petting dogs right now. I guess this is what I get for putting off Dr. Tsui's assignment.

"Come on," she says. "Trust me on this. Give me until Tanabata to change your mind. By then, you will have found the value in being human. I just know it."

I run my fingertip over the nickel, the metal growing warm against my skin. I don't know why I came back here or what I'm supposed to do now, and she's so bright and pretty, it's hard to think straight.

"Five weeks," she says. "You can hold on until then, can't you?"

I glance up at her, trying and failing to mask my surprise. Forming each letter with care, I write, *What do you mean, "hold on until then"?*

She mouths my message as she reads it. Grinning, she says, "Well, I'm guessing if *I* don't grant your robot vacuum cleaner wish, you're just going to go to some other, far inferior deity."

I'm not. She was my last shot. If this wish doesn't work out—which I'm almost sure it won't—I'm done. Done with disappointing my parents every time they call and pause for a moment after saying hello because a part of them is waiting for me to speak. Done with going to new doctors, only to get pushed out of my comfort zone, as if that wasn't what got me into trouble in the first place. Done with slinking from shrine to shrine, temple to temple, unable to take that first step because I'm afraid even if I manage to do everything right, *I'll still be wrong*.

"Okay," Benzaiten says, clapping her hands. "Enough jabbering. You're going to make your wish now, and I'm going to prove it to you. Right? *Right?*"

Five weeks. I can wait five weeks.

As soon as I nod, she cheers, jumping in the air and landing on the offering box in a supernaturally graceful move. Gesturing to the box, she says, "Well?"

God, she's pushy.

Dripping with reluctance, I toss the coin back in, ring the bell, and press my hands together.

I pray I will realize the beauty of being human and rediscover my voice.

Whatever that means.

I bow once more and look up. The girl clambers down from the altar, her white dress slipping off the corner. She lifts a hand. Between her index and middle fingers is my nickel, the ridges stained a lime green. She curls her fingers around a pendant on her necklace, the board tiny and new. Looking me in the eye, she grins and says, "Machi, your prayer has been heard."

CHAPTER FOUR

"LET'S GO OUT," Benzaiten says. "Get your boots."

I frown. Why does everyone try to get me to go places?

She crosses her arms until I collect my boots from near the torii. I hold onto them, hoping that'll be enough, but she gestures at my feet, as if to say, *Hello?*

I slide my boots on. Reluctantly.

"We're going to see the mortal world," she says. "I haven't been here in so long."

My lips press together. Her shrine is in the middle of nowhere. Unless she's thinking we're going to have a grand, life-affirming romp through the rundown corner store, she's setting herself up for disappointment.

"Come on."

She takes my hand, and before I can shake her off, a burst of wind hits me like a slap across the face. As a flash of light blinds me, the scene around me fades to white, its color seeping out like a reverse bath bomb.

Time slides past me like a slushy waterfall. I close my eyes and listen to the pounding of my heart, hoping everything will go away if I hold my breath long enough.

"Machi," Benzaiten says, her voice breaking the silence. "If the bones in my hand could be broken, you would be crushing them to dust."

I open my eyes. Her fingers are freakishly bent beneath the iron clasp of my hand. I release her, and she shakes out her arm.

"You're stronger than you look. Maybe your arms *aren't* too small." She raises her head. "Ja-jaaan! Look where I've brought us."

My eyes sweep across the streets. Neon lights shining from overhead poles cough weakly on the sunlit pavement. Fake sakura trees adorn every corner. Faces are everywhere, blurring together like images on the other side of a rain-spotted window. Most of the adults are holding hands—with other adults, with children, with an oversized sushi plush with arms that, unlike mine, really *are* small.

I blink. I have no idea where we are. We're certainly not at the shrine anymore. Or even in the same neighborhood.

But something about this place is nightmarish. Achingly familiar. I half-expect to see Angel standing beside me, arms crossed and eyeliner just beginning to smear, and, just beyond her, Sunny, fiddling with the top button of her blouse and tucking her hair behind her ear.

But when I look, there's only Benzaiten.

"Now you *have* to believe me," she says. "Right?"

I clench my jaw even as my insides go soft. I don't want to give in. This has to be a trick. We're in a hologram. She knocked me out and dragged my limp body here. I'm tripping on those drugs I told Dr. Tsui I've never taken.

"Seriously? You come to my shrine, pray to me, watch me do all these, quite frankly, amazing things, and yet you won't trust me when I say I'm the goddess herself? Why did you even pray to me, then?"

Because I didn't know what else to do.

But she's right. I can't deny it anymore. Benzaiten descended from the heavens, personally introduced herself to me, and decided to help me. And I didn't believe her. I almost never came back.

I take my whiteboard and write, *Am I going to be smote?*

She laughs. The sound is like bells, ringing above the clamoring of people demanding this food or that toy. "No, though I'm glad you finally understand."

I think faster than I can scribble. *Why are you here? Why are you so insistent on changing my wish? Why are you a teenager?*

"You're so funny." She flips her ponytail over her shoulder, nearly whapping me in the face. "I like being this old, and since you're roughly the same age, it works out. But I can appear whenever and however I want. With restrictions, of course."

I picture her shrinking down into a squat machine, her limbs folding inward and her golden eyes blinking beside the central power button.

Could YOU become a robot vacuum cleaner?

"I just said 'with restrictions,' didn't I?" She sighs. "You're so weird. But I kind of like that. Now." She stands. "Let's go."

Where?

"We're going to explore. See what's out here in the world. Or, at least, this lovely little place called Japantown."

I don't think I've ever used the word *lovely* unironically. I know Angel never did. No one could take a word, a phrase, a person, and twist it the way she could.

"Come on, Machi," Benzaiten chirps.

Suppressing a sigh, I stand and follow her.

"So," she says. "Don't freak out. We didn't go far. I mean, we're, like, in a completely different city, but—"

I stop dead in my tracks.

She glances at me. "Oh, don't look at me like that. Once we're done here, I'll just flash us back to the shrine. No big deal."

Teleportation. Magic. No big deal.

"Come along," she singsongs.

I stay a step or two behind her. A paper lantern hangs from an eave, shuddering every time the wind blows. A few feet away, a family struggles to slide teriyaki chicken off wooden skewers with their teeth, slick sauce dotting the sides of their mouths like thumbprints. I'm just starting to feel overwhelmed, panic brushing against my skin like glaze to a scrawny cooked chicken, when Benzaiten puts a hand on my arm.

"This way," she says, her eyes bright.

And just like that, I feel okay again. Or if not okay, a little less like I'm about to get skewered.

Her first stop is a little booth off the main street. A few children rush past us, screaming and running with their arms held out behind them. The nicer ones apologize when they knock into me, but not until they spot Benzaiten, their eyes wide as they take in the gentle curves of her face, the golden color of her irises.

I guess I should be relieved. So other people *can* see her.

For a split second, though, the tiniest part of me wishes they didn't. I don't want to share her.

I mean, it's not like I own her. I've been acquainted with the cheese in my refrigerator longer than I've been acquainted with her. Besides, she's a literal deity with thousands, if not millions, of followers. So nothing is ever mine, really. Not for long.

I let myself watch Benzaiten for another second, then look away.

The sign hanging from the stall reads 金魚すくい, and below it, KINGYO SUKUI. In front of a high counter is a rectangular plastic bin filled with water. A man sits behind the counter, his chin resting on his elbow. At the sight of Benzaiten, he perks up, then slides his elbow off the counter and gets to his feet.

"Hello," he calls out. "Did you want to play? Three dollars per person."

"What about goddesses?" she shouts back.

I shoot her a look, but the guy laughs. "How's about two dollars?"

She pulls my sleeve, dragging me to the booth. Once we come to a stop, she extends a hand. "Do you have five dollars?"

I give her another look.

"Come on." She pouts, pushing out her lower lip. When that doesn't work, she says, "I'll pay you back when we meet again, okay?"

Of course the first person interested in hanging out with me post-silence is a whimsical goddess who wants to take all my money.

Still. She made it sound like a sure thing. Like we're most definitely going to see each other at least one more time.

Struggling to ignore both her pouty face and the wary warmth blossoming in my chest, I put my whiteboard away, take out my wallet, and hand the guy a five-dollar bill. He hardly glances at me as he gives us two circular scoopers. I study one, running my finger along the top, a thin paper stretched across the round frame.

"You girls know how to play?" the guy asks.

"I don't," Benzaiten says, putting a hand to her chest. "Tell us?"

"Of course." He smiles and gestures to the plastic bin. Orange fish swim from one end to the other. "Each of you has a scooper. Oh, take these bowls too." He turns, picks up two bowls filled halfway with water, and sets them on the counter. "Scoop up all the fish you can. Be careful, though, because the scooper is fragile. Once it breaks, or after thirty seconds are up, you have to stop. You can keep the fish you get, if you manage to catch any."

I look back at the bin. Those poor fish. I'm sure some people take good care of them, but most probably don't.

I once played a different version of this game, one where I tossed a Ping-Pong ball into a cup and nearly gave the fish inside a heart attack. I named my prize "Fish" and did my best to care for it.

It died.

"Ready to play?" the guy asks Benzaiten.

"I was created ready," she replies, dragging me to the bin. We crouch, and when the guy starts the timer, we start scooping.

It's not as easy as I thought. Moving too quickly opens up a hole in the netting. There aren't that many fish, and the ones remaining are smart enough to evade the scooper. We also aren't the only ones here. A young child sits at the edge of the bin with his mother, his face crunched as he concentrates on catching something.

"Time's up, kid," the guy says to the child.

I look over. The boy's bowl is empty. His bottom lip trembles, but he lets his mother set the bowl back on the counter. She bows to the man, takes her child's hand, and leads him away as his head drops.

I peek at Benzaiten, then do a double take. Three golden fish are circling in her bowl. I guess she really is one of the Seven Gods of Fortune. Or she's just freakishly good at scooping fish.

"Time," the guy says. He raises his eyebrows at Benzaiten. "You're a natural. You've done this before?"

"Nope. First time," she says, straightening. As I stand, the guy takes her bowl. I set mine on the counter as she asks, "What happens now?"

"I bag them up just for you," he says, leaning closer.

I hold back a gag. He smells like stagnant fish water.

The fish flap their fins uncertainly as the man bags them. Holding them out, he says, "Come back sometime?"

"Maybe." She turns and tosses him a grin. "Thanks."

I wish I could ask him to pick his jaw up off the floor.

"Machi," Benzaiten says as she heads back to the main street. "Did you want these?"

I shake my head. I don't need a repeat of the Fish situation. I've grieved enough.

"Then keep up."

She breaks into a jog, somehow keeping the plastic bag still. There's not even a ripple on the water.

When she catches up to the boy from the booth, she slows. His hand is curled around his mother's. She taps them both on the shoulder, then bends down to meet his eyes. "Excuse me. I happen to have some fish. Would you like them?"

His eyes widen. "Weo-wee?"

"Really." She looks back at me before continuing, "*If* you promise to take good care of them. Put them in a nice tank and make sure to clean it. Okay?"

The boy nods hard enough to make me think his head is going to fly off. His mother asks, "Are you sure?"

"I'm absolutely sure." Benzaiten takes the boy's hand and wraps his fingers around the top of the bag. "I can tell they will be much better off with him."

"Y-yes," the mother says. "Yes. Thank you so much."

I watch Benzaiten in quiet admiration. She may have shown up out of nowhere knowing my name and wish and teleported us here in the blink of an eye, but something about this moment is different. For the first time, it doesn't seem like such a stretch, believing she's a deity. Or, at least, not mortal. There's something inhuman about her, a divine kindness I've only just begun to see. It makes me want to reach out and touch her like the bleeding woman who brushed her fingers along the edge of Jesus's cloak. She was healed in an instant, simply because she believed she would be.

Unfortunately, I don't think grabbing onto the flittering hem of Benzaiten's white slip will turn me into a robot vacuum cleaner. Especially since that apparently isn't even my wish anymore.

The woman shakes her head. "He's wanted those fish for so long. We have a tank and everything. I kept telling him we could just buy fish somewhere else, but he insisted on getting them here."

"I wanna save 'em," the boy says, staring at us through the plastic bag. His features blur, turning him to watercolor splotches.

"Then it all works out perfectly." Benzaiten gives the boy a solemn nod.

He nods again, less intensely this time. His eyes fill with tears. "Fwank you."

"You are so welcome." Her eyes are liquid gold as she steps back and stands. "Have a good day."

"We will now," the mother says. The boy is still gaping at the fish. "Thank you."

They glance back at her, then disappear into the crowd. Benzaiten keeps waving until they're gone.

"See?" she says to me. "Isn't the mortal world wonderful?"

Before I can reach for my pen, she points to something across the path and floats toward another stall, rambling about the colors and the smells and the people.

No. The mortal world doesn't seem all that wonderful. But she kind of does.

Kind of.

Crossing my arms, I watch Benzaiten sink into the crowd and tell myself it doesn't matter how many fish she catches with a paper net and gives away to a little boy. Someday, that boy will grow up and realize just because someone is there for him one day doesn't mean they'll be there the next. Just because something good happens once doesn't mean it'll happen again. Just because he loves those fish now doesn't mean he'll love them forever. Maybe by tomorrow, he'll realize taking care of fish isn't as great as he thought. Maybe by tomorrow, he'll decide he's sick of them. Maybe by tomorrow, he'll decide they're boring. And they, blissfully ignorant, will continue swimming in their tiny, pointless circles, waiting on an impossible miracle.

CHAPTER FIVE

"I BET THEY have kakigōri here."

I cross my arms. As if she needs more stuff. We've been in Japantown for about forty-five minutes now, and she's been toting around a plush daruma doll bigger than her torso for at least twenty. She managed to win other stuffed animals too but gave them to children whose parents just couldn't throw the ball into the oval hoop or toss a cheap wooden ring onto the right prize. I didn't bother pointing out that she was using my money, so those stuffed animals were technically mine. I don't care enough to steal toys back from children. Besides, I have to admit I like seeing her work her magic, enchanting everyone we meet.

Except once in a while, she reminds me so strongly of Angel, I'm afraid I'm going to be sick.

Everyone acted like Angel was some ruthless femme fatale because she always had a chip on her shoulder and a danger-ously specific insult on her lips, but there was a lot more to her than that. She was unquestionably generous around the people she loved. I never asked for a sip of her drink, but she always insisted on letting me have a taste anyway. When we went to the mall—always her idea; I'm not a shopper—she would buy me at least one thing, even if I swore I didn't need it. Back when she liked ice cream, she would give me the spoonful with the most cookie dough or chocolate chunks.

I turn my head and pinch my thumb until it goes numb.

"Do you like kakigōri?" Benzaiten asks.

I shrug, trying to get my mind off Angel.

"Never had it before? Then we should let you try it. They have all the other fun things humans like to do at festivals, so I'm sure there's a stall around somewhere."

She spins on the heel of her ballet flat and skips down the road. Pink and blue fluorescent lights hit her from every angle, making her look otherworldly. I suppose, though, that's exactly what she is.

It doesn't take her long to find a stall selling bowls of the fluffy, snowlike dessert. She scans the menu hanging at the back, her lips pursed as she weighs her options. I observe the other customers. One woman steps away from the stand with a heaping cup of deep-purple kakigōri, a spoon and a straw stabbed into the slopes of ice.

"Hmm," Benzaiten says, glancing at the person behind the counter. "You know, this isn't how you're supposed to make it. This is far too manufactured."

My eyes flick to her. She sounds like a jaded old woman. *Back in my day, they shaved ice the RIGHT way.*

My grandparents used to say things like that all the time. They would frown at our Honda, run their wrinkled hands along the leather interior, and say, *They don't make cars the way they used to.* If they turned on the news, the audio blaring, they would exchange a look and mumble, *What is this world coming to?* And every time they saw me doing homework on my laptop or quizzing myself with online flash cards, they would shake their heads and say, *Education is so different now.*

Different doesn't mean bad, I wanted to tell them.

But it would have felt wrong, saying that to people who had spent their entire lives being punished for not looking the way everyone else did.

We always understand too late.

"But we're already here," Benzaiten says, arguing with herself, "and I got excited at the idea of trying it. Plus, you haven't tasted it before."

I don't know what's so special about it. How is a bowl of fluffy ice supposed to make me see the beauty of humanity? The longer we stay, the more I realize nothing we've done so far has been for me. This is just a jaunt through the mortal realm for her.

"I think I want melon," she says. "What do you think?"

I shrug. I hope she knows I don't have infinite amounts of money. She's burned through about forty dollars already, and based on the prices listed on the menu, we're going to hit fifty soon.

I purse my lips. I hope she pays me back me before she gets bored and leaves me to figure out my life on my own.

"Melon is a safe choice," she says. "Mortals don't get how to properly extract flavors. In my world, everything is good. And free. Which, as you know, is not the case here. Money?"

I tamp down a sigh, but she doesn't notice, briefly distracted by a child tottering past, an alarmingly large bowl of bright-pink ice shavings in her chubby hands. A man catches up to the little girl, bends down, and takes the bowl. He gives her two spoons in return and says something in her ear. I imagine he's telling her he can carry the bowl to their table, and she will be in charge of the utensils.

They remind me a little of my father and me. We were close when I was younger, allies in subtle ways. Whenever my mother's parents complained about our house, which led my mother to complain about *them*, my father and I would play janken behind her back. He usually won.

I take my eyes off the father and child, but Benzaiten's still watching them. Sliding my whiteboard onto my knee, I write, *You have a soft spot for children.*

When she reads what I've written, her face blanches. She was always pale, her skin the color of a full moon, but even the rosiness of her cheeks drains away. She turns, her hair reflecting the soft pink lights around us, and runs her hands down her sleeves.

I start to write, but she cuts me off.

"Don't worry. I'll get an extra cup and put your share of the kakigōri in there. We won't have to use the same spoon."

I reach for her shoulder to tell her I'm trying to say something, but she shakes me off.

"Shush. I'm busy standing."

I erase the beginning of my message, frustration biting at my sides again. I guess I'm not the only one with things we can't discuss.

Why would that be such a sore subject, though? She's a deity. Of course she likes mortals still young enough to believe anything. If a child were to see her appear out of nowhere and claim to be a goddess, they would fall to their knees immediately. She wouldn't have to spend so much time convincing them of her worthiness. They would do anything just to make her happy.

Instead, she's supposedly trying to make *me* happy. Something I'm still not sure she can do.

I don't see how she can be so patient with children anyway. I was never good with young people. Or old people. Or people my own age. That's why it would be so much easier to just be a robot, sitting in the corner and recharging until I'm needed again.

I look back at Benzaiten as she steps up to the counter, her golden eyes brighter in the yellow light of the stall. On the other side, a guy gives us a blank stare.

"Irasshaimase," the guy says in a monotone. His eyes are fixed on something over my shoulder. I don't think he could look more bored if he tried. "Welcome. What can I get for you on this fine day?"

"It *is* a fine day," Benzaiten says, grinning. "Could we have a small melon kakigōri with two spoons and an extra cup?"

"Small melon," he says. He jots something down on a note-pad I can hardly see, my view obscured by the cash register. "Two spoons. Cup. Got it. Toppings."

She blinks. "Is that a question?"

He grunts.

"Ah." Her eyes dim to a dark amber. She seems disheart-ened by the ineffectiveness of her charm. "No, thank you."

"Kashikomarimashita." He does a halfhearted bow. "Please wait."

We watch as he pivots and starts up a machine behind him. It whirs quietly at first, then loud enough to make me grit my teeth.

The second she gets her kakigōri, Benzaiten claps her hands in delight and skips over to a nearby bench. I haven't seen any-one over the age of twelve skip, and since she's a goddess, she's probably about, like, a million times that old.

She sits, takes the second bowl, and starts dividing the des-sert. I don't understand why she would be willing to literally take a leap of faith, landing on the ground of the shrine and insisting she's going to change my life, only to shy away the second I ask her about herself.

As she hums yet another song I don't recognize, her voice quiet but unwavering, I pull my whiteboard out of my bag and set it across my lap. *How is sugary ice supposed to make me stop wanting to be a robot vacuum cleaner?*

She sighs. "Well, it's hard to help you when you won't tell me much about yourself. I wouldn't have even known your *name* if I weren't, you know, a beautiful, magical deity."

I give her a look.

"What? I *am*." She points at my bowl. "Eat."

Deciding resistance is futile, I jab my spoon into the side of the ice mountain and scrutinize the glittering green crystals, then the thin trail of condensed milk running along the sides. It's sweet, I realize as I put the spoon in my mouth, but I don't know if I would pay ten dollars for another.

Benzaiten studies me for a moment. "When did you stop talking?"

I roll the cap of my whiteboard marker around in my hand. *The eleventh grade.*

"I don't know what that means. Explain."

I crunch my ice, annoyed. I've gone over this story with every therapist I've seen. She's a goddess. She should be able to figure it out, or at least speak more politely, the way she did with that little boy. If I knew where we were or how to get home, I would leave her here.

I close my eyes.

No, I wouldn't. I wouldn't leave anyone.

Tightening my grip on my pen, I write, *It's been a year now.*

"A whole year?" She takes her spoon, turning it upside down and setting it on the tip of her tongue. "I imagine that has made your day-to-day mortal life difficult."

I shrug. It isn't as hard as people may think, though it was in the beginning. My parents went through all five stages of grief. First, they thought it was a phase, something similar to the time I refused to wear anything but graphic tees, denim skirts, and knee-high socks. I would grow out of it soon enough. That's what they told my teachers. What they told themselves.

Days passed, and their denial caught fire, burning all of us. They asked why I couldn't just *talk*. My throat was fine. I hadn't hit my head. They took me to my doctor, who confirmed whatever was stopping me from speaking was in my mind.

When we got home, my parents begged me to talk to them.

Say something. Didn't I hear the doctor? Didn't I hear him say I was perfectly healthy? Why wasn't I talking? Was I doing it just to spite them? Didn't I know how much stress they were under? Didn't I see how much I was worrying them? What were they supposed to do with a daughter who wouldn't talk?

The tone of our discussions shifted. I knew they loved me, didn't I? What if they let me stay home for a little while? Would I talk? It didn't have to be at school. What if they let me miss the first few days of the school year? A whole few days out of classes if I started speaking again. They missed my voice. They missed me. What about a week? Or what if they bought me something I wanted? Did I want something? No? What if they stopped checking on my grandparents so often? Would that make me happy? Was that why I had stopped talking? No? What about the school thing? Have I been thinking about the school thing? What did I think about my new doctor, the one meant to save me from myself? Did I like her? Did I feel a connection? If not, it was okay to switch doctors. They had a whole list of possibilities, all of whom accepted our insurance. Was I listening? Was I talking to the doctor? Was I feeling better yet?

The bargaining ended as the school year began, sinking us all into despair. They told me they loved me. They told me they didn't understand me. They told me they wanted me back. Where was I? What was going on?

Then the questions faded away. My mother cried. My father cried. I didn't. They wanted to reach out to people they loved, but who could understand? No one they knew had experienced this.

Whatever it was, it guided them to the final stage: acceptance. They pulled me out of school, enrolled me in online courses, and told me, in that weary tone I had come to know so well, I would have to take classes in the summer to catch up. They brought me to new doctors, eventually leading me to meet and connect with Sheryl. They liked her because I said more to her than I had to any other doctor, at least in writing. They still asked me questions, hoping one would break through and prompt me to speak just one little word, but they didn't slam their hands on the table or burst into tears when I pushed my food around my plate instead of answering.

It isn't bad, I write now.

Benzaiten takes a spoonful of the melted ice, neon green liquid sliding in its curve, and pours it over the top of the mountain. "What about when you need to get a job? Humans do that, don't they?"

There are jobs that don't require speaking.

"You're serious about this," she says, her voice soft. "Why?"

I don't talk. That's all you need to know.

"That's rude." She points her spoon at the spot between my eyebrows. "Do not forget your place, mortal."

How could I forget when she's constantly flaunting her status as a deity?

"I can't help you rediscover your voice if you won't open up to me."

I don't really care to ever speak again.

She chips away at the green ice in her bowl. "That's what I don't get. It's like you've given up, but you won't tell me why."

I don't write anything. I eat spoonful after spoonful of kakigōri, enjoying the way it chills my insides. Maybe I'll freeze to the spot, an ice sculpture in Japantown for all to see. Then, when someone finally swallows her fear and reaches out to touch me, I will shatter into a million pieces, shards flying in every direction. After the initial shock, everyone will move past me, leaving me to melt, forgotten.

"What did you expect to happen if I granted your first wish, as impossible as it was?"

I expected to become a robot vacuum cleaner.

"But what would you do?"

Clean.

Benzaiten lets the spoon hang from between her lips like a cigar. "You're on thin ice." She spins the utensil between her fingers, catching the attention of some passersby. It's the motion that initially captivates them, but they stay when they realize how lovely she is.

I'm used to not being the prettiest one in the room. When the three of us were together, Sunny and I accepted the fact that, nine times out of ten, we would not be the ones people wanted to know better. We talked about it sometimes, the two of us. It could have destroyed our friendship with Angel, could have torn us apart, but we swore we would never let it.

And in our defense, that's not what broke us. So I guess we succeeded in that one tiny, inconsequential way.

"You would clean," Benzaiten says, "and then what? Keep cleaning until you run out of batteries or get attacked by a raccoon?"

I don't think we have raccoons here.

"Not the point."

I roll my eyes.

"Ooh," she says, wrapping her arms around the daruma doll plush. "You know how daruma dolls are hollow? Do you think this one is too? Could I climb inside it? I've always wanted to see what it's like to be a daruma."

I blink slowly. I can't believe *she's* in charge of my wish.

I stand and take our bowls, dumping them in the nearest trash bin. When I turn, she's right behind me, her golden eyes and dark lashes all I can see.

She takes my hand, her fingers still cold from the kakigōri. I instinctively start to pull away, but she's holding onto me too tightly for me to extricate myself. I give a little tug anyway, but when she keeps her hand around mine, I find myself just the tiniest bit comforted.

She's got me. And she's not letting go.

I duck my head as she leads me to a quiet alleyway. After checking the area for observers, she exhales. Wind whispers at our feet, then curls around us in a gentle swirl. As everything fades to white, I close my eyes and try to memorize the way her hand feels in mine.

CHAPTER SIX

I ALWAYS TELL myself I don't need much.

It's been that way ever since I was little. When I first started school, my mother armed me with a pencil, a wide-ruled composition notebook, and a beaten-up canvas bag she had gotten for free with a purchase of a dozen eggs. I was self-conscious enough already, but upon reaching my classroom, I saw everyone else in my class had backpacks. Whenever we lined up all our bags on the side of the carpet, mine stuck out, drooping to one side, one strap snaking out like a pale, limp arm stretching toward something out of reach.

I didn't say anything to my mother. I told myself I didn't need a backpack. My old bag was perfectly usable. That's what I told all the people who asked why my bag was so ugly: *It works just fine.*

Then one day, somehow, my mother found out I was the only one without a backpack. On the way home, she said, *Why didn't you tell me? I could've gotten you a backpack.*

I didn't need one, I said.

But I was crying in relief.

I changed in some ways as I grew up, but that one thing, the conviction that I don't need much, has always remained. I don't need my voice. I don't need friends. I don't need a goddess, especially one who won't even grant my original wish. I can make it on my own.

But then I let myself go for a moment, and when I come crashing back to Earth, I'm there. Needing.

I don't *want* to need Benzaiten. I'm not even sure I'm quite there yet. I just sometimes think, when she's chattering about fish-scooping and kakigōri and how happy that little boy was, maybe it's not so bad. Being with her.

That's a dangerous thought, though. More dangerous than the thought of becoming a robot vacuum cleaner.

She offers to flash me into my apartment, but I decline, choosing instead to take the long, scenic, gives-you-just-enough-time-to-ponder-the-mysteries-of-the-universe way home from her shrine. She must assume it's because I'm not a fan of fast-travel, or because I'm on a sugar high from the kakigōri, but after taking her hand and getting so close, I don't think I can be around her anymore.

As I pass a flower shop with geraniums drooping in the window, I decide there's no point in bonding with Benzaiten. Even a goddess can't change my mind in five weeks, five months, five years, or five decades. It's best to keep my distance.

If she hadn't made me revise my prayer—which probably means she won't leave me alone until she's convinced she's granted it—I wouldn't go home at all. I would hide out someplace far away. I would live among nature, befriending the deer and tending to the mushrooms. I would bake bread in my clay oven and trade the best loaves at the small market, simply pointing at the fruits and vegetables I wanted to purchase, never speaking to anyone. No one would know much about me, and I wouldn't ever get close enough to learn about them. That way, we could never hurt each other's feelings. We would just live our separate lives. Forever.

I glance down at my phone. It's not even noon.

Shifting my weight from foot to foot, I argue with myself

about my plan for the rest of the day. Ideally, I would go home and do nothing. But my next appointment with Dr. Tsui is coming up, and I still haven't gone to any of the places on his list. If I can handle getting whooshed out of a shrine and into an unfamiliar town by a deity with golden eyes, I can surely use my own two feet to get to an animal shelter.

Huffing through my nostrils like an angry dragon, I clench my hands into fists and start walking.

I don't know what he wants from me. Just as watching Benzaiten give fish away to children isn't going to make me want to stop being a robot vacuum cleaner, awkwardly offering my hand for a dog to sniff isn't going to make me want to talk again. Everyone keeps pushing me to be different, to be better, but I don't know how. I only know how to be myself, and I'm not even good at that.

The Yip Yap Shelter is smaller than it looked in the Yelp pictures. Its exterior has been painted white, and its logo—the silhouettes of a cat and a dog resting their fuzzy foreheads together, the negative space forming a heart—has been mounted just beside the glass door. I read the PULL sticker above the door handle at least four times, afraid I'm somehow going to wind up trying to push it.

I lift a hand, my fingers inches from the handle. I don't know why I'm so nervous. It's an animal shelter, not a party. It doesn't even look like anyone is there. No one is at the counter. Maybe it's closed.

A flash of motion from inside nearly sends me tripping over my own feet. I look up in time to see a man plop himself down on a stool behind the cash register. He appears to be just a little younger than my parents, in his late forties or so, though it's hard to tell with his clean-shaven face and bright eyes.

He's also looking right at me.

Well, okay. I guess I have no choice but to enter.

When I open the door—pulling, thank God—a silver bell tied to the inside handle lets out a light *ding-dong*. The sound reminds me of Benzaiten's laugh.

"Good morning," the man says. "Or, well, afternoon? What time is it?"

I give him a tight-lipped smile in lieu of an answer.

He checks his watch. "It looks like we're at exactly noon. So good noon. Welcome to the Yip Yap Shelter. Is this your first time here?"

I hesitate, as if I have to think about it. After glancing over my shoulder at the closed door, I nod.

He tilts his head. I can tell he's trying to puzzle out whether I'm mute or just socially awkward.

Both. The answer is both.

"Well, I'm glad you're here," he says. "Do you have any pets? Or are you thinking about getting one?"

I shake my head. I still don't see the point of this. I have no reason to be here. I'm not going to adopt an animal. I could buy something for my neighbor's cat, but that would be weird. I feel like apologizing to this man for wasting his time.

His laugh is soft, melting like rice paper on his tongue. "You don't have to look so sorry. It's okay if you came here just to spend some time with animals. It's one of the best forms of therapy, if you ask me. Which you didn't."

I tighten my grip on the handle of my bag. I should take out my whiteboard.

"I'm Andrew, by the way," he says, standing from his seat and extending a hand. "My family and I own this shelter."

I eye his hand. He seems nice and all, but I don't want to touch him. I didn't even want to touch Benzaiten at first.

Taking my cue, he pulls his arm back. "Okay, well, if you need anything, I'll be here. You can stay here as long as you want."

I toss him another awkward smile.

The shelter is about the size of a small living room. There are two dogs, one on the larger side and one small enough to fit in a purse, and a few cats. Rats sniff around the edges of a nearby cage. I can see a couple of tanks in the back, the fish swimming aimlessly.

I crane my neck to take a look at the cage. Two rats chase each other while another sleeps in the corner, its white fur pressed against the edge. I wonder if the animals get sad when one of them is adopted. If they wake up from dreams of the ones who have disappeared, or if, by the next morning, they have already forgotten.

The two active rats give up on their pursuit, slump against each other, and close their eyes. Like they know because they're together, they're safe.

If Benzaiten can't make me a robot vacuum cleaner, maybe we can compromise and turn me into a creature instead. With my luck, though, I would be placed with a bonded pair of rats, ostracized and forced to spin on a wheel by myself for the rest of my three-year life.

Maybe that wouldn't be so bad.

"This," Andrew says, edging around the counter and gesturing to a ginger cat in a large crate, "is our resident grump."

I eye the cat. It eyes me back.

"Most people don't want older cats, especially when they aren't big fans of interacting with humans. But I introduce him to everyone who comes in anyway."

I tilt my head in a silent *Why?*

"He needs the socialization. Besides, I keep hoping someday, someone will see him and adore him just as much as my daughter and I do."

So he has a daughter. I bet she's normal. I bet she talks.

The ginger cat's tail flicks once as the man crouches beside the crate. Andrew leans in, touches the cat's forehead, and says, "I love you too."

I look away.

WHEN I GET home, I reach for the notebook from Dr. Tsui to finish my assignment, running a thumb over the yin-yang symbol. Turning to the first page, I make a little check next to the words *animal shelter*, printed in Dr. Tsui's small, blocky handwriting. Then, just out of curiosity, I take a peek at the first prompt: *What is your happiest memory?* ☺

I roll my eyes. Of course. I shouldn't have expected anything different from a journal specifically for therapy.

I have to admire the creativity, though. I've been to a lot of therapists, from ones specializing in cognitive behavioral therapy (as if I can change my way of thinking), dialectical behavior therapy (as if I can figure out a way to cope), humanistic (which was my least favorite; wow, I have the power to change my own life? Gee, thanks, Doc. I never knew), and now, Dr. Tsui's psychodynamic psychotherapy, because surely, my unconscious is holding onto something deeply traumatic—but writing in a prompt journal is a new one.

I chew my nail. I know I don't *have* to write anything.

But I can't stop thinking about that cat. That cat and Benzaiten and Sheryl and Angel and Sunny and everything else that makes me feel like my eyes are going to pop out of their sockets from the pressure. Every time I think of a potential good memory—the time Angel and I filmed ourselves cooking macaroni and cheese, narrating like we had our own cooking show; the time Sunny and I created a shared document where we could dump all our angsty little poems we wrote in the margins of our school notes; the time the three of us went to the mall, even though I hate shopping, and got caught in a downpour so bad we walked out looking like waterlogged rats—all I can do is sit back and watch invisible cigarettes burn holes through the good, leaving only ash and the acrid smell of smoke.

Sheryl would want me to write in this journal. She would be so proud.

Wow, she would say. *You mean you went out with a new friend, visited an animal shelter, AND met its owner? That's great, Machi. Do you think you could do the other assignment Dr. Tsui gave you? Could you try writing in that journal?*

Why? What's the point?

I keep chewing my nail and stare at the closed blinds.

I don't have anything else to do.

At least when my parents were here, I could lose myself in the busyness of their lives. Without them, I have nothing but myself.

So I open the notebook, pick up a pen, and start writing.

Prompt #1:
What is your happiest memory? ☺

~~This is~~
~~I don't~~
~~Well, I guess~~
~~It's funny because~~
Okay, I don't know what I'm doing.

I keep thinking I'm doing this for you, Sheryl.

Oh, God. Am I writing to you now? I guess I am. Does it even matter if you're never going to read it? How could you? You left.

Anyway, happiest memory, I guess.

I was in the seventh grade. I didn't have friends, but it wasn't like how I don't have friends now. In the seventh grade, I was used to having no one. I got along fine with my classmates. I even had some inside jokes with them. Once class was over, though, so was our friendship. We didn't check on each other. We didn't ask personal questions. Everything was about that single class, those individual moments. We never bothered to string them together to create a cohesive picture of the other, and that was fine.

I had friends in elementary school, back when we had to give those paper or cardboard valentines to everyone. I hated those packs of twenty-something cards because in every one, there had to be a particular design that was flirtier than the others. Most of the cards would say something like *You Cheer Me Up When I'm Blue*, paired with an anthropomorphic blue crayon, or *Your Heart Is Your Best Koala-ty* with a marsupial doodle hanging from the letters. But there would be one set of cards with something like *You're Absolutely Radishing* or *Bee Mine*.

I don't think I have to explain what drawings accompanied those. You're a doctor.

Sorry. I got way off track. My memory has nothing to do with valentines.

Friendships were hard in middle school. We all hated each other. We all hated ourselves. That's why we acted out so much. Why we bullied people whose only transgression was talking just a little too loudly or caring about grades just a little too much or dressing just a little too conservatively. Why we reached and grabbed and pulled at everything we saw.

Some of us veered one way, plunging into goth subcultures and listening to classic alt-rock bands. Some of us poured our extra aggression into sports, imagining the baseball was every bad thing we had ever done and hitting it hard enough to make it vanish from sight. Some of us became obsessive in our studies, talking about PhD programs and career trajectories. Some of us let our passion for music sweep us from beat to beat, then song to song, then day to day.

I didn't do any of that. I just sat in the classroom and went home. I was a member of the No-Club Club, also known as the Go-Home Club. But really, those little moments, those inside jokes? They were enough for me. I don't know if you can believe me, but they were.

Until Serena.

Before Serena became the girl who was expelled because she showed up to art class visibly under the influence, she was the girl everyone loved to hate and hated to love. She was a terrible gossip, but, perhaps even worse, she was also incredibly sweet. The daughter of a locally famous fashion designer, she wore only the cutest clothes. Whenever she waved to anyone—and she waved to everyone—she would show off nails painted the same color as a piece in her outfit.

It was December, and I stood in the girls' bathroom, picking out an eyelash from the bottom of my eye.

Yes. This is what I was doing during the happiest moment of my life.

I freed the eyelash and made a wish before blowing it off my fingertip. Then I started washing my hands with the lemon-scented foaming soap. The kind that feels like diluted shaving cream. I was letting the water run over my palms when one of the stall doors opened. I hadn't known anyone was in the bathroom with me.

Good morning, she said too loudly.

It was the afternoon.

Um, hi, Serena, I said.

Because I talked back then. I even joked around with my classmates sometimes, which is, I realize, hard to imagine now. And admittedly, Serena fascinated me. Every time I thought I had her pinned down, she did something unexpected. The week before we met in the bathroom, I heard she had kissed a boy from another school. Someone older. When people asked for the details, she simply shrugged and said, *He wouldn't want me to talk about it. He's too mature for gossip.*

Then she started rambling about some other girl in our grade.

She wasn't *mean*, though. Her rumors were harmless, like *I heard this girl is dating this guy, and they're so cute together*, or *Someone told me this guy is having a surprise birthday party, and I want to bring those chocolate cupcakes from that bakery near my house*, and if she ever heard one of her friends saying something cruel about anyone, even the people we knew she didn't like, she would put a stop to it immediately.

I was ruminating on all of this, all the little Serena-related tidbits I had been subconsciously collecting, when Serena's hiccup startled me out of my thoughts.

You know my naaaame. Serena giggled. *I know yours too.*

Do you, I said. It wasn't a question.

Yeah. She was really, really close. I could spot the dried glue from her false lashes. She was the first person in our grade to wear them. *Your name feels so cool to say. Maaa-chee.*

Oh. Yes. That is my name. You DO know it. I'd thought she was bluffing.

You and me, she whispered, *we should be friends.*

I blinked hard. It's not like I had *dreamed* of being her friend, but I sometimes wondered what it would be like, getting close to someone so vibrant and dynamic and alive. It would feel, I thought, like getting swept up in a teen movie, complete with exclusive sleepovers and makeovers transforming me from quiet, mousy girl to respectable crony of the (in)famous middle school idol.

Why? I asked softly.

Serena didn't have time to answer.

Ser? One of her friends stepped into the bathroom and took one look at Serena. *Oh, God. Now? Are you for real?*

Serena's giggles scattered around the bathroom, hitting the walls and dribbling out the door. *Hi. Look who I'm talking to.*

Hurry up. We're going to be late. Oh my God.

Okay, okay. She waved to me. *Byyye, Maaaa-cheeeee.*

I think I said goodbye. To this day, I can't remember. She left, pulled out by the arm and still smelling of something I couldn't recognize.

She wasn't at school the next day. Or the day after that. After winter break, the administration was silent, but the students were not. The wheels of the rumor mill were spinning fast enough to keep the school running for years.

She never came back.

I'm sure if you were to read this, you would give me one of your *Oh, Machi. I care about you, but you so greatly worry me* looks. You don't see how this could be a happy memory. I had an eyelash in my eye. I was approached by a girl I hardly knew, then never saw her again.

It's a happy memory because it was before anything happened. I didn't need friends. I swear I didn't. But the possibility of having one? The concept that Serena, daughter of a fashionista, the girl who said hello to everyone without a trace of malice, could want to be my friend? That was what made me happy.

What about after? What about when I had real friends instead of girls who made promises they likely didn't remember by the time they left the bathroom?

No. Those aren't happy memories. Not anymore.

CHAPTER SEVEN

TODAY IS MY grandparents' funeral.

I don't want that to be my first conscious thought. I wish I could wake up again, better this time. Even shaking off the sticky threads of a nightmare would be preferable. Maybe this is my penance, all this guilt and gloom. My punishment for not being there.

I hold my phone above my face, half-hoping I'll drop it on my head. The final anvil of Reasons Why I Suck.

Turning phones on silent for the funeral, my newest text message says. Call your mom or me twice in a row if you really need something. It should go through.

I consider replying with a thumbs-up, but that seems highly inappropriate. I set my phone back on the bed.

My mother's going to cry. She cries at every funeral, so I imagine attending one for her own parents is going to leave her sobbing. She's an avid user of tissues. She doesn't let a single tear fall down her cheek. When she forgets her pack of tissues, she insists on asking everyone around if she can borrow one. She almost single-handedly finances the tissue business, and though I sometimes take her hand to comfort her, that usually makes her cry harder. But that's not why I didn't go to the funeral.

My father is going to drop his voice into his lowest register, forcing each word to rattle out from his chest like someone is playing xylophones on his rib cage. He will wear his face of stone, his mouth set and his eyes down. At funerals, he is the silent one, one hand on my mother's back as she weeps her way through the mortuary. He doesn't want to talk to me because he's so busy stuffing himself into the Stoic Husband mold. I dislike the way he acts at funerals, but that's not why I didn't go either.

I sit with my burnt toast and banana. I consider spreading peanut butter over the bread and slicing up the banana to make my meal less sad, but there's no point. As I chew, I let myself wonder what will be said. What the funeral will be like.

The only two young Japanese Americans in their town, my grandparents practically grew up together.

It was a love story that began in their youth and carried them through the years like the notes of a nostalgic song, I can hear the emcee saying at a wooden podium, half-choking on the heavy incense.

No one will mention how that love story ended. How the bass of the song faded, and nobody noticed. Then the treble line cut short, and still, nobody noticed.

Maybe they'll make it sound romantic. *They died only days apart.* That's what some people say they want, isn't it? A love so strong, the two can't bear to be without each other. But was it really a matter of not being able to bear it? I guess we'll never know.

My mother blames herself. Every time she dropped her spoon in her (not-expired) yogurt and ripped a tissue from its box, we could hear it: *How could I have been so ignorant? Why didn't I feel it, somewhere in my soul?*

My grandparents died days apart, but they weren't found for at least another week.

She hates knowing the neighbors found them. The neighbors didn't even like them. No one in that town did. My grandparents were the only Japanese Americans who hadn't given up and moved away.

After my mother got the call, I spent a lot of time wishing I could tell her I was sorry. She had escaped the town she hated so much, the town that hated her. She had married someone with a face her high school classmates despised. She had given birth to a child with a face her high school classmates despised. She had thought, *Life will be better for my daughter. One day, I'll come back and show that town how wrong they are.*

And then I messed it all up.

I wish I could wake up again, better this time.

I DON'T *HAVE* to go to the market. All I need is bread. But it's the day of my grandparents' funeral, and I'm not there, and my mother probably hates me, so why not get some honey oats?

My parents usually go to one of the mainstream grocery stores that take up the entire block, but I can't get to any of our usual places unless I want to walk until I can't feel my legs.

I instead head to the small market near our house, Let's Grow Already. Most of the produce is organic and therefore more expensive, but I'm only getting one thing anyway.

When the sliding doors open, a burst of air hits me in the face. For a second, I feel like Benzaiten's teleporting us to Japantown again. Even once I've stepped inside, the air blowing over my head, I can't stop thinking about her. I don't know if she's waiting for me to return, if she'll call me when she wants to see me again, or if she'll just appear in my house one day and scare the living daylights out of me, but she said we'll meet again. And I believe her. Even if I still wish she had just let me become a robot vacuum cleaner.

Shaking my head, I make my way to the bakery and cereal aisle. I'm just reaching for a loaf of honey-oat bread when my phone buzzes. Still searching for the flimsy expiration date sticker on the bread, I tap the green button on my screen and press my phone to my ear.

"Machi?" my mother says, as if she may have called the wrong person. And as if I would give her verbal confirmation. "Are you out?"

Sometimes, she asks me questions. I can't tell if she wants to test me or if she genuinely forgets I won't respond.

I take the bread off the shelf and hug it to my chest like it's my emotional support loaf.

"The funeral is over." My mother sniffles. "There was andagi."

There's always andagi at funerals.

I roam around the store. I'm not ready to go home. I don't know why the office supplies aisle is sandwiched between the prepackaged snacks and the freezer section, but I'm going to examine every single item in this store if it kills me.

"The neighbors were there," my mother continues.

That's surprising. I didn't think they cared.

I turn the corner and stop dead. Sitting at the end of the aisle, right at eye-level, is a familiar yellow bird character.

My steps are slow, as if I expect it to hop to the edge of the metal shelf and take flight. I reach for the plush, my fingers closing around its plump side, and check the tag.

Toridachi.

"I think we'll have to send them something." My mother won't stop sniffing. "We gave them money, but they deserve more."

Toridachi. Stupid yellow bird. It's just another character meant to sell cheaply made merchandise to satiate children's "gimme" desire for a few days. Then the thirst returns, stronger. The yellow bird needs more.

Wow. I've officially sunk low enough to project my problems onto a children's toy.

My fingers tighten around the side of the plush, my nails pressing into its stuffing. I tell myself to release. Release. Release.

"We're really lucky to have them," my mother says.

I drop the plush back where I found it, take out my phone, and type a message to my father.

"Text from Machi," my father says in the background. He pauses as he skims my message, then clears his throat. "She says, 'Did you forget about the racism?'"

"Machi," my mother snaps.

I feel the bread, my fingertips pinching the crust. Today is her parents' funeral. She lost both of them at once.

Except she didn't. A few days separated their deaths. But we didn't know that, did we?

"Machi. No matter how you feel about this place, I don't like hearing you talk about it that way. This is where I'm from."

Squish. Squish. Squish. Squish.

"And besides, what right do *you* have to say something like that? You aren't even here."

The line goes dead. From its shelf, Toridachi stares.

DR. TSUI'S IDENTICAL triplet figurines haven't moved.

I don't mean on their own. (I can believe in goddesses, but sentient toys are a different story.) I just mean they remain on his desk, their hands on their instruments and their eyes cast down. I wonder if they came as a set, the three of them packaged together in bubble-wrap veils, or if they had to be purchased separately. Would they be incomplete without each other? If only two were put away, would there still be space for the third?

Dr. Tsui smiles, the corners of his eyes crinkling like tissue paper under a gentle thumb. "I'm so happy to hear you were able to visit one of the places on the list. What was it like there?"

I slowly run my eraser along my whiteboard, my explanation of my trip to the Yip Yap Shelter disappearing. Placing my marker on the white surface, I write, *It was okay. The man seems nice.*

Dr. Tsui's eyes run across my message. Nodding, he says, "I'm glad. Do you think you would be willing to try visiting another one of the places on the list? Or if not, would you go to the shelter again?"

I press my tongue to the backs of my teeth. *Why?*

He hesitates. "You've been hurt, Machi. I understand why you may not want to interact with people anymore."

I bite the inside of my cheek. He probably says that to all his patients, but it feels personal.

"Connection is what makes us human."

I never said I wanted to be human, though.

I keep thinking about that Toridachi I saw at the market. I know I should be focusing on my argument with my mother, if it can be called an argument when she was the only one talking, or even the next time I'll see Benzaiten, but it's that yellow bird that haunts me the most.

Angel had her childish moments. For a while, she was obsessed with every little-kid food she could get her hands on: macaroni and cheese, mini pizzas, gummy candies, and those little ice cream cups we used to get at school. The only one that stuck around longer than a couple of weeks was ice cream, and even that craze ended after she ate so much Spunky Punk ice cream, she threw up in a trash can on the way to the bus stop.

We haven't touched ice cream since.

Or maybe she has. It's not like I would know.

She never cared for Toridachi, though. Never found it even a little cute.

Is it better to be loved for a moment, then forgotten for the rest of your life, or to never be loved at all? Better to be her best friend for years, then cast aside, or some innocent cartoon character adored by everyone except the one person you want most?

"Try to keep going to the shelter," Dr. Tsui says, "or anywhere else you want to go, and just spend some time around people. Then, when you're ready, you can start working on communicating with them—using your whiteboard, if that's what you're most comfortable with."

Writing to strangers on a whiteboard. Going to Japantown and eating frozen sugar. Neither Dr. Tsui nor Benzaiten has been able to change my mind. Benzaiten has almost five whole weeks left, and Dr. Tsui has however long before he gets tired of me or leaves like Sheryl, but the timeline doesn't matter. I don't think I'm going to turn into a Serena-level chatterbox by the time this is all over.

Dr. Tsui leans back in his chair. "What are you thinking about?"

I glance up at him. Somehow, I don't think I can tell him I'm comparing him to a Japanese deity, so I write, *I got into an argument with my parents yesterday.*

"An argument? Over text?"

I shake my head. *They called. I texted my father, and he read the message to my mother. She hung up on me.*

"What was the argument about?"

The funeral. I pause. *When I was little and we got into fights, I would write these long apologies and leave them on the table for them to find later.*

"When you were little." He sets his clipboard on his leg, clicking his pen. "Writing is a way of communicating too. One you've been using for a long time."

I nod. I've always expressed myself better through writing than speaking. Every time I tried to apologize or hold an important conversation, my words would lodge in my throat like peppermint bark, piling up and leaving me to choke through my sentences. It was so much easier to write. No one could interrupt me. No one could shoot me down mid-argument, smashing me under their thumb as if pressing down on a robot vacuum cleaner's OFF button.

"Can you tell me what you're thinking?" Dr. Tsui asks.

I shake my head.

He presses his lips together. "Okay, well, I know I said it wasn't mandatory, but have you taken a look at the journal? Have you felt like answering any of the prompts?"

I think of the first prompt. My unofficial letter to Sheryl.

I turn to the three figurines on his desk and slowly shake my head.

Prompt #2:
Who is the person you trust most?

It's sad to think it just might have been you.

I mean, if I mull it over for more than a second, I know it's not you. It should probably be my parents, who have cared for me for seventeen years and didn't give up on me even when they should have.

But I thought of you, Sheryl, because I trusted you. I told you so much. I don't know why it was you. Out of all the doctors I saw, why *you*?

Maybe I knew you were going to leave.

I always choose those kinds of people.

Before you, though, I think my answer would have been Angel. She's the closest thing I've had to a confidante.

I shouldn't say *thing*. She wasn't a thing. She's a human being, and her name is Angel.

I just realized how weird that is, calling her a human being and identifying her as Angel in the same sentence. Angels aren't supposed to be humans, right? They're divine creations. Celestial beings.

She's not the otherworldly being, though. Benzaiten is.

But I don't really want to write about Benzaiten. I don't even know when we're supposed to meet up again. I guess I just show up whenever I feel like it. I'm the one who made the wish, so I have to meet her halfway.

What if I don't want to meet her, though? What if I don't want to meet anyone anymore?

Anyway, back to Angel. I told you about her before. Not much. I tiptoed around her. I think a part of me worried if I said too much, you would start liking her better than you liked me.

I remember telling you how Angel and I met in the sixth grade and how it would be another three years before we became best friends. Our friendship wasn't a slow burn; it was a contained grease fire. And in our freshman year, the water finally hit us like a tidal wave, leaving us roaring in its wake.

I remember almost nothing about the class I took the summer before sixth grade, aside from the times Angel and I created another inside joke like children forming paper snowflakes or proposed a game to pass the time. She knew more card games than a Vegas dealer. Our classmates marveled at the way she shuffled and flipped the cards from one palm to the other like a magician. But we knew there was no sleight of hand. She always played fair—when it came to cards, anyway.

I once asked how she had mastered so many games, but she only shrugged. I could feel it, her open-book policy slamming shut, protecting the one forbidden page.

When summer evaporated, though, so did our friendship. We didn't exchange numbers. I wasn't on social media, so she couldn't look me up and probably didn't care to try. It was nice while it lasted, but it, like that class, like that summer, was over.

Later, she told me she wondered about me sometimes. I called her a liar, but she swore it was true, and I believed her. Of course I did.

I don't remember how we reconnected. We went to the same high school, but every time I search for that first memory, the moment we locked eyes and recognized the other as that awkward girl from three years ago, I can't find anything. One day, the word *angel* would summon an image of a heavenly being. The next, all I would ever think of was her face. Her laugh, sometimes as small as a whisper but usually loud enough to shake the walls. Her nails, nice when she was in a good mood but torn to shreds every time she fell apart. Her hands, which grasped mine like they had been reaching for me all this time, sifting through the years we had spent apart.

We shouldn't have been friends. Everyone saw that.

Especially us. But we defied the odds. I had never experienced a friendship like that. When we were lying on the floor, telling each other secrets or making noises just to keep ourselves awake, I thought, *This. This is what it's supposed to be like.*

It wasn't just the two of us, though. Come sophomore year, our friendship evolved. It stretched to accommodate a third person. You know about her too, though by now, maybe you've forgotten her. Maybe you've forgotten me.

Her name is Sunny. She and I were close too, but just as we all understood most people who approached us would be interested in Angel, we all understood Angel and I were the real best friends.

So yes. Angel was my best friend and one of the people I trusted most—which is why it hurt so much when everything fell apart.

But you knew that already. You knew it all.

CHAPTER EIGHT

I AM IN a mess of my own making.

I've been taking an English and a math class, but I have so much downtime, I'm almost an entire month ahead of schedule. By the time most of my classmates catch up, it'll almost be Tanabata.

Which is why, after rolling around in bed for a while, opening and closing the blinds until I was afraid I would break them, and reorganizing all the books on my shelf, I decided to go to Benzaiten's shrine.

A decision I now regret.

Why are we here?

Benzaiten glances at my whiteboard, then back up at the dark-brown building before us. The double doors remain closed, though a metal sign claims it's CURRENTLY OPEN. Above the doors, squished between an owl design and an hourglass engraving, is the museum's name: THE GRAND MUSEUM OF MODERN HISTORICAL IMPORTANCE.

"That is quite the name, isn't it?" she asks, reading along with me. She fixes her ponytail, halving the hair and tugging the two pieces apart to tighten the tie. "Well, art and other creative ventures are part of my domain, and I know humans have wonderful artistic abilities. Maybe seeing fellow mortals' talents will help you understand the importance of remaining human."

Okay, but why this particular museum?

"I don't know. I have this strange feeling about this area."

Aren't you supposed to AVOID places with weird vibes?

"No. Certainly not. That would be incredibly boring." She marches toward the front doors. "Let's go."

As soon as we enter, a man pops up.

"Oh my gods," Benzaiten says, putting a hand to her chest like he scared her half to—well, whatever the deity equivalent of death is.

"So sorry, miss," the man says, his voice smooth as he dips into a bow suited for a British soldier. He has clearly startled people before. But when he looks up, his eyebrows shoot to his hairline. "Oh."

I suppress the urge to roll my eyes. Yes, she's beautiful. We get it.

Benzaiten's laugh swirls around us, striking the pop-up man in the chest. He almost stumbles back as she says, "You startled me. Now, how much is a ticket?"

"For you and your"—he shifts his gaze to me—"companion? There can be no charge. You are modern art itself."

Well, not *that* modern.

"Oh, you." Benzaiten puts her hands to her cheeks. "No, it wouldn't feel right to enter without paying. I must support the arts."

I tune out the rest of the exchange. I haven't known her for a week yet, but I'm already over all the fawning. My focus drifts to the rest of the museum. It's set up like a movie theater, the lobby smattered with chrome creations and experimental abstract art I can tell I won't understand. To the left and right are corridors to other exhibits.

"Machi." Benzaiten slips something into my hand and calls out to the man, "Thank you. You're a gem."

I unfurl my fingers and take a look at the admission ticket.

A dollar bill design has been printed on a paper-based card, the material thicker than printer paper but flimsier than cardstock. The word *Art* has been stamped across the front in jet-black ink, likely to show she has paid. Or has had her ticket paid for.

The ticket is the most interesting thing about the museum. Even Benzaiten, patron deity of the arts, can't seem to understand some of the pieces here. She can find the beauty in the horse made of cigarette butts and glass shards, but the longer she stares at the museum's current Piece of the Month, the more her mouth tightens.

"I don't get this one," she declares after a minute.

According to the placard mounted beside the easel, this piece is by an up-and-coming artist with a name made up of only consonants. It was created when the artist got a friend to slap him across the face. The slap sent his head flying onto the easel, supposedly leaving a mark of a thousand different emotions on the canvas.

Which is the long way of saying the easel is blank.

"In any case," Benzaiten says, pivoting on her ballet flat, "I appreciate its originality. Machi, do you like art?"

I shake my head. I was shoved into an art class in elementary school, but it didn't go so well. The teacher called me a good-for-nothing because I cleaned clay off the tables with a crumpled paper towel. She snatched the ball from between my fingers and got me a new one, laying it flat, grabbing my hand, and slamming it onto the single-ply sheet.

Too slow, she said. *And use a whole sheet instead of that little scrap.*

About a week later, I forgot to make a hole to hollow my clay cat. She caught me before I could put it in the kiln and asked, teeth gritted, if I remembered clay pieces will explode if they don't have a hole. If I *wanted* to ruin everyone else's hard work. When I shook my head, she took a fist and smashed my clay, denting the cat's back and sinking its spine to the table.

I didn't tell anyone. The art teacher did that to all of us. She hated every single student in that class. She quit in a fit of rage mid-semester and didn't come back.

That's a pattern, I've realized. Everyone leaves. It's always so suddenly.

I look over at Benzaiten. She turns from the blank canvas and takes my hand.

"Come with me," she says.

I try to pull my hand from hers. I've just barely gotten used to her touching me when she teleports us places. I'm not ready to start clinging to her like we're codependent elementary schoolers the teacher has expressly forbidden from sitting together in class.

"Machi," Benzaiten says, still holding my hand. "Let go a little, okay? It's an art museum, not a battle arena."

I think I would feel more comfortable in a battle arena.

"Trust me," she says.

Why? I almost ask.

Then I realize I do.

I don't know why. I barely know anything about her, and she still doesn't understand changing my wish won't change *me*.

But maybe a small part of me wants to be the person she thinks I am. The kind of person who *can* find the beauty in everything and *doesn't* doubt at every turn. Maybe a small part of me misses being taken along on adventures, no matter how purposeless they seemed. Maybe a small part of me knows doing anything with anyone is better than sitting at home on the peeling loveseat and eating plain toast alone.

So I let her lead me forward.

Once we've managed to extricate ourselves from the sea of

eyes following Benzaiten and that one artist who insisted Benzaiten be her muse—*Just don't make me look pasty like they did in the Edo period*, she replied—we're back at the front entrance.

"Where to next?" she ponders aloud. "How about an art store? Aren't you feeling inspired to create wondrous works of your own? Which is, I may add, something a robot could never do."

I shake my head. She clearly hasn't been keeping up with technological advances. But considering she called my phone a "tippy-tappy device," I don't open that can of worms.

She sets her jaw, folding her arms across her chest, and starts walking. "Fine. We can wander for a while and see if something catches your eye."

A couple of minutes later, we stop. At the end of the block, a single car bumper lies on the sidewalk. Tire marks streak across the road. Most of the scene has been cleared, the police work finished, but a girl sits at the corner, alone. Her knees are bent, her legs forming upside-down *V*s over the pavement. She holds her head in her hands.

My fingers twitch. Even when I pull them into a fist, my hands won't stop shaking.

For a split second, it's like looking into a mirror.

After everything with Angel and Sunny, I spent a lot of time sitting. A lot of time sleepwalking. A lot of time stagnating. I stayed in my room and sat on my bed, set my head on my hands, and felt the weight of the world on my palms.

I was never one to decorate my room, but that summer, I got rid of everything I had ever put up, stripping the few photos of Angel and Sunny from the wall and hiding them deep in my bookshelf. I kept the blinds closed and picked at the paint on the wall, ignoring my parents when they begged me to please, please explain what had happened. They knew it had something to do with Angel and Sunny, but the details weren't clear, and they didn't know my former friends well enough to ask. Every time they wondered if they should try tracking down Angel or Sunny, I started hyperventilating until they promised they wouldn't.

I stare at the girl by the road and take a step toward her.

Benzaiten's hand clamps down on my arm, making me jump.

"No," she says.

I slide my bag off my shoulder and take out my whiteboard, but Benzaiten just says it again, her shoulders stiff: "No."

As Benzaiten looks away, a man in a crisp suit turns the corner, nearly knocking into the girl. She calls out to him, but he doesn't notice, straightening his tie with one hand. A moment later, a person in a bright-yellow feathered chicken costume lopes toward us from a nearby building. The girl hesitates but yells out for help. The chicken doesn't even pause.

"Let's go, Machi." Benzaiten spins on her heel, but I shake my head. "What?"

I don't get it. The girl looks older than the children we've encountered, but she can't be more than twelve or thirteen. It's hard to tell from this distance, at least fifty feet away, but she doesn't seem dangerous. She looks small and sad, and she may need medical attention. I would think Benzaiten would be the first one at her side. She's trying to help *me*, after all, and I can almost guarantee this girl is a lot less hopeless than I am.

"Machi." Benzaiten's voice is cold. Her eyes have cooled to a faint saffron shade, her pupils fossilized in amber. "Let's go."

At least tell me why, I write, but before I can show her the board, voices bounce against the nearby buildings. A horde of college-aged people laugh and chatter about some movie they saw. They're headed straight for the girl. I take a step, ready to intervene if they give her a hard time, but they don't give her a second look. They don't even give her a first one. Instead, they walk right through her.

Through her.

One moment, the girl's hand is extending, her fingers stretching. Then they have passed her, their steps never stuttering, their conversation never halting. The girl remains on the pavement.

The girl appears to flicker, a shaky image on a projector. Her hand, reaching for people halfway down the road, falls to her side. Her fingers vanish for a moment, then fade back in.

Great. Now I'm seeing things.

"Machi," Benzaiten says again.

I take a step forward, but she grabs my wrist and jerks me back too quickly. My head spins. I withdraw, pulling my hand toward my chest.

Her eyes soften. "I'm sorry. Are you okay?"

I don't look at her. My wrist stings. Of course it was a mistake to let her touch me.

"Please," Benzaiten says. "Can we go?"

I raise my head. Tension arcs off her as she brushes her ponytail over her shoulder just to keep her hands busy.

Taking out my whiteboard pen, I write, *What's going on?*

She doesn't meet my eyes. "You aren't losing your mind, if that's what you were thinking."

Explain, I write. The girl gets to her feet, using the base of a streetlamp to support her unsteady legs. She hugs the pole, her head dropped and her hair melting down her thin body.

"She's dead, Machi."

I turn fast enough to nearly give myself whiplash.

"Her physical body was taken away, but her spirit remains here." Benzaiten's hands run along her sleeves. "When human beings don't understand their deaths, and especially when they have strong negative emotions tied to the way they died, they are unable to cross over to the next world. They're stranded here as spirits."

The girl hasn't moved. She looks so much like a normal human. I never believed in ghosts. But then again, I never believed in goddesses either.

"I see spirits all the time." Benzaiten raises a hand from her sleeve to fix her hair, running her fingers through the ends of her ponytail. As the strands spring back into place, her eyes flick to me, then away. "I would think you can only see this girl because you're beside me."

She sees spirits all the time. Does that mean they're everywhere? People who can't grasp the concept of death, who hate what happened and can't find peace, walk the Earth just like the rest of us? Forever?

Isn't there a way to help her?

"No." She turns. "We're going now."

I glance back at the girl. Her arms flicker as she clings to the streetlight.

"I'm thinking we could stop by an art store. I know you said you didn't want to, but sometimes, you don't know how much creative soul you have until you're in a store full of art supplies, you know?"

She's talking a mile a minute now. I stop walking to write. She takes a few more steps before realizing I'm no longer with her.

There really isn't anything we can do?

"I said no," she tells me, and then, all at once, she's furious. "I *told* you there's nothing I can do. Why don't you believe me?"

My lips part instinctively, but I don't speak.

Her irises flash deep orange and gold, a fast-motion explosion. "You know, I try to push you in a nice way. Get you out of your comfort zone. But you're not getting *me* out of my comfort zone. You don't even *need* to get me out of my comfort zone. *I'm* helping *you*, remember? So *stop*, Machi. Just stop."

I shrink back. The edge of my whiteboard cuts into my side, below my bottom rib. My heart thunders in my chest. I can hear my breath in my ear. I can't take my eyes off her face, where her emotions are layered one over the other, rage rippling through her like a mounting earthquake.

She looks so much like Angel, it takes my breath away.

I'm still trying to remember how to breathe when she returns us to the shrine. Then, before I can even consider apologizing, she's gone.

I stand at the edge of the path. I'm not stupid enough to think she's going to reappear. I know once she leaves, she's not returning. But I stand there anyway, holding a staring contest with the hand-sized Benzaiten figurine placed on the altar.

I don't know what I did to upset her so badly.

The real Benzaiten. Not her figurine.

A flicker of a smile pulls at my mouth. She would have laughed at that.

Or maybe not. It's not like I know her.

I've just started to turn when something flashes in the corner of my vision. I whip around, one hand wrapped tightly around the strap of my bag. My eyes scrape along the sides of the road. For a split second, I'm certain I see a pair of eyes, impossibly blue, the color of the clearest sapphires. But then I blink, and it's gone.

I wait another minute, scanning every inch of my surroundings, the faint chime of a bell on a store door around the corner marking each passing second.

Nothing.

Hi, Mom,

Remember when I used to leave you apology notes? I can't do that since you're not here, and you would probably rip it up anyway, so I'm writing this on my laptop, your email address in the "To" line.

I probably should have done this earlier. Not just because of our fight. Because of everything.

I've been getting into a lot of arguments lately. It feels like all I ever do is make everyone around me mad. I don't mean to. I don't know why I'm like this. I've been going to therapy for a year now, and I'm not any better. In fact, I think things have only gotten worse. Ever since Sheryl left, I just don't see a point.

I still think your email address is hilarious. You didn't realize you had to use the same email whenever you logged in, so you mashed your fingers on the keyboard, then had to contact customer support because you couldn't remember your own creation. Ah, the early days of the internet.

I always wondered why you didn't make a different email. When I asked, you told me it was because you already signed up for newsletters and eBills with that account. I said I would help you switch over, but you declined. Now I wonder if it's because it's your reminder: "This is what happens when you don't think things through."

Maybe that's a reach.

I didn't mean to make you hang up the other day. It's been a couple of days now, and we still haven't really spoken.

I'm sorry I wasn't at the funeral. I can't imagine what it's like to lose your parents.

Things were complicated with them. They were always pushing us to move back. I didn't get why. In a twisted way, I think I understood it better when I was younger, and as time went on, I lost touch with the part of me that wanted to move just to *make them happy. Because how could they want us there, in that town, where you spent eighteen miserable years putting up with ignorant people? The other children asked so many questions: Why did you look like that? Why didn't you have the latest toy? What was the point of folding paper? How was that fun? Were you making a fortune teller, at least? Or a plane? No? Then you were boring and weird.*

It didn't get better in high school. If you were lucky, people ignored you. If you weren't, the only guys interested in you were the ones who thought "yellow fever" was something to brag about—an inside joke, a conquest.

You rarely talk about it, but I remember the one time you did. It was right after the holidays. Your parents had been bugging you to move back home the whole time, right up until we left them at the airport. Back then, I didn't realize how much it bothered you. I was too busy selfishly thinking about how moving there meant my Christmas presents wouldn't get smashed in my grandparents' suitcase.

When you saw me standing in the doorway, you wiped your tears as best you could and said you were fine. I was old enough to know you were lying.

If Dad had been around, you probably would have talked to him instead. I realize now how often you would hold your tongue just to keep me from tasting the poison in your mouth. But he was already back at the office, finishing up something that, apparently, couldn't wait until after the holidays. You needed someone, but all you had was me.

The story trickled out of you like blood. I did my best to patch you up, but I've never been good at making anyone feel better.

You told me you were proud of yourself for leaving. Proud of yourself for insisting that your parents fly to our town if they wanted to see us. You swore you weren't going back.

But you did.

You don't have to say it's because you can't stop picturing them in their old house, their souls gone and their bodies growing cold. I know. And I'm sorry, but that doesn't mean you have to act like everything is better. You can love the town for being their home and not for the way it made you hate your face. You can be thankful for the neighbors and still hate them for spitting words at you every January, when you and your parents set out kagami mochi instead of a light-up HAPPY NEW YEAR sign.

You can say your parents made mistake after mistake, from the moment they decided to have a child in a town like that to the last time they called you up and pressured you to move home for the tenth time that month, and still miss them.

I wish I could tell you all of these things. But now that I've gotten to the end of my apology, I realize you won't listen. You don't want to hear these things. You'll delete this email because you were never good at handling grief. So I'll save you the trouble and erase this message before I even send it.

I am sorry. For a lot of things. More than I will say.

Love,
Machi

Delete.

CHAPTER NINE

I DO SEND my mother an apology, but it's a paragraph-long text instead of an email essay.

"Machi," my mother says when she calls on Saturday morning. "I got your text. I'm sorry for hanging up on you. That's all I wanted to say."

I sit on the floor, watching old reruns. I've been doing that a lot. Reading books, listening to songs, half-focusing on episodes I've already read and heard and seen. I'm sick of the unfamiliar. I want to know exactly how everything ends.

I text my father again. I'm sorry. I should have gone.

"Well," my mother says once my father has read my message aloud, "I'm not about to disagree with you." She takes a breath. "We're cleaning out the house now. I had no idea there was so much stuff. I don't know how this old house held it all."

I wish I could ask her what it's like to be back. When she enters her childhood bedroom, turned into a guest room and never used once she left, what does she feel? Are her yearbooks still there? Has she flipped through the pages and touched the inch-high portraits of every kid who called her names or pushed her down or told her to go back to her own country? When she tries to fall asleep, does she feel the ghosts of her parents beside her? Does she imagine them angry, their mouths twisted as they say it took her until their deaths to come home?

What if their ghosts *are* there? What if, at this very moment, they're curled up next to her, flickering like the girl outside the museum?

Maybe they're not with her. Maybe they're with me. Maybe every time they see me picking up my whiteboard marker instead of opening my mouth, they shake their heads, even more disappointed with me in death than they were in life.

So many people, including my mother, have endured worse than I have. They don't lose their voices. They don't withdraw from society, leaving school and holing up in their rooms. They don't force their parents to pay for doctor after doctor.

There are days when I visualize what it would be like to open my mouth and talk. My mother asks, *How was your appointment?* and I reply, *Fine*, like it's nothing. Like every other seventeen-year-old does when a parent asks a question.

We used to be so much better than that. I didn't consider my mother my best friend, especially not once I got close to Angel and Sunny, but I trusted her with everything. I even thought one day, if I ever got married, I would seriously consider making her my matron of honor instead of Angel—though that was partly because I had the feeling Angel's plans for a bachelorette party would kill me before I could ever walk down the aisle.

It wasn't just because of my fear of what Angel could do, though. It was also because my mother understood me in a way no one else could. She had never been as shy as I was, even before I stopped speaking, but she knew what it was like to feel alone. Her differences were more immediately visible than mine, her face the only Asian one in the crowd of pre-schoolers shouting "Jingle Bells" at the winter program, but she knew, driving me home as I cried about my old tote bag or the dodgeball game where someone beaned me with a ball hard enough to make my bones ache, exactly what I needed to hear.

"Anyway," my mother says now, "I should go."

I listen to the *beep, beep, beep* as she hangs up.

I DON'T KNOW if two days is enough time for Benzaiten to forgive me, but I figure if she's really going to grant my (revised, unwanted, straight-out-of-a-self-help-book) prayer, we should probably stop avoiding each other.

In the early afternoon, I return to the shrine and take a nickel from my wallet. When I was buying bananas the other day, I had to ask the cashier, via whiteboard, to give me change in nickels and pennies. He was not amused. I wished Benzaiten had been with me. He would have emptied out the register.

She catches the coin just before it falls through the slats of the offering box. "Are you going to insist on trying to pay me every time you want me to appear?"

I shrug. I don't know how else to summon her.

She holds out her hand, and when I open my palm, she drops the coin. I put it back in my wallet and take out my whiteboard.

"Can I go first?" She sits on the offering box, fixing her dress to hang just above her ankles. "I'm sorry."

I blink. That's not what I was expecting. On my way here, I was kicking myself for not writing out an apology on paper ahead of time to save us the trouble of awkwardly standing around while I scribbled out my woes.

"Can you not look so surprised?" She flips her ponytail over her shoulder. "Deities can express their regrets, you know. Mostly over more devastating things, like the time Ebisu accidentally destroyed an entire—well, that's not important." She huffs. "I'm sorry, okay?"

Me too. I didn't mean to hurt you.

"I know. I know I should have explained what was upsetting me, but I didn't." She leans forward, resting her elbows on her knees. "I don't do well with child spirits."

Because you care so much about children?

I can understand that. No one likes knowing a person's life has been cut short, but it must be especially painful for someone who cares about young children the way Benzaiten does. I haven't forgotten how her expression softened the moment she saw the boy running his scooper through the water, his motions too deliberate to catch the fish he wanted so badly.

"It's more than that," she says, rising from the box. Her eyes glisten. "I mean, of course it's a reason why. But it goes beyond that." Her ballet flat touches the stone path but makes no sound. "It seems you aren't the only one with buried secrets after all."

We stand, hardly half a foot apart. I watch her, my eyes skimming along the dark lines of her hair, the curve of her shoulder as she lifts a hand to brush her bangs out of her face. She won't look at me.

"I also lied." Her golden eyes flick to me, then away. "A little."

I give her a questioning look, not bothering to write on my whiteboard.

"It hurt, seeing the girl by herself." She takes my hand and examines it like it's her own. I stiffen, but her touch is too gentle for me to justify pulling away. "I didn't want to leave her. Of course I didn't. I told myself a spiritual leader would find and rescue her, but I can't stop thinking about her. I need to go back. Will you come with me?"

I nod, already erasing my board and sliding it into my bag. As much as I don't like knowing she lied, I have to admit it's a relief. If a goddess couldn't help that girl, who could?

She runs her index finger along my knuckles, her fingertip rising and falling. "Let's go."

For a split second, I feel a pang of regret.

I obviously want Benzaiten to help the girl. She shouldn't have to sit out there alone.

But what if we can't help her? What if Benzaiten tries and nothing happens? What if she calls her deity friends, all the other Gods of Fortune, the girl seeing as many gods as I've seen therapists, and every single one fails her? What if the girl keeps fading faster and faster, and no matter what we do, it isn't enough, and one day, she's just . . . gone?

I close my eyes, and though I only meant to steady myself, Benzaiten takes the flutter of my eyelids as a sign of acquiescence. The wind picks up, butterfly kisses on my cheek. By the time my eyelids lift, we're back at the corner. The air smells like smoke and leaves. Somewhere in the distance, electronic music blasts from speakers. If we were any closer, we would feel the ground shaking.

The girl rests against the same streetlamp, her legs crumpled beneath her and her head propped up on her arms. She's fainter now, her body nearly translucent. If I look closely, I can see the green paint of the streetlamp through her abdomen. Every few seconds, she glitches like a buggy video game character, parts of her disappearing and reappearing.

Benzaiten takes a deep breath, her eyes fixed on the young girl. "I can do this. I can do this. I'm Benzaiten. I can do this."

I nod, the best encouragement I can give.

"Machi." Her voice trembles. She says it again. "Machi. I don't want you getting close to her. You've never been around spirits before, but even if they seem harmless, they're here because of their unresolved trauma. They may unintentionally hurt you."

I reach for my whiteboard to ask what she means, but she's

already moving, her steps fast and even, her dress swishing above her ballet flats. She doesn't slow until we're within ten feet of the girl. Then her movements are quiet. Careful.

"Hello, child," Benzaiten says, crouching beside the streetlamp.

The girl lets out a sigh, her voice wobbly. Her breath clatters up her throat like a train on an old track as she tries to speak.

"Shh. It's all right. You're tired."

The girl's eyes are huge, pushing the rest of her features toward her chin. I'm certain she's about to cry.

God, I know how that feels.

But instead of reaching up to wipe her tears, she shoots her hands out, lightning fast, to snatch Benzaiten's sleeves. She's frantic, an inhuman sound scraping out of her as she yanks the goddess closer.

I don't think. I just leap forward. At the sound of my boots on the pavement, the girl spins around. Her desperate hands reach for me, and as soon as her fingers touch my skin, I'm gone.

IN THE DANCE studio, she is a snowflake. In the dance studio, she is special. In the dance studio, she is home.

She loves every minute of dance class, but her favorite part is when Madame Franklin turns on the wintry music, piano notes gliding from the ceiling speakers, and lets the girls dance, a cooldown before they return to their parents. She imagines she is pure crystal, or whatever snowflakes are made of, and it doesn't matter if her bun is too tight and her mother has poked too many bobby pins into her scalp. She is beautiful.

She liked elementary school, but everything about middle school is worse. She hates her teachers. She hates her class-mates. She hates her body.

But then Madame Franklin teaches her how to use dance

steps to memorize formulas. Madame Franklin says it doesn't matter what other people think of her as long as she is working to better herself. Madame Franklin says she can see so much grace in the way she moves, and she realizes maybe life isn't so bad.

Except.

Except there is one thing Madame Franklin can't fix.

It was an open secret before she knew what an open secret was. Her mother knew, certainly, but so did the neighbors. The teachers. The bartenders at every counter in a five-mile radius. They all feel sorry for her.

Sometimes they say it. The neighbors stand outside in the open hallway, gossiping between drags of thin cigarettes.

That poor woman and her daughter. Stuck with such a deadbeat. He told me the other day he was going to pick her up from school, but guess who I saw with that girl when they came home? Not her father. That's for sure.

More often, she sees it on their faces. Her elementary school teachers were more concerned, calling her parents for conferences and never registering anything but resigned disappointment when her father failed to show. Her middle school teachers know only because of an incident at the one conference her father actually attended, but she doesn't like remembering what happened then.

When she was four, she thought if she stayed up long enough, he would come home and be better.

When she was seven, she thought if she studied hard enough, danced well enough, he would come home and be better. So she studied harder. Danced better. Harder. Better. Harder. Better. She just wanted him to see her. Be with her. Clap for her. She would be more interesting than the taste of liquor. More surprising than the twist of lime. More charming than the twenty-something-year-old who liked cosmopolitans.

and sipped with four fingers touching the straw. She would be all he ever wanted.

For years, she has pushed herself, dancing until her feet are close to cracking and bleeding into the crevices of her shoes. She dreams of only one thing: being Clara in the one-night special performance of *The Nutcracker*, put on in early June to kick off the local Winter in Summer Festival. She asks Madame Franklin to give her extra lessons, and though it makes the other studio girls hate her, she doesn't care. She knows what she wants, and she isn't going to stop until she gets it.

When she is twelve, Madame Franklin squeezes her hands, tears in her eyes, and says, *You're ready.*

And she is. She tells everyone. She tries not to talk about ballet with her friends too much because they don't get it, but she can't contain herself. They scream with her, and they don't even care if it's just a Christmas special in June. She brags about it when she's stuck in the elevator with the woman who smells like vanilla extract. She finds her father, catching him just before he leaves for work, and finally says it: *I'm Clara, Papa. I'm going to be Clara.*

He takes her in his arms and lifts her into the air, the best dance partner she will ever have. He twirls her, and she is a snowflake again, so carefree, so special. When he sets her back on her feet, her cheeks are wet.

He promises he will be there. He will be in the front row. She tells him he can't be in the front row because it's reserved for the teachers and the press. *The second row then*, he says, and she believes him.

The day of the showcase arrives. Her father isn't home yet, but she isn't worried.

The evening arrives. The vanilla neighbor has to drive them to the venue because her father has the car and didn't manage to get back in time to pick them up, but she isn't worried.

The hour before curtains arrives. Her father isn't in the audience yet, but she isn't worried.

She steps onto the stage. She scans the crowd. She locates her mother. Her lovely mother with the pale face and the tremulous smile. The spot beside her is filled, but not by her father. It's someone whispering in the ear of the man next to her. She thinks she recognizes her as one of the other girls' mothers.

She isn't worried.

She is crushed.

Sorrow sends the ribbons in her hair fluttering through the sweating summer air. Grief anchors her when she spins until the audience is dizzy. Fury launches her up to the skies, making her wonder if she will ever come back down. She puts everything she has into that performance. She dances like it's the last time.

The rest of the cast emerges to take their final bows. And then he is there, all the way at the back, a wilted rose clutched in his hand. She can see his apologies scrawled over his face, and it makes him blurry. The curtain falls.

Gorgeous. Showstopping. A star-making performance. No one could take their eyes off her. She is one to watch. That's what they say.

But she doesn't care about them.

Her mother finds her first. Her mother always finds her first. Her mother's voice is high and quivering, uncertain hands around a wound bleeding too fast to fix. Then her father is there, and he's saying he's sorry. He's so sorry. He lost track of time. He will make it up to her. He promises he will. Just like how he promised he would be at the performance.

He smells like beer and sweat.

Madame Franklin says not to get into the car with him. She says to stay for a little while. She even pleads. But her mother insists they get home because she is tired. They are all tired. And very proud. Yes. Very proud.

Her father is still apologizing when they get to the car. Her mother sits in the passenger's seat, as always, because she doesn't know how to drive. Her father is saying he is so, so sorry. Every time he says it, he adds another *so*, and soon she's thinking, *So. So what? Suck on your* so. *Sew your* so *shut.*

But then she's crying because she wants his *so*. She wants his *I'm so proud* and his *I'm so happy* and his *I'm so much better now*. And then she's thinking about the way *so* sounds like *snow*, and then how *snow* sounds like *show*—

And then her father is weaving more than she was at the climax of the ballet. Is it because he is *so* drunk? Or because he is *so* sorry? He is reaching for her, trying to give her the rose he had forgotten to hand her when he found her. He had been twirling it nervously the whole time, and she hadn't said anything because she didn't want his stupid rose. She just wanted him.

Her mother screams. There are words, maybe, but they don't sound like anything in particular. The pitch clashes with the screech of tires, the honk of the other car's horn, the shouting in the street.

She thought she would never fly higher than she did on that stage, but she was wrong. She thought she would never feel more fear than when she couldn't find his face in the crowd, but she was wrong. She thought this show would fix everything, but she was wrong.

She thought he would be there and she would be enough, but she was wrong.

She lies on the street. She imagines she is making a snow angel, though she has never made one before. She is beautiful. She is a snowflake. She is special.

She can't keep her eyes open. Her eyelids are so heavy. She

can't hear anything. Her ears are full of snow. Her lips form the word *Papa*. Then the snowflakes fill her mouth.

She closes her eyes.

BENZAITEN TAKES THE girl's hand, severing the connection. I stagger back, but the sudden motion throws me off balance. I stumble to the pavement. The impact stuns me, leaving me on the ground with a throbbing tailbone.

"Shh," Benzaiten says to the girl. "Shh." She takes the girl in her arms, simultaneously restraining and embracing her, and looks over at me. "Are you all right?"

I can't decide whether to nod or shake my head.

"Hold on. I need to get her under control first." Benzaiten's eyes tear away and fix themselves on the girl's face. "Shh-shh-shh. It's okay. I'm here. I hear you."

"Ahhh," the girl moans. Drops of moonlight fall from the girl's face but dissipate midair.

The goddess holds the flickering girl. "I'm here. I'm listening. I have you."

"Aaah." The girl covers her face. She takes a shaky breath. "Papa."

The girl leans her head on the goddess's shoulder. Together, they weep.

CHAPTER TEN

I DON'T LIKE to think about it, but not long after I fell silent, my parents and I were almost in a car accident.

We were on our way to a doctor's appointment. Of course. It was before Sheryl, but after I had been declared physically healthy. It was quiet in the car. I didn't say anything, obviously, but my parents didn't either. They just stared straight ahead, their jaws clenched. I was in that haze, not asleep but not entirely conscious either. I was drifting from my body, out of the vehicle, hovering above the car like a plastic bag taped to the sunroof.

I remember what I was thinking: I was imagining what I might have been like if, rather than tumbling into a friendship with Angel, I had waited for Sunny instead. She was more like me. Me before Angel. If it had been just Sunny and me, maybe things would have been different. She wouldn't have ditched her study group, taken me by the hand, and raced out of the library just to dance in the rain. She would have hunkered down right beside me and helped me make flash cards. The kinds written on multicolored index cards, linked together on a sturdy metal ring. I wouldn't have spent summers café-hopping, accompanying Angel on her quest to find the coffee shop with the best refreshers; I would have gone to Sunny's concerts and clapped my hardest after every one of her solos, telling anyone who would listen, *That's my best friend.* Maybe if it had been Sunny, I never would have gotten close to Angel at all, and Angel wouldn't have even known anything about Sunny.

But it hadn't happened that way. My best friend had been Angel, and Sunny had joined us later, completing our mortal, once-untouchable trinity. And my mouth was so bitter with regret.

I wasn't paying attention when the near-accident happened. All I knew was one moment, I was biting my lip. The next, the car was swerving, and my father was swearing, and my mother was shouting, and when I looked up, there was a huge truck barreling toward us, the blare of its horn slicing the morning air, and all I could think was: *I'm okay with this.*

I'm okay with this because there's no point in anything.

I'm okay with this because this is probably the most exciting thing that will ever happen to me.

I'm okay with this. And I hope Angel and Sunny aren't.

A sick thing to think. I thought I knew it then, as the words were drifting through the fog. I thought I knew it immediately afterward, as the truck passed us and my father pulled over to the side of the road and my mother thanked God again and again. But only now do I truly realize it. How twisted, how selfish I was to have wanted something like that to happen when this girl *truly* suffered. When she *truly* died.

Is that wrong? To feel like, because someone has gone through something worse, my pain no longer matters? To feel like my prayer—whether it's to regain my voice or become a robot vacuum cleaner—is meaningless compared to a girl's simple wish to be seen? To live?

Benzaiten still has a little under four weeks to change my mind.

This girl has no time at all.

But I'm still hurting. I'm still aching. I'm still waking up disappointed. In myself. In my life. In everything, all the time.

Angel once said no good comes from comparing trauma. If you're hurting, you're hurting. That's all there is to it.

Can I trust her words, though, when she's a big part of why I'm hurting?

The pavement is uneven and cold beneath my boots. Maybe it's just because I know what happened on this very road, but something about it feels eerie, like I'm standing on the edge of this world and the next.

When I look over at Benzaiten, she's sliding a ten-dollar bill out of her sleeve. I have yet to figure out how money appears there.

"Could you get her something to eat?" she asks me. "Whatever's close and easy to hold."

I glance at the girl. I didn't realize spirits could eat.

Shaking off the shock, I start searching for food like a nervous wood mouse. I'm afraid I'm going to wind up wandering the streets for hours, lost in an unfamiliar neighborhood, but when I turn a corner, I spot a cart set up by the road, a cardboard sign hanging from the front.

"Ice cream?" the vendor asks, eyes on her phone.

I take a step back. It just had to be ice cream. It isn't the same brand as Angel's former favorite, but it hurts to see anyway. And I hate that it hurts. I don't want to be doomed to remember forever. I don't want to shut down my own thoughts every time I see something I can connect to her or Sunny. I don't want all the pain to pile up, one speck of lint at a time, until I collapse under the weight of it all.

"We got chocolate, vanilla, strawberry, and nee-oh-politan," the woman says.

I'm pretty sure it's nee-ah-politan. I remember because Angel practically cried over thinking it was Neopolitan for fifteen years. *Like Cosmopolitan, you know?* But then *cosmopolitan* reminds me of the woman the girl pictured with her father at the bar.

"Hello?" the vendor waves a hand over my face. "You there?" Not really.

I point at the Neapolitan. I don't know which flavor the girl likes. The vendor returns my change, hands me a small ice cream carton, and slaps a flat wooden stick on the lid. I dip my head, feeling the ice chipping along the edge of the cardboard.

When I reach Benzaiten, she thanks me and accepts the carton and spoon.

"This ice cream is three flavors in one," she declares, as if giving an oral report. "Mortals are so indecisive."

The girl has quieted down. She flickers in and out of sight, her skin deathly pale, but she manages to curl up beside the goddess and eat spoonful after spoonful of ice cream.

I do my best not to stare, but it's hard. Every time the girl blinks, I'm afraid her eyes are never going to open, and she'll be only a husk, her mouth going slack and her arms falling limp at her sides like the straps of my old bag.

"Is it good?" Benzaiten asks, her voice kind.

The girl nods, then opens her mouth for more, craning her neck to see how much is left.

When she's about halfway through the carton, a college-aged boy passes us, whistling a pop song. I look up. He glances at us, then does a double take, his whistling cut short. He narrows his eyes but doesn't seem to quite see the girl. He turns and resumes his whistling, louder this time.

"Don't worry," Benzaiten says as he disappears around the corner. "He doesn't think a cup of ice cream is floating midair. As long as she's holding it, he won't be able to see it."

I lift my eyes to her, but she's still watching the girl.

"The food is helping her regain spiritual energy," Benzaiten continues. "Once she recovers, she may become visible to other mortals, especially because she's close to me."

I nod. A few people pass, but they don't pay attention to any of us. Not even Benzaiten.

"Rest," Benzaiten says to the girl, who closes her eyes and appears to fall asleep on the goddess's lap. Benzaiten takes the empty carton, sets the spoon at the bottom, and moves it to her side. "Are you all right? That was a nasty fall earlier."

I shrug. It wasn't that bad. The things I saw were far more painful.

"When spirits are spiraling like that, their memories splash everywhere. They can't think rationally. That's why you saw her"—she runs her hand along the girl's hair—"final moments."

The girl's face is soft as she rests, her expression peaceful. I hate myself for thinking she looks the way she did when she lay on the street. Dying. I saw her memories as if I were a third-person observer *and* through her own eyes, simultaneously. I saw her grief, her pain, her stress, her momentary happiness, from every angle.

Benzaiten hums, her voice strong but quiet as she holds the girl's head in her lap. "She has entered a meditative state. It isn't quite like sleeping, but it serves a similar purpose. She isn't used to it yet, so she may not stay this way for long. Hopefully, when she opens her eyes, she will have recovered more energy."

My eyes fall to the girl. Her outline has grown brighter. Her fingers loosely grasp the hem of Benzaiten's dress.

I slip my bag off my shoulder and set my whiteboard on my lap. *What happens when she wakes up? How do we help her?*

The space between Benzaiten's eyebrows narrows as she frowns. "I am expected to send her to the spirit world."

What does that mean?

Behind her, a rat crosses the street. It doesn't look or act like a street rat, or even like the rats at the Yip Yap Shelter. Its body is sleek, its movements methodical. When it reaches the other side and turns, I swear it's staring at us.

"It means I'm supposed to stabilize her and transport her to the world where spirits and deities roam," Benzaiten says, pulling my attention away from the rat. "Some mortals work there too, but it's primarily meant for those who aren't from your world."

I look back at the edge of the street, but the rat has vanished.

After one last glance at the road, I write, *What happens to her then?*

The goddess clenches her teeth, her jawline sharpening. "She is put under the spiritual council's supervision, and the members of the council determine where she goes next."

I try to imagine what a spiritual council would be like, but all I can picture is a bunch of people under white sheets, eyeholes punched through so they can still read their spiritual agendas.

I take my time writing my words, fixing the letters to put off asking the question. *Is there something wrong with that? You seem unsettled.*

She brushes her bangs to the side. "That is what I am expected to do. I never said it's what I want."

The girl stirs, her eyes opening. Her gaze latches onto me first before sliding over to Benzaiten. She sits up, her movements slow, and studies her own hands, then the goddess's face. "What happened to me?"

"It's all right, child. You're safe with us." Benzaiten's smile is gentle. The girl drinks it in. "I am the goddess Benzaiten, and this is my friend, Machi."

I twitch at the word *friend*. I don't know what else she could have called me—assistant, maybe, or amenable hostage—but I bite my tongue until it feels like it could fall out of my mouth.

"We're here to help you. What do you think we could do?"

The girl shakes her head. The memories seem to return gradually, a reverse leak back into her bones. Her arms pull her knees closer to her body. "I just want my mama and papa." Benzaiten's eyes flash, a miniature spark, but the girl doesn't notice. She rocks forward, then back. "I want to dance for them again."

"I'm sorry," Benzaiten whispers.

I erase my board and place it in my bag. I don't want to think about her parents. If they're alive, they must blame themselves. The girl loved her father so much, it hurt. Even her mother's quiet, steady love wasn't enough. Her poor mother. Her poor father. A selfish part of me wishes we had never seen the girl at all.

"I know," the girl says. She takes her index and middle fingers and sets them on her knee, forming an upside-down *V*. She lifts her index finger until it runs parallel with the road. The other finger remains straight down. They look like the legs of a ballerina. "Then could I dance for you instead?"

Benzaiten's eyes warm, molten gold. "Of course."

Even with the goddess's support, the girl struggles to stand. I toss the ice cream carton in the trash. I've just dropped my arm to my side when the girl looks up at me. The desperation swimming in her pupils sends a shiver down my spine. I tell myself it's just from the chill of the ice cream container.

As I watch, my arms clamped against my rib cage, the girl extends her free hand.

I haven't touched anyone's hand, aside from Benzaiten's, in at least a year. And the worst part is knowing I will never remember whether it was Angel or Sunny or what we were doing or why or whether it was because they were laughing or because they were crying or just *because*.

The girl flickers.

So I take her hand.

She's cold. Inhumanly so. But something about that feels right.

Together, we stumble to the outdoor stage, a simple wooden block in an empty field. No chairs have been set out.

Once the girl reaches the center of the stage, Benzaiten and I stand in the open space, the grass tickling my ankles. Above us, the sun hides behind the clouds.

The girl takes her position. She lowers her head, one arm curved out and the other gently arched over her head. She rises onto her toes, then lifts her eyes to the skies. She twirls. She dips. She leaps. Her feet are soundless on the stage. Mid-performance, as she sails from one spot to the next, a ray of sunlight bursts out from the clouds, striking her just so.

That's when I see it. What she could have been if she had grown up. Her limbs are longer, and her neck is graceful, her features accented by the faintest dusts of makeup. She is stretching toward the sun, reaching for the light, her fingers so close I can almost believe she'll make it.

The girl moves into her final pose, so small at the center of the wooden stage, and the illusion shatters. My eyes sting as Benzaiten and I clap. Benzaiten takes her dainty fingers and places them in her mouth to let out a sharp whistle. Then she steps up and joins the girl onstage.

"You were amazing," Benzaiten says. She wipes away a tear, glistening silver, and bows. "It was an honor to watch you."

I nod. I wish I could say more, but even if I could speak, I don't know what I would say. There's something indescribable about the way the girl dances, something that can't be put into words. The curve of her back, the line from the start of her leg to her pointed toe, the purposeful and fluid motion from one position to another—it was all so beautiful. And she was so alive.

"Now what happens?" the girl asks. She should be winded

after such a dynamic performance, but her chest is still, neither rising nor falling.

Benzaiten doesn't answer at first. She holds her arms close to her chest, her eyes murky. I search them for meaning but find nothing but barely restrained anger.

"I need to send you to the spirit world," she finally says. Her hands clench at her sides. "I need to do it."

I watch her for a moment. I can't understand why she seems so reluctant to send the girl to the council. She said that's what she's supposed to do, so why wouldn't she just do it? There's a reason why people create rules. Why things work the way they do. Why robot vacuum cleaners don't beep angrily until they get their way. The girl clearly doesn't belong here; she was falling apart when we found her. So why not just let her go?

Because it's hard.

Letting go.

The girl looks up at Benzaiten, fear glinting in her dark eyes. "What is it like?"

"There is a council meant to protect you. I will do everything in my power to ensure you are happy with their decision." Her fingers wrap around her thumb, straining like they want to tear themselves apart. "I want to do more for you, but I can't. I can only do this."

What else could she do, though? I don't think the girl expected Benzaiten to bring her back to life. She just doesn't want to stay here anymore, stuck in limbo. Sending her on is the kindest thing to do.

"Okay." The girl nods. "Thank you."

Breathing slowly, I take her hand. She turns to me, tears in her eyes. I squeeze her palm, and she tries to squeeze back. Her fingers buzz against mine. A drop falls down her cheek, shining until it hits the wooden floor and melts away.

"I am so proud of you," Benzaiten says. "You are such a beautiful soul. You deserved much, much better."

Tear after tear trickles from the girl's closed eyes. "Thank you."

Benzaiten places both hands on the girl's head, inhales, and whispers a string of words I can't make out. The girl's edges illuminate, subtle enough at first to make me think it could be my imagination. When the glow grows too bright, I close my eyes. Something flashes white, and when I look back, the girl is gone.

Benzaiten says nothing. Her hands fall to her sides, but a moment later, they fly up to the back of her head. She slides out her tie, her hair pouring over her shoulders.

"Are you happy now?"

I flinch—but she isn't speaking to me. Her eyes scan the open field. I do the same, but all I can see is stillness.

Then, in the corner of my eye, something silver skitters into view. A rat. Is it following us?

"I know you're here." Benzaiten's thin fingers return to her hair. She puts it back in a half-up, half-down style and sets her hands on her hips. "There's no point in hiding."

"Never said I was hiding."

I startle and turn as a figure appears behind the silver rat. He steps forward, squinting in the light. His hair is dark, but his eyes are darker. For a heartbeat, they appear blue, two spots of a contained ocean. Stubble dots his chin, but he doesn't look older than twenty-five.

He's also holding a large hammer.

I slide behind Benzaiten, peeking over her shoulder. Her arm extends, a barrier against the man.

"Relax," he says. I can't tell if he's speaking to me.

"We'll be fine." Benzaiten's arm stays steady. "Once you leave."

He takes his hammer and sets its head in the grass. As he leans on it, I realize it's a rice mallet. Though that doesn't make him any less frightening.

"You have no right to be here," Benzaiten says.

The rat scurries to the man's side and sits beside his boot. It doesn't seem much like the rats at the Yip Yap Shelter. Its nose doesn't twitch. It doesn't skitter from side to side. It's unnaturally still, its head raised to its owner's face.

"Thought you were staying away from the mortal world."

"Yeah, but then I realized *you* were in the other world, so, you know." She lifts her shoulders. "Decided to get away."

His eyes soften. Light shines through his irises, turning them a deep cerulean. "We don't have to be enemies."

"Except we do, and we are." She crosses her arms but steps to the left to block me from his sight. I crane my neck, curious now. "You have no reason to stalk me. I did the right thing."

"You did," he says, and I can feel her momentary shock like an arc of electricity. "You did well."

The pleasant surprise fizzles out. "I don't need your praise."

"All right." He switches his mallet to his other hand, letting it cut through the air before placing it on the ground. He steps to the side until we can see each other and gives me a solemn nod. I have the stupid urge to nod back, as if we're classmates passing each other in the hall: *Hey, man. Hey, dude.* But I was never the type to greet people at school anyway, the way Serena was. I really only spoke to Angel and Sunny.

"Leave." Benzaiten's dress waves in the breeze, her sleeves the softest part of her. "I said I never wanted to see you again."

He opens his mouth but says nothing. He nods again. In a flash of white light, he disappears. I search the grass, but the rat is gone too.

Benzaiten takes a step forward and pivots to face me. Her expression is somber, her eyes a stagnant gold. "If you ever run into him, Machi?" She leans close. "Stay far, far away."

Prompt #3:
What event in your life made a major impression on you?

Well, how much time *do* you have, Sheryl?

I don't know why I'm still writing to you. This is supposed to be my journal, after all. I guess it just makes me feel better. Especially since I still look you up every once in a while, only to find absolutely nothing new. Where are you? Where did you go? Why aren't you coming back?

I guess I'm doing this because I don't have anything else to do. I finished more of my homework for my online classes. Benzaiten was in a weird mood after our last outing (it's a long story), and I didn't feel like going to the shelter, especially after seeing that rat (again, it's a long story).

So here I am. Thinking about things I don't want to remember.

I don't think I ever told you about this, but something else happened between the time I met Angel and the time we actually became friends.

I'm not sure why I mentioned Angel. She doesn't have anything to do with this story. And I mean it. There isn't some psychologically deep reason why I brought her up. There is really, truly no reason. Except, I guess, it just goes to show how she once occupied every space in my mind, blighting memories she wasn't even in.

In the sixth grade, my classmates and I had to go on this camping trip. It was meant to create long-lasting bonds and prepare us for the harsh realities of the outdoors or something, but it mostly taught me how greasy my hair could get in a day or two.

Throughout our all-day hike, which was even more miserable than it sounds, the group leader kept stopping to point out invasive plants. At one point, he even ripped some out with his bare hands and released a tremendous roar. I was surprised he didn't stuff them into his mouth just to add to the ambience.

There was one part of the hike we all hated. It was a tunnel, but not the kind you hold your breath in. You know what I mean, don't you? We did it all the time in elementary and middle school. When the bus would plunge into a tunnel, we would all take our deepest breaths and see if we could hold it until the bus emerged from the other side.

This tunnel wasn't like that. It was low and narrow. We could only walk one at a time, and all around the tunnel, the foliage was thick. Suffocating. Psychologists could use it to clinically diagnose claustrophobia and nyctophobia. A two-for-one.

I didn't know anyone in my class that year, so I spent most of the hike listening to other people. Two classes went on the hike at once, totaling about fifty kids, so I had a lot of good eavesdropping options.

See, that's another thing I don't get. I was specifically listening to the group of kids behind me, up until I lost interest in whatever game they were talking about. Then I switched to the people preceding me, and I guess that's when it happened?

Always check on those in front of and behind you, the hiking leader said, but no one really did it. There were only so many times you could check on other twelve-year-olds before they lost their patience and told you to mind your own beeswax.

We entered the tunnel as a line of fifty. We exited as a line of forty-four. And guess who the forty-fourth person was?

Okay, look. The hiking leader was a six-foot-something guy in army pants and a white tank top. He had skin that glistened under the beat of the sun. His scruff could have cleaned burnt eggs off a cheap metal pan. He knew martial arts and claimed he could channel his energy with enough focus to shoot a bird out of the sky with just his eyes. And we all believed him.

I don't remember approaching him. It's all a blur until his

eyes—you know, the ones he used to gun down a bird—landed on me. I said, in a voice reaching dog-whistle pitch, *S-some of the people behind me a-are, um, missing?*

With a stony expression, he radioed someone, jogged back to the tunnel, and returned us to the camp. The whole way back, we scanned our surroundings for our classmates, certain they were hiding behind a nearby boulder or in a clump of ferns, just waiting to jump out at us.

But there was no sign of them.

The search stretched into the evening. I sat outside the showers, waiting my turn. Rumbling, chopping sounds climbed above us. We all turned our faces skyward to the rescue helicopters.

I cried. I didn't want to, but I couldn't help it. I thought I, at twelve, would have blood on my hands for the rest of my life. In the years to come, they would tell the story of the girl who lost her classmates, and every new batch of children would pass judgment, their disdainful words piling onto my shoulders.

Some of the girls held my hands, their hair wet from the campground showers. They told me the choppers would find the hikers. Or if they couldn't, the hiking leader would.

Why didn't we become friends? I sometimes wonder.

It was just before dinner. My grumbling stomach was a betrayal. I didn't deserve to eat. I didn't even deserve to be hungry. I was a monster.

The hiking leader burst into the campgrounds. *We found them.*

I can't recall what happened afterward. I know I apologized profusely, but the hikers didn't want to hear it. They claimed they thought it was fun, hanging out in the tunnels and telling secrets until they got hungry. Not trusting the nearby plants, they decided they would have to kill one of the boys and eat his flesh. They had just started mentally divvying up Will, the leanest and therefore most nutritious guy, when the hiking leader popped his head around a tree and practically cried from relief.

Everyone thought the cannibal conundrum was hilarious.

Boys will be boys, one teacher joked to the other.

But Sheryl, I've been wondering: How about *girls will be girls?* What would that look like? Does it mean kissing boys on the cheek when they *do* you a favor because boys go crazy when you do it? Does it mean stepping in when a girl seems uncomfortable around someone because you know exactly how she feels?

I want it to mean that. Or, better yet, I want to destroy the concept of boys being one thing and girls being another. What about the people who don't identify as either?

I hope someday, I can be strong enough to believe there is no *boys will be boys* or *girls will be girls.* But right now, *girls will be girls* means only one thing to me: they will take your heart, sew it together with strings of secrets, then plunge the scissors deep into you, purely because they know they can.

I don't want to think like that. I don't. But I'm trying to be honest here. Especially since you're never going to read this.

All the exciting things happened when I was younger. Then, slowly but surely, my life ground to a stop.

CHAPTER ELEVEN

I STARE AT the PULL sticker above the handle to the Yip Yap Shelter for a solid five seconds before summoning the courage to open the door. When I step inside, the man at the front, Andrew, is still chuckling, his eyes glittering.

"Sorry, sorry," he says. "I'm not laughing at you."

I give him a look. It sure seems like he is.

I thought I would be good and return to the shelter, the way Dr. Tsui wanted, especially since I still haven't told him I've written in his journal, but I should have known the first visit to the shelter was a fluke. Andrew may have introduced himself using only his first name, like he's my friend, or at least a cool uncle, but he thinks I'm just as much of a joke as everyone else does.

Or maybe I'm overreacting. Maybe he laughed because he trusts me with the sound, trusts me to hold the free flow of his voice as his eyes crinkle at the corners, and believes I'll find a way to laugh with him someday, even though that day isn't today.

Meeting the girl spirit didn't make me magically see the beauty in humanity. But watching her go from that despairing weed of a soul on the side of the road to the shining star of the stage made me think maybe it's not impossible to change.

Maybe.

"No," he says as I take a step back, my boot edging closer to the door. "Really. I'm sorry. I was just laughing because I was thinking about my daughter."

I tilt my head.

"When we first opened this shelter, about four years ago now, she had trouble remembering how to open the door. Eventually, she found this place that prints stickers and made one to put over the handle." He shakes his head, an affectionate smile on his face. "She's such a goofball."

I wonder how old his daughter is. I would guess she's younger than I am, based on his age and what he's said about her, but I'm sure twenty-something-year-olds have trouble with push-pull doors too.

I make a small circle around the shelter, studying the animals. The ginger cat gives me a flat look.

"I think you would like her," he says. "My daughter."

Even if I did, she wouldn't like me.

"She's probably about your age," he says.

I whip around, my eyes running along his face. I only met Angel and Sunny's fathers a few times. I search his features for any sign of them, for even the slightest hint of a bold girl with the world's best poker face or a sweetheart with a wild side, but there's nothing familiar there.

Misinterpreting my panic, he gives me a solemn nod. "It's okay. I get it. I'm a stranger, and you just came here to look at animals. I'll be quiet."

I blink. I don't want him to think I'm upset with him, but there's no way I can explain what I was thinking, especially when the ballerina is still twirling through my thoughts, stretching a hand out toward a world unknown, and I'm just . . . me. A girl physically capable of speaking, of smiling, of saying I like how much he talks about his daughter and how I wish my parents could be that happy with me, but unable to so much as open my mouth.

And just like that, I can't stand to be here anymore.

Chewing my lip, I turn on my heel, duck my head in a pathetic attempt at a thank-you, and stumble out of the shelter, the PULL sticker glaring at my back.

For the first few steps, I think Andrew is going to chase after me, one hand outstretched.

Wait, I imagine him saying. *I get it now. I understand you perfectly.*

But he just watches me leave.

I THINK HIS name is Daikokuten.

After ditching Andrew at the shelter, I spent a few minutes sitting on the loveseat and moping. Then I picked up my laptop, opened a browser window, and, deciding I was sick of the mortal world, launched into some divine research.

I didn't know what to expect when I entered the words *Japanese god rat* and *Japanese god hammer* in my browser, but Daikokuten was the first result. Known for his affiliations with rats and often depicted with a rice mallet, he's one of the Shichifukujin, or Seven Gods of Fortune—just like Benzaiten. There's nothing about any kind of falling-out, though, no recorded reason why she would hate him so much. She didn't even want to talk after telling me about him, flashing me back to the shrine and warning me, again, to stay away.

I can ask questions, can turn to the internet, can open tab after tab, but I still don't get all the answers I want.

Dr. Tsui said connection is part of being alive, and though he acknowledged it can also be scary, something no other therapist besides Sheryl has ever admitted aloud, I don't know if he understands just how petrifying it can be.

Because while I'm not about to declare myself the president of Benzaiten's fan club, there's something about her I can't help but like. I would never admit it, both because I'm still not changing my mind about my original wish and because she would hold it over me for the rest of my mortal life and beyond, but a small part of me is curious to see where she's going to take me next.

I think curiosity is just as important anyway. Just as human. I've been curious all my life, wondering why everyone else had a bag, a best friend, a hobby or a passion or a dream, and I didn't. My only dream is being a robot vacuum cleaner, and that's not happening. Not if Benzaiten has anything to say about it. And we all know she has a lot to say about everything.

It's already been more than a week. I'll admit I like and trust her a lot more than I did when she leapt from that tree and landed in front of me like a fluttering parachute, but the goal isn't for me to like her.

I close my laptop, grab my bag, and head out, wondering if the flutter in my chest is nervousness or just the faintest hint of excitement.

BY THE TIME I reach the shrine, Benzaiten is already there.

"Bonjour," she says, hopping off the altar. "I was waiting for you."

There's nothing quite as strange as watching a Japanese goddess speak French as she clambers down from an altar, nearly knocking over a figurine of herself.

"In today's episode of 'Help Machi See the Beauty of the Mortal World and Find Her Voice,' I thought I would do something different." She tosses her arms in the air. "We're going to a party."

I shake my head. No, we are not.

She drops her arms. "Come on. I get the sense you're not a party animal, but it's part of being human. Think of all that stuff you see in teen movies. Don't you want to try that?"

My breath hiccups in my chest.

I *did* try that.

I close my eyes. I can feel the thud of the bass in my body, can see the flash of the neon lights pushing against my eyelids.

I take out my whiteboard but erase my message three times.

Are you saying you want me to get wasted and wake up in an alleyway?

Benzaiten sighs. "No. I would never want that. You know what I meant."

I grind my teeth. *I'm not going.*

"Machi." She places her hands on her hips. "Yes, you are. You prayed and asked me for help. You even gave me a five-week deadline."

She gave *herself* a five-week deadline.

"So here I am." She throws out her arms. "Helping."

This is not helping. I'm not arguing about this.

"No, you're not. Because I'm a goddess, and what I say goes." She takes my hand. "Come on. I even made the effort to find a party in your area. I mean, we're flashing over there because I do *not* feel like walking that far, but still. It'll be fun."

She tugs. I stay put. She tugs harder. I plant my feet. She stomps her ballet flat on the center of the path like a child. "Machi. What is the big deal? It's one party. I'm going to be with you the whole time. What do you think is going to happen?"

I clench my jaw harder. I wouldn't be surprised if my teeth shattered.

I want to think I'm wrong. Things have changed. It would be okay. But just by hoping, I know I've ruined any chance I had. That's how it works, especially in a town as small as mine.

"Half an hour." She shakes her head, her ponytail weaving around her shoulders. "If you're not having fun, we'll leave. I won't fight you."

I listen to the sound of my breath in my ears.

I didn't know if Benzaiten would be able to help the

ballerina, but she did. She made that girl feel more seen than she ever did in life. Maybe I need to trust Benzaiten to do the same for me.

When I raise my head, Benzaiten's watching me, her golden eyes shimmering.

"Just one party," she says. "Half an hour."

That's not even as long as a session with Dr. Tsui. I'm sure going to a party with a deity isn't exactly the type of connection he thought I would make, but it's something.

Pressing my lips together, I take the smallest step forward.

She throws her arms in the air with a "Whoop!" and grabs my hand. Before I can decide whether to scowl or smile, she whisks us away.

At least, I tell myself as the color pours back into our surroundings, it's in a neighborhood I don't recognize, with perfectly paved sidewalks, modest houses painted inoffensive shades of brown, and palm trees lining the spaces between each block. I don't know how Benzaiten could have learned of this party, but then again, I don't know how anyone learns of any parties. It's an afternoon social at a pool, and I tell myself it's fine. I'm sure everyone has better things to do in early summer than attend some stranger's pool party. No one is handing out beers at the entrance, and people aren't splashing neon paint on each other, mouths open and eyes closed. I have divine protection. It's fine. I'll be fine.

But I can't stop shaking as we cross the street.

Benzaiten stops at the edge of the pavement. "Machi? Are you okay?"

I beg her, with my mouth pinched shut, to change her mind and say, *Nah, this party is boring. We should do something else instead.* I don't care what it is. We can go back to that museum and study the blank canvas for hours. That would be a lot better than this.

But her eyes are hungry. As pain circles her pupils, I realize she wants to forget the young ballerina. She hasn't mentioned the girl, but I see it in the way Benzaiten moves. She's too graceful, her steps deliberate. And she wants to forget him too, whatever he is to her. Daikokuten. She drives her gaze into me because she doesn't want to catch sight of him again. If he's here, she doesn't want to know.

"Half an hour," she says again, and with that, we step through the open gate.

I never thought I would crash a party, and with a goddess, no less. But for the first few minutes, it isn't so bad. Benzaiten weaves her way through the hordes of teenagers, mesmerizing almost everyone she passes. Even those with arms around someone can't help but take a few glances. One guy in a state university hoodie temporarily suspends his make-out session just to get a good look at her, his beer sloshing onto the floor.

I am also there. Not that anyone notices.

I can feel anxiety building in my chest. My eyes sweep around each room of the house. I keep expecting to see someone I know. We're not in my neighborhood, but I swear I've seen some of these people before, at the convenience store or in the halls, albeit without red plastic cups.

What if someone recognizes me? What if someone goes, *Machi? What are you doing here? We thought you dropped out.*

To which Benzaiten will say, *Oh, no. She didn't drop out. She moved to online school and got so weird and desperate, she came to my shrine and made a wish to be a robot vacuum cleaner. She's doing great, though. Seriously. By the way, I'm a goddess.*

"Machi," Benzaiten says. "Stop thinking so much."

If only it were that easy.

It's not like Benzaiten was ever lacking vivacity, but in the thick of the crowd, she comes alive. She spins and twirls and pulls me from room to room, giggling and humming and going on and on about something funny Bishamonten did. Unintentionally funny, she adds, because he's just so awkward.

Listening to her reminds me of when Angel and Sunny would talk about all these people I didn't know, classmates I had never spoken to before or girls Angel had met on dating apps or peers Sunny had performed with the other night—not that she had invited us, too humble to even mention her many, many recitals.

I don't think I'll ever stop thinking about them. But, I realize as Benzaiten winds around the couch and stops to watch a rerun playing on the TV mounted on the wall, that doesn't have to be a bad thing.

I take a moment to breathe, flexing and unflexing my fingers at my sides. Maybe things will be different this time. Just because everything came crashing down last time doesn't mean it will now.

I smile as Benzaiten dances along to a song winding out of a Bluetooth speaker. I can't tell if she somehow heard this trap beat up in the heavens or if she, as the deity of music, knows every melody before it's even made.

"I *love* this song," she shouts above the music.

I don't. But that doesn't really matter. If she loves it, maybe someday I will too. That's how it worked with Angel.

Laughing, she lifts our arms and spins me in a circle. I'm mid-turn when my heart stops, my entire body going numb.

I thought if they were here, I would know immediately. I thought if they were here, it would be a slow-motion moment, their faces flooded with the glow of a spotlight. I thought if they were here, our eyes would lock, our jaws would drop, and time would freeze, suspending us in time, pushing everyone and everything else aside until it was just the three of us.

But it's nothing like that. In fact, I don't even see *them* first. It's Angel's boyfriend I recognize.

He doesn't see me, and neither do they, but it's enough. It's more than enough. It's a thousand branching pathways all converging, slamming together into this one moment at this one party with this one goddess, decent for a while until I'm turning on my heel and running. It's the kind of running that would be funny if it weren't so animalistic, so carnal, so desperate. Anyone who sees it will know. Whether they have done it themselves once, or more than once, or they will do it one day, it doesn't matter. They understand, moving aside to make way for the girl who runs. Runs because she can't take being left behind again.

Dear Dr. Tsui,

I'm typing this on my laptop like it's due in an hour. I kept trying to figure out what to do with all of this. All of this *what*? I don't know. All of this *everything*. Does that make sense? Probably not. I don't know. I feel like I'm losing my mind. Which is funny for me to say, considering you think I already *did* lose my mind. Not that you would ever say that. You've been very patient with me. Very kind. You gave me a journal, and I, as far as you know, have never put my pen to a single page.

Except I have. I've written in it three times. I'm also writing this so I can print it out and place it in the pages and give it all to you. Everything I've written. I wrote to Sheryl at first. The therapist I saw before you. I'm afraid you'll be a little hurt by that. That I was writing to her instead of you, in a journal you gave me.

I never even thanked you.

Thank you, by the way.

God, I can't stop typing.

I'm afraid if I stop, I'll never do it again.

Do what?

I don't know. Type? Write? Breathe? I don't know, Dr. Tsui. I don't know.

I've already written about Angel. A part of me is afraid you won't care enough to read what I wrote about her, even though I, in my opinion, am really putting myself out there. But whatever. If you want to know about Angel, read my response to my second prompt. Or don't. Your reading, like my writing, is not mandatory.

I want to tell you about Sunny. I want to tell you because if I don't, I'm going to explode.

Sorry, I know I've never mentioned Sunny, never even

written her name on my whiteboard, but frankly, there's no good place to start.

But while there are a million places where I could begin the story, it can only ever end one way.

Sophomore year has this strange feel to it. It's hard to describe. You know how some people have synesthesia, that phenomenon where one sense is linked to another? A certain letter or number has a color or a personality. Saying the word *antidisestablishmentarianism* tastes like butter at the beginning, but by the end, it's maple syrup.

Well, my sophomore year was glossy. Blurred. Soft at the edges. I was coming down from my first summer with a best friend, which meant an entire two and a half months of doing nothing and everything, singing along to songs we claimed we hated and heading to malls just to try on clothes we claimed we also hated. Angel briefly dated some girl, but she ghosted Angel a few weeks into their relationship. Angel wasn't even sad. It made her braver. So when Josh Daniels let his eyes linger on her too long, she was ready.

I'm going to have him, she told me, and in my mind, it was a done deal. I was prepared to give him my Best Friend speech, in which I would tell him I may seem quiet, but if he hurt her, I wouldn't hesitate to make his life hell on earth.

For Josh Daniels, it wasn't such a done deal. He flirted with Angel, sure, but they had one class together. All the other hours of the school day were his to use as he pleased. And he was very pleased to use them.

Of all the girls he juggled, Sunny was the one with the most promise. She's smart. Freakishly so. But she doesn't brag about it or guard her homework like it's her life's essence. She's willing to help everyone, giving tips to the guy sitting behind her and the girl still stuck on an algebraic equation she learned three years ago. She's the best violinist we have.

Everyone expects her to get a scholarship to some fancy school far away. She might have already accepted an offer. It's not like she would have told me. She has an offbeat sense of humor, her jokes landing two out of three times, but every time something falls flat, she somehow manages to laugh hard enough to make us all forget we weren't rolling from mirth in the first place.

I'm not proud of this, but Angel and I had a bad habit of scoping out the other girls. It's how I knew Sunny was the most likely candidate. And yes, I hate phrasing it like that, but it's how Josh Daniels saw girls. I'm *stepping into the character's shoes*, as one of my former English teachers would say. This girl was good to have around at a party, but sober, she didn't know how to hold a conversation. That girl was cute and sweet, but she was hardly more than his cheat sheet in Spanish class. This girl seemed like an implausible option, but she had a hot, divorced mom.

Again, not my words. Maybe after this, you should find Josh Daniels and get that boy some therapy.

In early October, Josh Daniels made his choice. And it wasn't Angel. It wasn't Sunny either. It was hot-mom girl. (Note: They didn't last. I heard she spent, like, fifty bucks on matching Halloween costumes, but they had broken up by then.)

To no one's surprise, Angel was enraged. She called him out whenever she saw him. That was fine. Everyone expected that. I was the only one who listened to her when she cried over the phone. I think that may have been the ice-cream phase.

The other girls were fine. They got over him, which is good. No one should be heartbroken over Josh Daniels.

But whenever I saw Sunny, she was alone.

Not literally. She had lots to do. I passed her in the hall and found her tutoring someone, charging no fee. I sat outside the orchestra room and listened to her play. I didn't have to see her to know she was the one drawing the bow across the strings with such a modest hand. So she wasn't alone; she was *alone*. Just as sophomore year was soft, she was lonely. Sweet but detached. There was something missing, and I thought it might be us. Angel and me.

So I told her. I said, *I think we should try hanging out with Sunny.*

That could have gone wrong. Very wrong. Angel didn't like suggestions, even from me. Sometimes even especially from me.

But she just shrugged and said, *Sure. Where is she?*

It shouldn't have been so easy, but it was. Just like that, we were friends. When Angel had a crazy idea, Sunny and I teamed up to shoot it down. We usually ended up doing what Angel wanted in some way or another, but at least I had an ally. When Sunny was drowning in self-doubt, Angel and I were there to yank her out, metaphorically shake her by the shoulders, and tell her to snap out of it. And when I . . .

Well, anyway. It was good for a while. But there's something so impossibly irresistible about Angel. When she takes your hand, you don't care what she does. She can drag you across hot coals, and you'll laugh until your cheeks melt off.

Maybe that's what Angel liked about me. A part of me was always turning away, not ready for whatever she wanted to do next. And not only not ready but not willing to compromise. I knew where to draw the line, and once I drew it, I wasn't moving it for anyone. Not even Angel.

Sunny wasn't as unyielding. She let Angel guide her away from the violin, the math, and toward the wild side. Which was good, at first. Sunny was dedicated, but it hurt her a little more every day. She told me as much when she and I were sitting together, facing forward and telling secrets like a priest's confessional screen separated us.

There must have been things happening behind the scenes, but obviously, I couldn't have known about them. Once in a while, I felt a pull in my stomach telling me something about Sunny or Angel was off. But I was happy; I didn't care. So when Angel gathered us for an announcement, I didn't know what was coming.

Clear your schedules. I found an eighteen-plus club that doesn't care if you look older than, like, twelve, so we're going.

Cool, Sunny said.

Wait. I shook my head. *A what?*

An eighteen-plus club.

What is that?

She took my cheeks in her hands. *You're like a baby.* She squished my face before letting go. *It's like a nightclub, but the minimum age is eighteen instead of twenty-one. And the security is slack. They won't care if we're a little under eighteen.*

Sure, if by *a little* she meant *two or three years*. Sunny wasn't even sixteen yet.

I didn't like the idea. I think. Perhaps I did. I wasn't as easily swayed as most, but something about the idea of sneaking into a club in clothes I would have to borrow or buy, Angel and Sunny by my side, was thrilling. For a second.

I remember what Angel and Sunny wore that evening. Angel was dressed to the nines in a leather jacket, a lacy black camisole, and dark-wash jeans. Sunny wasn't comfortable in anything but jeans and a T-shirt—it was either a T-shirt or a gorgeous dress for her violin concerts with no in-between— but Angel had made her pull the sleeves down to reveal the rounded caps of her shoulders.

I couldn't describe my own outfit if you paid me. I do recall almost breaking my ankle when we stepped onto the sidewalk, but that's about it. Angel led the way, as usual, but Sunny and I weren't far behind.

I could feel my heart slamming the bottom of my chest cavity in time to the beat pounding inside the club. I was positive we were going to get caught, seconds away from being asked, *How old are you?* I kept wondering how I was ever going to explain the situation to my parents. They would ground me forever. Longer than forever. They would find me in the afterlife and tell me I couldn't haunt anyone after ten. The school would discover what we had done, and we would get kicked out. Angel would be fine because Angel was always fine. She had marketable skills. Sunny would be more than fine. She was set for life as soon as she picked up her violin, as soon as she was placed in the most advanced classes. But what would I do? What was I good at? Nothing really. Not without them.

We can't do this, I said as I stopped, wobbling on borrowed heels.

We can, Angel said, *and we will.*

Machi, Sunny said.

Who's Machi? Angel asked. She quirked an eyebrow. *I only see Strings and Heels.*

Right. I forgot to say Angel gave us code names. It was supposedly a layer of protection, a way to halfheartedly hide our identities. Sunny, the violinist, was Strings. Because I was incapable of standing straight in anything but boots, I was Heels. And Angel was Lilith. None of this is important to the story.

Sorry. Sunny shook her head. *Heels, don't you think this could be fun? Just once, don't you want to let go?*

Yeah, but we can let go at a party we can actually attend without breaking the law.

Angel crossed her arms but uncrossed them to adjust her bra strap. *Listen. Strings and I are going. You're either in or you're out.*

She wasn't saying it to be mean. I think. She wasn't pushing me away. I think. She wanted me there because she loved me. I think.

She lifted a hand.

I took it.

The bouncer hardly looked at us. He opened the door and mumbled either *Have fun* or *Get drunk*. His voice was a grumble, the music surging out from behind him and into the streets.

We will, Angel said, and she pulled us inside.

You'll be surprised to hear this—or, I guess, read this—but I actually liked it at first. The techno beats were annoying and there were way too many bodies, but it was like the nightclubs in movies and TV shows. People weren't drinking, allegedly, but they were doing everything else. A couple danced like they were at prom, their hands around each other and their movements too slow for the song. Someone in the corner couldn't stop sniffling, stars in her eyes and dust on her upper lip. And Angel, Sunny, and I were at the center of it all.

We danced. Angel talked. Sunny jumped along to a song she said her mother never let her play on her phone speakers. I thought maybe it wasn't so bad.

But then it got bad.

I can't tell you why. It was such a sudden switch. One moment, I was fine. The next, I was sure something bad was going to happen. Something so bad. The lights splattered the floor like neon blood. The girl in the corner watched us with glowing eyes, her lips nothing but a scarlet gash. The bouncer was probably on his way to drag us out by our hair, incandescence streaming through his rippling arm muscles in colorful rivulets.

It was wrong. Everything was wrong.

I tried to turn, to search for something familiar, but everything was whirling around me, voices loud and slow, melting into each other and pooling at my feet.

I do not exist, I thought to myself. *I am not real.*

I couldn't breathe. The world was too fast for me to handle. Angel's face. Sunny's hands. My heart was screaming to get out. Get out get out get out get out.

You're either in or you're out, Angel had said.

And I was out.

Oh, Machi, I can hear you saying. *I'm sorry.*

Yeah, me too. But that isn't the end of it. I hate to use the old adage, but that was actually just the beginning.

The details are fuzzy. How did I escape the club? Did they call out for me? They must have, because they loved me and were worried about me. They must not have, because I was ruining their fun and they weren't sure what was happening until they saw me jam my shoulder against the door and stagger into the open air.

I expected to fall to my knees and cry because I couldn't breathe. But I was walking, my legs functioning without my brain. The lights were hazy. The pedestrians around me were fake. Was I drugged? Dehydrated? Losing my mind?

I found myself at a tourist trap store across the street. It had license plate key chains with all the popular names. *Machi* was never on those things, but I wouldn't have wanted one anyway. Near those key chains was a spinning rack of oversaturated postcards that smelled like glue, and beside it sat a shelf of cheap maps and guidebooks no one would use more than once, if at all.

Welcome, a worker chirped. He took one look at my face and changed gears. *I mean, uh, konnichiwa. Irasshaimase.*

I considered telling him I understood him the first time, but my words dissolved in my mouth like a capsule held under the tongue. I huddled near the back of the store, and there I found Toridachi.

Dr. Tsui, I don't know much about you. You could be more of a Toridachi expert than I am, taking time out of every day in December to vote for Toridachi in that Best Mascot of the Year contest I keep seeing online. But if you, by chance, don't know about Toridachi, let me explain: It's a little yellow bird character with black button eyes and a tiny pink beak. It began as a temporary character of the month for some larger franchise, but no one expected how much children would love that bird. Soon, it was everywhere, sweeping across stores and taking over every aisle. Toridachi toasters that made plastic-smelling toast. Toridachi coin purses with a beak that opened and closed with a clasp. Toridachi TV shorts, animated and fully voiced.

I thought Toridachi was cute and all, but I didn't get the hype until I was crouched in the mouth of the tourist trap, staring at that stupid bird. Then I was reaching, touching the merchandise because it was so yellow. So happy. So cute. It didn't sneak into 18+ clubs or break down when it was supposed to be living it up. It was Toridachi, and that was enough.

I don't know how they found me. One of them must have been tuned into me somehow, searching for the Machi Radio Signal. Was it Angel, our connection inexplicable but undeniable? Was it Sunny, who sometimes knew exactly what I was thinking, down to the last word? Does it even matter when I wound up losing them both anyway?

Machi, Angel said, kneeling with her knees pressed together. *Why are you sitting next to all these yellow ducks?*

I must have replied, but I don't remember what I said.

Angel got us a ride home. I don't remember that either. She said she would check on me later, but I'm not sure she followed through. It was Angel, so I want to believe she did.

I spent a lot of time in bed. My parents thought we had shopped for too long or it was too hot or I had messed up my sleep schedule again. I didn't tell them what had happened. Just like I didn't tell them about the art class, though they must have wondered why I never brought any pieces home.

I told Sheryl some of this, by the way, but it wasn't in nearly as much detail. Sorry you have to read all of this. I should have given you the concise version. I guess I'm just remembering these things, and I want to throw them onto the page like I'm a tortured artist and you're my well-paid audience.

Oh, and it's still not over.

It could have been. I must have thought that was it. How humiliating. They wanted to have fun, and I ended up freaking out on them. But you know what? They were so understanding.

I'm not being sarcastic. Maybe they were upset for a few hours. Maybe Angel didn't call. Come Monday, though, they were checking up on me. *Are you okay? Hey, Machi. I know that was rough. I can't say I get what happened, but I can try. Do you want to talk about it? You worried us.*

I thought they were the best friends I had never even asked for, and again and again, I waited for everything to burn down.

Angel didn't stop wanting to do things. She was restless. She had a thirst for more. More adventures. More code names. More everything. She chased down dreams and acted on impulse and did stuff now and regretted it later. But she didn't force me to join her. Sunny went along, and they left me behind. I didn't want to drink with a guy Angel met outside her building, but Sunny did. I didn't want to buy some questionable stuff with money she had slowly stolen from her parents, but Sunny did. And they didn't make me feel bad about it. I thought that meant they respected my decisions, but now I realize it meant they didn't care.

The summer was a sleepy slog. We were almost juniors.

Junior year is always rumored to be the hardest, but I thought that meant academically. I guess I can't know for sure if that's true because by the time the fall semester rolled around, I wasn't there.

Angel was dating an older guy, some graduate from a high school we'd never heard of, and through him and his friend group—who seemed to hang out together for the specific purpose of dating each other—Sunny found a boyfriend of her own. It was perfect, really, and sometimes, Angel wanted to make it triply perfect. She wanted me to meet their other friends and snag a guy too.

It was a Friday. Our storms always happened either on the weekend or just before it. It's like the three of us avoided drama, holding our breaths on Monday, biding our time on Tuesday, checking our calendars on Wednesday, itching to scream on Thursday, and then letting it all out just as the school week ended.

Angel showed me a picture. *What about this one?*

I'm sorry, I said for the fortieth time. *I'm not interested.*

I didn't yell it. I didn't snap at her. I didn't roll my eyes or pinch the top of her hand. So I don't know why that was what set her off.

Yeah, of course you're not. Her voice was cold.

Do you want to hear something sad? I knew that tone, and every time I heard it, it plunged me into frigid water. I could feel panic rising, eating through my veins, because I didn't want to fight. I wanted her to love me because I loved her. I wanted to hold her hand until the end of time, and whenever something threatened that, even if it was only a moment of irritation, I was terrified.

Every time before, it had turned out to be nothing. Nothing we couldn't overcome in a few minutes. And it really did take only a few minutes, until that day.

Sunny, Angel said. *We're going to the lookout. Probably getting drunk. You coming?*

Yeah. Definitely. Sunny looked different. She had looked different for a while.

I'd invite you, Machi, but we wouldn't want you to freak out again.

I was already frozen, but I imagined myself turning blue beneath the ice, colder than cold. We hardly ever discussed what had happened at the club. Once twenty-four hours had passed, it was expired. A relic. There was no need to touch it. We saw its aftereffects, the mutual decision to pull back and let me have my own life, but I thought it was a good thing. I thought it meant she understood me better.

Oh, I said. *Oh, yeah. That's okay.*

Sunny turned. She stood beside the window. The sun shone onto her earrings. The light refracted, blinding me. Maybe that's what was different. Maybe she hadn't worn earrings before. She clasped her hands. *It would be weird, I think. If you came. Because we're dating the guys, and it's like a double date, you know?*

I know.

But it's not personal, she said, the space between her brows forming a triplet of creases.

Sunny. So polite, even just before a kill.

I imagine that's how it worked at her performances too. She would greet the other violinists, dipping her head and blushing when they complimented her dress or her violin, and they would think, *What a cute girl*. Then she would get on the stage and play so well, no one could ever dream of measuring up. The people before her? Forgotten. The people after? Too stunned to play right, the notes coming out ragged and squeaky. She was sweet in the moments up to her complete destruction.

I know, I said. *It's fine. We can hang out some other time.*

Unless you ruin that too, Angel said.

It seemed sudden. So sudden. But in retrospect, I saw it. The way Angel grew bored of me. She must have liked it at first, having a friend so wet behind the ears. She could coddle me, enjoying quiet days where we would lie beside each other, our heads pressed together, and breathe until we fell asleep. She could push me out of my comfort zone and feel that burst of joy all proud parents get when they watch their children thrive. She could slow herself down or pull me beside her, and once in a while, it seemed to physically hurt when we had to part ways for the day, even if we would see each other in the next twenty-four hours.

But then she realized how fun it was to be with someone who could match her speed. She didn't have to haul Sunny anywhere. Sunny was ready to go. She didn't scream it like Angel, but anyone could see her enthusiasm, from her clean shoes to her eager hands to her calm but anticipatory expression. Who could blame her? I know, better than anyone on Earth, how good it feels to be with Angel. How special it is to be seen, recognized, loved by someone like her. It's fun, and it's addicting, and it's everything you wish it could be when you dream of a best friend, and you would know because you spent so many years dreaming. Even if you tell everyone you never wanted friends.

Angel, I said.

But she had lost it.

You're boring, she said, calmly first. Then louder. *You're BORING, Machi. Everything ABOUT you is boring. Your voice is boring. Your face is boring. Your personality is boring. The things you say? Boring. The things you like? That stupid bird you were staring at in the store? Boring. Everything. About. You. Is. Boring.*

Was she whispering? Screaming? How would I know? I wasn't there. Not really.

Angel, Sunny said.

Angel wheeled around to face Sunny. *You know it's true. You KNOW it's true.*

I swallowed. It hurt. I looked at Sunny. It hurt. I saw her mouth open. I saw her mouth close. It hurt. It really, really hurt.

Let's go, Angel said.

Then they walked away. Sunny didn't look back once, and a small part of me was proud of her. The old Sunny would have, and Angel would have hated it.

I was stunned enough to watch them leave without putting up a fight. I didn't say a word.

Why? Why didn't I speak up? Because I was shocked? Yeah. Because I was hurt? Fine. But I could have said something, couldn't I? What if I had said, *Wait, Angel. You know what? I'll go with you on that triple date. What's the worst that could happen?*

Sure. I could have said that.

But that wouldn't have changed anything.

If I had gone on that date, I still would've been the same person. I still wouldn't have known what to say to a strange boy with strange friends. If he had touched my thigh under the table, I wouldn't have smiled and batted my eyes at him, the way Angel would have. I wouldn't have blushed and hidden a smile, the way Sunny would have. I would have jumped up, stumbled out of the booth of whatever café Angel had been hearing all about, and left, just as I had at the club.

Because I do not know how to be like everyone else. I have never, in my life, known how. And that means I will never, ever be good enough. For anyone.

I don't think I've said this before. Or if I have, pretend you didn't know, just so I don't feel stupid for telling you again. Okay, ready? Here it is:

Angel and Sunny were the only ones who truly under-stood me.

Oh, Machi, I'm sure you're thinking. *People say that all the time, but they never mean it. I'm sure if you just opened your eyes and took a look around, or if you would just let people see you for the person you really are—*

No. You're wrong.

I tried. I tried so hard. I did my best to be the person every-one wanted me to be, but no matter how hard I tried, I just wasn't *like* other people. I didn't stay up late to buy concert tickets. I didn't gush over crushes. I didn't sneak out to go skinny-dipping at two in the morning. I was only ever myself. Because I only *knew* how to be myself. And Angel and Sunny were the two people who made me feel like that was okay. Like that wasn't boring. Like that was special.

So if, in the end, I couldn't be enough for the two people who were once the only ones to ever accept and love me, even when I felt like a completely different species from everyone else, then what was even the point of being anything at all?

I don't remember how I got home, but when I did, the house was empty, and that felt right somehow. I didn't speak because no one was there, and what could I have said anyway?

I screamed into my pillow until I lost my voice, and then I couldn't say anything at all. Every time I tried to speak, I just made this little squeak, like I was nothing but a tiny rat stuck in a too-small cage.

Then my parents came home, and I realized it was nice not to talk. It was nice to listen, even when all they were say-ing was *Machi? What's wrong? What happened? Talk to us*. The longer I was quiet, the more natural it felt, and soon, I couldn't imagine speaking ever again.

I went silent elsewhere too. Deleted my social media. Let people wonder—if they wondered. I was a mystery, a fever-dream fragment of a person. *What ever happened to that girl? I don't know. No one does.* Then all I had left was the texting app that comes on every phone. I left that one avenue open, just in case they missed me one day.

They never did.

And there's something funny about that, isn't there? I've been bullied by a teacher who destroyed any love I could have ever had for art. I've been one wrong step away from ending up as part of a Reddit write-up on the unresolved mystery of a handful of middle schoolers who got lost in the woods because I couldn't just look over my shoulder once or twice. I've been conditioned to never bring up my Japanese roots, lest I become the target of the town's mockery, the way my mother and grandparents once were.

But none of those things broke me.

No, what broke me was that one day. That one conversation. What one girl said to me in front of one other girl one time. And isn't that sad? Isn't that pathetic?

But hey, at least it isn't boring, right?

Dr. Tsui, do you want to know another thing I never told Sheryl? Another thing I never told anyone?

Choosing not to talk made me interesting. It made people worry. It made people pay attention and speculate and ask and find themselves baffled by my inability to answer. And, of course, no one could accuse me of saying boring things if I never said anything at all. So I was silent, and I stayed silent, and I decided that's how I could keep myself from ever feeling the way I felt that day.

So are you happy now? Sad? Have you lost interest in me? Am I boring? You can tell me. I've heard it all before.

CHAPTER TWELVE

TAP, TAP, TAP.

I lie on the floor, my head resting on the printer. It's not comfortable, but I like the heat.

Tap, tap, tap.

I haven't figured out if I can hear knocks at the front door because the layout lets the sound bounce around the apartment or because the apartment is just that small. My parents and I don't need much space. It got a little crowded when my grandparents were here for Christmas, but that's not a problem anymore, is it?

What an awful thing to think. I'm an awful person.

"Machi. It's me."

I turn to the printer and think to it, *What would you do if a goddess were knocking on your door?*

"Hey. I know you're in there."

The printed pages of my letter to Dr. Tsui lie in a neat pile beside my hand. I could reach over and read them if I wanted, but I don't. I hope I never have to read those words again. I didn't even proofread, which is dangerous. What if, at a crucial moment, Dr. Tsui laughs because I wrote *nightcub* instead of *nightclub* or *boned* instead of *bored*?

"I'm trying to be polite, but I'm losing my patience."

Deities are often characterized as impatient and reckless,

but I don't understand why. Time is nothing to them, so why are they in such a rush?

Also, how did she find my apartment?

"Machi."

She crouches beside me and turns off the printer. I turn it back on. She turns it off.

"Machi, what are you doing? What happened?"

She's so close. I'm tempted to set my head on her lap, the way the young ballerina did, but I manage to restrain myself.

I look her in the face. Her eyes are soft, a glimmering gold. They remind me of glitter glue. I wasn't much of a glitter-glue person when I was young, but I see the appeal. People like things that throw off bits of light. We can't help but stare.

"I can't believe you made me leave the party," she says, her tone light. "Do you know how long it's been since I was among so many mortals?"

I close my eyes. I could fall asleep.

"Machi." Her fingers brush mine. "What happened?"

My whiteboard is somewhere too far to reach. I threw my bag down as soon as I got in the door and started typing. I don't know what time it is, and my perpetually closed blinds and curtains block out all the light, no matter how bright or dark it is outside. I don't know how she got into my apartment. Maybe she teleported. Cheater.

"What is this?"

The papers rustle, unhappy with the sudden disturbance. A voice in my head urges me to snatch the pages out from between her delicate fingers. She doesn't need to know. I didn't write that for her.

But didn't I? Didn't I have the feeling she would find me? Now that she's here, it's impossible to determine. If she hadn't come, I wouldn't have expected her to, but because she's beside me, I knew she would chase after me. It's Schrödinger's goddess.

"Machi," she says. "Can I read this?"

I don't hesitate. Just as every path led to that party, to Angel and Sunny and their boyfriends, every path leads here. To this apartment, in this room, with this printer.

I nod.

She reads silently, taking her time. It feels like forever before she lifts the first page and sets it on the floor. I stare at its corner and imagine it slicing me open, a fatal papercut. I'm ready for the vulnerability hangover.

Fwip. She puts the papers facedown, one by one. She doesn't speed up.

When I read, I tend to zone out upon hitting the center of a book. The little complications interest me, but I need to know the end. I rush, scrolling or flipping the pages until I reach the conclusion.

Fwip. She places the final paper on the top. She tucks her fingers underneath the stack and flips it. The words stare at the ceiling.

If I spoke, I would say, *So that's the story*.

There's no reason why I would say it. It's not necessary. Just filler words. But it would make me feel better. And God, I need to feel better.

"Machi," Benzaiten says.

She pulls me up from the ground, wraps her arms around me, and cries.

I SIT WITH my hands squished between my knees, watching the blood leech out of my fingertips.

Dr. Tsui takes one hand, lifts his glasses, and rubs his eyes. He touches the edges of the pages. "You even printed this to fit in the notebook."

It's true. I formatted my typed entry to make the margins match the edges of the therapy notebook. It felt stupid, but I wanted the pages to sit just right. I wanted to run my fingers along the edge of the book and have everything match up. Benzaiten didn't understand why I did it, why I found a sort of poetic justice in cramming something so messy into precut pages, but she didn't say anything. She let me fiddle with the notebook, her tears such a pretty silver.

"I'm sorry," Dr. Tsui says. "I'm sorry that happened. It makes sense why you felt you couldn't speak anymore. Why you worry about opening up to people again. That must have been incredibly difficult."

I pick at my nails. Tightening my grip on my whiteboard marker like I'm trying to smother the truth before it leaks out through the pen, I write, *A lot worse has happened to so many other people. What right do I have to go silent because of one incident?*

He takes a moment to collect his thoughts. "Do you feel it was just that one incident?"

I look away. Then, slowly, I shake my head. Staring at the triplet figurines, their bows drawn, I write, *It was a lot of little things. Then everything.*

He nods. "I can tell they meant a lot to you. No matter how it happens, whether it's to time, miscommunication, or something else entirely, losing someone is never easy. Especially when that 'someone' is two someones you once considered your best friends."

I swallow, my throat tight.

Benzaiten spent some time crying for me. It was a very strange thing to witness. I sat there, my hands pressing into the floor, as she held me close. Then she told me she was sorry. She asked about the party, and I explained, writing the words on my whiteboard with too much care. She apologized and hugged me again. Then she stood and wandered around my apartment, taking me with her on a tour of a place I've lived since birth. I've never heard someone say the words *mortal* and *curious* so many times in the span of a half hour.

She made me promise to come back to her shrine soon, and I will. Not today, though. Once I survive this session, I plan to sleep for the rest of the day.

"Who is Benzaiten?"

My head snaps up, panic pulsing through me like I just downed a bowl of kakigōri.

He holds up the notebook. "You wrote about someone named Benzaiten a couple of times. Who is that?"

I break out in a sweat. I forgot I mentioned her. What did I say? I can't remember anything but those printed-out pages.

Serena. I wrote about Serena. And Angel. When did I ever write about Benzaiten?

At the sight of the stricken look on my face, Dr. Tsui returns the notebook. I have to keep myself from snatching it from his grasp, making a concentrated effort to turn the pages one by one instead of frantically flipping through them.

She's not the otherworldly being, though, I wrote. *Benzaiten is.*

Then, one entry later, *Benzaiten was in a weird mood after our last outing.*

Oh my God.

"I don't think I've ever heard that name before," Dr. Tsui says. "Is this someone you've met recently?"

I swallow. Then, pushing the notebook beneath my whiteboard, I grab my marker.

What should I write? What *can* I write? How can I explain this?

"You mentioned something about a wish," Dr. Tsui says, switching tactics in the wake of my silence. "You told her you were wishing for something? Could you tell me what it was?"

I flex my fingers around the marker. I can't dodge his questions forever. That's what I did at the beginning, and look where it led me. Instead of opening up one story at a time, I held it all in until it broke out of me in a Jack-Kerouac-writing-*On-the-Road* kind of mania.

It felt good, though. Saying something without *saying* something. Being heard, first by Benzaiten, and now by Dr. Tsui.

Taking my time, I write, *My wish was to become a robot vacuum cleaner.*

When I turn my whiteboard around, I stare at the floor, unable to look Dr. Tsui in the eye.

He's quiet for a moment. Then he says, "I think that's something worth exploring."

No. Please no. I can't do this. I already feel like a cracked-open coconut, truth leaking out of me and dribbling along his plush carpet.

I shouldn't have shown him anything. Not anything about Benzaiten, obviously, but not anything about Angel or Sunny or Serena either. I should have known opening up was a mistake.

"But," Dr. Tsui continues, "I know you already shared a lot today. How about you think about telling me more about your wish next time, and for today, we'll just focus on what you intended on sharing with me? Would you be willing to discuss Angel and Sunny?"

No. That's worse.

But if I say no, he'll ask about my prayer again, and I don't want to think about that either. I don't want to think about anything.

Erasing my words one mark at a time, I nod.

"Thank you." Dr. Tsui gives me a few seconds to calm down, setting one arm on the armrest of his chair. Then, tilting his head, he asks, "Do Angel and Sunny know?"

I look up, the threads of my thoughts still wrapped around

Benzaiten. My eyes dart to the figurines on the doctor's desk. The three sisters.

I turn my head.

"Do they know you've stopped talking?" he asks.

I shrug.

"If it were up to you, would you want them to know?"

I take the whiteboard pen and flip it between my fingers. *I don't know. Would it get them curious about me? Or would they take pleasure in knowing they destroyed me?*

He pushes out his chin like he wants to lean closer but doesn't want to frighten me. "Do you think that's what they did? Destroyed you?"

I chew my lip. *I don't know how else to explain it. What did they do if not destroy me?*

"Led you to where you are now?" he suggests.

But that feels a lot like the same thing.

I'VE ONLY JUST started to get a nickel out of my pocket when Benzaiten appears.

"It's been two weeks. Haven't you learned yet?" She puts a hand on mine. "I know when you're here. You don't have to lob coins into the box."

I drop my wallet into my bag. She wraps her fingers around my palm and pulls me to the offering box. Taking the black cord with the prayers out from under the neckline of her dress, she touches each pendant.

"I know you're not feeling great, but I hear them." She tucks the prayers away. "The child spirits."

She scoots to the side. I sit on the timeworn edge of the offering box.

"I can feel them calling to me." Her eyes darken, burnt-orange and troubled. "I try to ignore them, but it's getting harder."

I wonder if helping that one girl has opened her up to hearing all the others. Like how meeting one person who lit up my life has made me start looking for them, for anyone, everywhere I go. Even if I know I'm only ever going to get burned.

"I want to find them," Benzaiten says. "And I want you to come with me."

I pull back. I didn't think she would want me to accompany her. I'm the reason why she wound up getting pulled back into spirit-saving in the first place. She should hate me.

Maybe she's being nice because she feels bad about dragging me to the party.

Or maybe she just wants me there.

And maybe I want to be there.

I tilt my head in a wordless *Why?*

She looks away, her irises melting like caramel left out in the sun. "There are lots of ways to get lost, you know. Lots of ways to get found. Sometimes, when you're at your most lost, you find everything you didn't know you were looking for."

I try not to roll my eyes.

It's not that I'm against looking for the spirits. As hard as it was to learn of the ballerina's past, as sad as I was for her, I can't help but believe we were connected in some way, even if I was the only one to feel it.

Sometimes, I wonder if that's why Sheryl was able to reach me. She didn't go silent the summer before her junior year, at least as far as I know, but she was only ever the loudest person in the room if I was the sole person sitting with her. She reached me because she understood me in a way the other therapists, the ones who *only* talked or *only* listened, never could.

I just don't see how helping spirits is supposed to get me to find the beauty in life. Even if I *do* bond with them, they're still dead. They're going to leave too. In some ways, they already have.

"Machi," Benzaiten says. "Of all people, you should know how good it feels when someone finally finds you."

I glance up at her. I feel like I'm on the verge of understanding what she's trying to tell me, but I just can't get there yet. Maybe the pieces will fall into place once we find the next spirit.

But even if I never grasp what Benzaiten's trying to tell me, even if, by Tanabata, she still hasn't managed to change my mind, at least some other souls will have been saved.

I put my hand on hers, and just like that, we're gone.

Our surroundings slowly take shape, forming the walls of a house. At first, I think I must be hearing a faraway train or the hum of a radiator.

Then I realize someone is crying.

In another room, out of sight, a woman weeps.

"This way," Benzaiten says, her face solemn as she leads us down a hallway. Even after the woman's sobs fade, I swear I can hear them, just barely.

The girl in the corner of the room is faint. She curls up against the wall, her eyes stretched wide. She sticks out an arm and watches it flicker. She can't be more than seven.

"Child," Benzaiten says.

The girl lifts her eyes to the goddess. "I can't sleep."

"I understand." She kneels beside the girl. I sit about a foot away. "It's all right. I'm here. Nothing bad will happen."

"I can't sleep." Her voice totters from one word to the next. "Don't let me fall asleep."

Every time she speaks, her body fades. Her voice distorts at the end of each sentence like she's speaking through a malfunctioning walkie-talkie. I can feel her shoulders straining from the weight of her memories. If she doesn't get help soon, she's going to be crushed.

Benzaiten knows what I'm doing a second before I do it.

She says, "Machi," but it's too late. I reach out and touch the girl's hand.

HER MOMMY AND daddy say she was a sleepy baby. They say she always smelled like milk and baby powder. She doesn't think that sounds very nice, but they promise her it was. They used to brag about how she slept through the night from day one. It didn't matter who was trapped in the conversation. It could be a stinky stranger in the elevator, a man smelling of sweat and old food, and her parents would find a way to talk about her, their sleepy angel.

At sleepovers, she's the first to fall asleep. She misses some TV show everyone talks about at school, but she doesn't care. She would rather watch the backs of her eyelids.

Her parents take her to the pediatrician—that's the fancy term for a doctor—to check that everything is A-okay. The doctor gives her a thumbs-up and says some kids are just natural nappers. That's her. Princess of the Natural Nap. No, wait. Queen. No. Princess. Queens are old. She doesn't want to be old.

On Christmas Day, her parents surprise her with the best present ever: a drowsy kitten toy. It doesn't do anything but sleep, but its body moves as if it's breathing. She keeps it by her bed on its little pillow and matches her breathing with the kitty's, their sides moving up and down together.

Then, at the beginning of summer, when her mommy and daddy take her for her checkup, her doctor says he's worried. She doesn't like when doctors are worried. That usually means she's sick, like when she had the stomach flu and threw up. Twice.

The doctor runs a bunch of tests. She has to get hooked up to beepy things and get needles stuck in her arms and go into big, loud machines, and in the end, they say she has sleeping problems.

She doesn't get it. So she likes sleeping. What's the problem with that?

Her mommy and daddy try to keep her on a strict sleep schedule—that's the fancy term for controlling everything she does and never letting her sleep, even when she really, really wants to—and she does her best to do what they say, but she's so sleepy.

One day, while her daddy is working overtime, because mommies and daddies can come home and go to sleep late and not get in trouble, her mommy picks up the phone and goes on and on about grown-up things like cooking and the news. Her mommy is being boring, so she goes to her room, even though she's not supposed to, and flops onto her bed.

Ahhhh. She loves her bed.

She closes her eyes and pretends she's the kitty her mommy and daddy gave her for Christmas. She wishes she could hug it to her chest, but they put it away after the doctor got all worried about her, as if they thought hiding the sleepy kitty would make *her* less sleepy. Now it's on a shelf at the tippy-top of her closet. She probably can't even reach it unless she stands on a chair.

Rolling over in bed, she stretches a hand in the direction of the kitty, hoping she developed superpowers and can summon her toy with just one hand. Then, when that doesn't work, she frowns, slides out of bed, grabs her chair, and drags it over to her closet. Even when she stands on the seat, her fingers can't quite reach the kitty. She'll have to jump.

She doesn't like jumping. Not nearly as much as she likes sleeping. But if she wants her kitty, she'll have to, as her daddy says, suck it up.

Well, her daddy doesn't say it to *her*. He isn't *mean*. In fact, he told her not to say that. *Suck* is a bad word. Sometimes.

But sometimes, it *isn't* a bad word. Vacuum cleaners suck, but that's okay because they're supposed to suck. Except her mommy gets angry when they suck up stick-on earrings and hair ties. Then her daddy has to unplug the vacuum cleaner and pull them all out.

Anyway, she's sucking it up now.

Focusing on the kitty on the top shelf of her closet, she gathers her energy and leaps with all her might.

And misses.

Her fingers don't even brush the kitty's soft fur.

Then she's falling, her body moving all on its own, like when the doctor hits her knee with the little hammer and her leg kicks out, even when she doesn't want it to.

She tries to reach for something, but her fingers swipe through empty air. She scans the spinning world around her, searching for the kitty or her mommy or her daddy or even the vacuum cleaner, but there's nothing. Nothing and nothing and nothing.

When she crashes to the ground, her eyes are wide open.

Above her, the kitty doesn't even notice. It just sleeps on.

I DRAW BACK, my hand numb as I wrap my arms around myself. Benzaiten wipes the tears from my cheeks. When I look up, she holds my gaze for a moment in a silent apology.

I don't know why she's trying to say sorry. I was the one who reached for the girl. I just couldn't bear the thought of making her relive those memories. Not alone.

Benzaiten turns to the girl. "I know you don't want to close your eyes, but you have to get some rest."

"No," the girl whispers hoarsely. "I don't want to sleep."

Benzaiten's voice is gentle. Subdued. "It isn't quite like sleeping. It's storing your energy so you can feel better."

The girl shakes her head. "No, no, no."

In the days after the fallout with Angel and Sunny, I needed to hold onto something, anything, to keep myself from tumbling into the abyss. I searched for evidence of our friendship. Physical proof that we had once been close, and I was not always boring. I ran my fingers along the blouse Angel had bought me at the mall. I touched the glossy cover of the book Sunny had given me for my birthday. I kept the broken paper wristband from an exhibit we had visited for Sunny's extra-credit project and clung to empty plastic cups from the museum gift shop.

This child wanted to do the same thing. To take comfort in something familiar when everything around her was changing. And even that one little thing was too far out of reach. No wonder she doesn't want to sleep. She's missed out on so much already. If she closes her eyes, maybe when she opens them, everything she ever knew will be gone.

And what a betrayal it is to love something so much, only for it to be the very thing you can never have again. Not without conditions. Not without hoops to jump through, without rules to follow, without wondering if you're doing it right this time. You never realize how lucky you are to love something, to love someone, until you no longer can.

I stand, my movements slow to avoid scaring the girl, and raise my head to the closet. The cat toy is still there, in the exact same position as it was in her memory. I wonder if her parents even realized what she was so desperate to have.

Standing on my toes reminds me of the young ballerina. I close my eyes for a second. Benzaiten said she would be okay. I want to believe her.

When I grab the cat, I realize it's still on, letting out a muted *shhhnnuf* sound as its fur-covered body rises and falls. I run my finger over its head, then return to the girl's side, my eyes never leaving her face.

"Kitty," the girl whispers as I set it on her knobby knee. Tears slip down her cheeks, the thin trails gleaming silver.

Benzaiten takes the girl in her arms, placing the child across her lap, and hums a lullaby. Her voice ebbs and flows, creating a steady tide of sound. The girl quietly rests her head on Benzaiten's knee. Then, little by little, she closes her eyes.

Benzaiten and I sit in silence as I study the girl's room. She doesn't have much on her walls, but a scribbly drawing of a fairy hangs on the back of her door, the wings pink loops. She has more pillows in this room than I have in my entire apartment. I spot a sleeping bag in the gaping closet. She has tossed clothes into a hamper, missing about twenty-five percent of the time. Someone will have to go through all her shirts and nightgowns one by one, realizing how small this girl was when she died. How small she will stay forever.

I don't know how people can possibly handle death. I wasn't close to my grandparents, but I still couldn't bring myself to go to their funeral.

The girl's eyelids lift after about ten minutes, the edges of her body stronger. She looks into Benzaiten's eyes. "Is it time for me to go?"

Benzaiten's jaw clenches, but she only nods and helps the girl to her feet. The girl reaches for her sleeping cat toy, but her hands pass through. Her bottom lip trembles. Benzaiten takes her hand, making the girl's body glow.

"Try again," Benzaiten says quietly.

The girl picks up the toy and hugs it to her chest before setting it back on its pillow.

"You're safe now," Benzaiten whispers, her eyes wet.

The girl takes one last look at the cat, then at us. "I know."

Benzaiten prays over the girl, one hand on her hair. Light fills the room. I turn away until I hear a hiss and a snap. When I face Benzaiten, her arms are empty.

She sits back on her heels and covers her face. Her ponytail weeps down her spine. I extend a hand, but she doesn't see it.

Her arms fall to her lap. She stares at something beyond me, her eyes dark. "Why do you always show up at the worst moments?"

I turn. The man with the mallet, Daikokuten, stands in the doorway. He keeps one hand on the doorknob. A rat sits at his feet. He doesn't look much like the pictures I found online, his face too young and narrow and his eyes devoid of the joy carved into each statuette, but Benzaiten didn't resemble any of her depictions either.

"It hurts me as much as it hurts you," he says.

Her lips jerk into a snarl. "Yeah, right."

"You know it's true."

She's silent. Her eyes find my hand on her knee. She looks away. "I could have taken really good care of her."

She said something like that before, with the ballerina. I still don't understand what else she would be able to do for them besides help them cross over.

Daikokuten rubs his chin. "I'll make sure she's okay. I promise."

"Your promises mean nothing to me."

The tension is heavier than the little girl's eyelids as she fought off sleep. I stay still, my focus caught between them.

"You shouldn't even be here," she says.

His eyes are black. "Neither should you."

"Just leave."

The rat runs in an anxious circle around his left boot. It clambers up to his free shoulder, but he only watches her. "Benzaiten."

"Get *out*," she half-shouts.

He takes a step back and waits. When she does nothing, he looks to me, dips his head, and vanishes.

Benzaiten stands, keeping her face turned away. She picks up a picture on the girl's dresser. Her mother and father smile for the camera. The girl, only an infant in the photograph, is in the middle of a hearty laugh, her eyes crinkling at the sides.

"I never told you who he is," she says. "Did I?"

I shake my head. She never *told* me, but I know.

"His name is Daikokuten." She sets the photo back on the dresser but keeps one hand on the frame. "He ruined everything."

CHAPTER THIRTEEN

SOMETHING ABOUT THE flip of her fingers along the ridges of her dress tells me she's nervous. I didn't think goddesses could be nervous. Especially not Benzaiten.

"It was a long time ago," she says. "Everything was."

It didn't feel right for her to tell her story in the girl's house, so we returned to her shrine. We now sit on the offering box near the altar, my knee touching hers.

"Daikokuten and I were, well, in love." She wrinkles her nose. "I guess."

I'm not surprised. In the open field and at the house, I could feel the complexity of their relationship, more intricate than netsuke. It wasn't only hate carved into hate; the animosity that crackled between them ran deeper than mutual distaste.

"Deities like us aren't required to lead the dead to the spirit world. There are others who do that. But we wanted to help." She tilts her face to the sun. "That's one of the things I liked about him. He wanted to help."

A gentle breeze dances along the shrine grounds. It twirls through her dress. She closes her eyes.

"I didn't like sending them to the spirit world. I don't have full control over what happens there. The adult spirits can handle it. They've fought their way through decades of life. They comprehend what's happening, at least as much as any mortal can.

"But how could the children understand? How could they speak for themselves? If the council responsible for their safety doesn't make the right choice, doesn't place them in the right home for care and rehabilitation, what are they supposed to do? Suffer? More than they already have?"

Her hands won't stop trembling. I take one, and the other joins our mess of fingers a moment later. Sadness twists through her hair, wilting flowers pulling her to the dusty earth.

"I wanted to keep them. I thought if they stayed with us, if we helped them understand, they would find peace, and we wouldn't have to send them away. They could be with me until they were ready.

"We had so many. Enough to make an entire American football team. We remembered all their names. We tried not to play favorites, but the young ones were always so helpless. They wanted me. They *needed* me."

She pulls her hands from mine and stands, restless. Her ballet slippers tap against the center of the stone path, but she still makes no sound. Her hand brushes the pendants on the black cord, each prayer clinking against the next.

"Kenichi was the youngest one." Her arms ascend to her waist, forming an empty cradle. "He was a baby. Based on what I had heard of mortal children, I expected him to be a nightmare. I can't tell you how many parents have prayed to us, pleading for their babies' cries to ease or for a few more hours of sleep.

"He was different. Kenichi never fussed or grumbled. He was the happiest child I have ever known. He smiled like a red panda. He cooed like a sweet-faced carrier pigeon with a love letter in its beak. He loved me so much. I could feel it every time I held him."

She ventures too far away, her voice nearly lost in the hollows of the shrine. I rise from the offering box and follow her.

"We got into an argument, Daikokuten and I. I don't remember what it was about, but I assume it was his fault." She turns, half-smiling. Her eyes scan mine like she's searching for something, but I don't know what she wants. "But even if I was in the wrong, he had no right to do what he did.

"I had stormed off to cool down, and when I returned, they were gone. All of them. He had taken the children to the council, and he had the audacity to stand there, alone, and act like he had done the right thing.

"I looked at him and asked, 'Where are they?'

"'I told you,' he said. 'You couldn't handle them, so I brought them to those who can. They'll know what to do.'

"'But not Kenichi,' I said. 'Not the baby. Right?'"

She puts her hand on the thin trunk of a tree, the one from which she leapt that first night. Her fingernails rest against the bark like she's threatening its life, but then she relaxes. Her hand slips. She brings it to her side.

"Do you know what it's like to look into the face of someone you loved, someone you thought you knew, and realize you can never go back to the way things were?"

I say nothing, but my fingers twitch at my sides, reaching for Angel's hand, for Sunny's, for anyone anywhere, even if I know they will always be the one to let go first.

"You do," she says softly. Her hand curls around mine. "It hurts, and every time you peel off a piece of yourself in the hopes of healing, you find more hurt. It goes deeper and deeper, and it feels like it will never stop." She looks up, her eyes a thousand shards of stars, each one shattering into smaller pieces, then smaller pieces still. "Doesn't it?"

I nod. I have to tell myself to stop nodding because if I don't, I'll nod forever. *Yes, yes, yes, yes. That's exactly how it feels.*

"I ran to the council. I begged. *I* begged. I *begged*." She says it over and over, not believing her own words, her own actions, her own tired, ungodly desperation. "But the council members said it was for the best. That's what I was supposed to be doing. Giving the children to them.

"So they were gone. And so was I."

The sun is setting. The colors melt into each other, pink crying into orange. How does it feel to have a sky weep just for her?

"I swore I wouldn't get attached anymore. I wasn't going to open myself up to hurt like that ever again." She raises her head, her eyes wide. "I didn't even want to help *you*."

I press my lips together. That's the first time she's ever said that. But it's probably not the first time she's thought it.

"I had to, though," she says. "I didn't feel like I had a choice."

Why? She's never explained.

Before I can reach for my whiteboard, she starts talking again.

"Now you know why I didn't want to get involved with the lovely ballerina. I'm already too involved in your world."

I touch the strap of my bag. I shouldn't have asked so many questions. I spent so much time resenting the people who needed to know the whys and hows, only to turn around and do the same thing to her.

"If you're going to apologize, don't." Her eyes find me. "You have a good heart, Machi. I hope you know that."

She squeezes my hand once, then disappears in a burst of white light. As it fades, I catch a glimpse of eerily familiar blue eyes. Watching.

As I walk back to the bus stop, I keep glancing over my shoulder.

But I am always alone.

THE LAST THING I want to do after hearing the saddest story of a goddess's centuries-long life is listen to my parents talk about how dusty my dead grandparents' house is. But if I can't be a good daughter by speaking and attending funerals and going to school like a normal person, I can at least put up with a little grumbling.

"When we get home," my father says into the phone, "I'm never complaining about cleaning our apartment again. If I do, just remind me of this house."

My mother scoffs. "It isn't that bad."

"Yeah? *You* try dusting the old bookshelf and inhaling a spiderweb."

"Who dusts with his mouth open?"

He moves the phone away. "What are you talking about? You were doing that same thing not even five seconds ago."

I smile. They're ridiculous. Eighty percent of the time, they're relatively serious, but in that other twenty percent, anything goes. I once opened their bedroom door to ask if I could go out and found them lying together on the bed, watching online juggling tutorials, my father's old tennis balls in their hands.

"I'm just glad this is the last house I should have to clean," my father says.

They both stop talking for a minute.

They never sat me down to walk me through their love story, but I've managed to cobble together enough of a narrative. They met in college, either through mutual friends or at a party, and formed a study group. Everyone dated everyone in that group. It was like the ensemble cast of a TV show. My parents were the only ones who stuck together.

Upon learning his mother had passed away when he was in high school and his father in his freshman year of college, my mother wept. She asked what he did when the holidays rolled around, and he said he stayed at the dorm. Then she wept again. My mother, ever the crybaby. In that way, she reminds me of Benzaiten, who has cried for every child she has met.

Including, somehow, me, when she read my letter to Dr. Tsui about Angel and Sunny.

I don't know if my mother warned him before bringing him to her hometown for Christmas. I hope, for his sake, she did. It's hard enough to meet a significant other's parents. It's much harder to meet them by staying at their house for the holidays in a town where the neighbors are discriminatory at best and flat-out racist at worst.

When my parents married, they moved to my mother's hometown. It made the most sense in every logical way, but emotionally, mentally, it must have been horrid. That's why, when they decided to start a family, they moved here. Away from the town of people who once gave my mother—and only my mother—rice instead of Halloween candy because they figured that was all she ate.

Here, they could forget their pasts almost entirely. My father could be more than the man who had to clean out his own home, plan his parents' funerals, and sort out all the financial obligations while his classmates got drunk on dollar beers and wine coolers. Returning to my mother's childhood home and cleaning the way he did so many years ago must remind him of those lonely days. All the time he spent packing up things he knew his parents would want him to have but didn't keep because he was always a minimalist. All the papers he had to sort through. All the people he had to call.

I think of Benzaiten and how she never told me what happened with Daikokuten and the child spirits until today. How I didn't tell Dr. Tsui anything about Angel and Sunny and still don't want to talk about Benzaiten. How my parents tried to wipe their own slates clean and raise me in a town where I never feel out of place. Not because I look Japanese, anyway.

But our pasts never really disappear. They come back again

and again, sometimes when we least expect it. All we can do is hold on and pray for a better future.

I take my phone and tap out a message.

"Machi texted me," my mother says. "'I bet the spider you inhaled tasted better than anything Mom could cook.' Hey!"

My father's laughter fills my ear. After one more second of irritation, my mother joins in, her giggles like bubbles.

"That's true," my father says. "That's very true."

Sorry, Dr. Tsui. I'm not answering the prompt today.

For the record, though, nothing relaxes me. I am eternally sad, anxious, or both.

It feels strange to write to you now after writing the first three entries to Sheryl. It's like I'm talking about my ex.

I saw a lot of doctors before Sheryl. You know how there are womanizers? People who jump from partner to partner? I was beginning to feel like a doctorizer.

The first one didn't know how to handle me. She told me to close my eyes and explain what I saw, but what could I do? I didn't talk, and all I ever saw was the insides of my own eyelids.

The second was the embodiment of the yin on this notebook. Everything was negative. We were passive beings in our own lives, buffeted by the winds of fate, and in the end, our existence was meaningless. Thanks, but I'm enough of a pessimist as it is. I don't need someone to wait for the world to end with me.

I saw the third one once. I don't remember what was wrong. I just don't think we were a match. That happens a lot, right? It isn't just a me thing?

The fourth one let me stay quiet the entire time. Do you know how long fifty-five minutes is? I do. He told my parents he couldn't help me, and though it stung, I had to admire his honesty.

The fifth one was a teddy bear of a man. He had my parents sit in on sessions so they could feed him bits and pieces of my past. The things they knew. The events they thought led up to my silence. The whole time, he made little comments, these *I sees* and *oh, mys* and *hmm-hmm-hmms* that did nothing to help. He reminded me of an uncle at a distant cousin's graduation party. We were there because we had to be, and neither of us was particularly thrilled about it.

Then there was Sheryl.

I'll refrain from writing out long descriptions of her office, though I spent enough time staring at her walls and her desk and her mug of cake pops to paint you a detailed picture. The one thing I'll say is this: I couldn't understand the point of those cross-stitches and framed decorations with happy suns and motivational quotes. Reading them has never put a smile on my face or inspired me to do better. They just annoy me.

Or, well, they did at first. After a while, though, I realized Sheryl straightened them before every session to make them face me, as if she knew I didn't believe them but hoped I would someday. I still don't know if I ever did, but over time, something about them felt genuine. Because *she* felt genuine.

Are you jealous yet?

I'm kidding.

I knew I would like her from the first time we met. She had a soft, sweet voice. It could have sounded patronizing, but it was Sheryl, so it wasn't. She didn't mind laying out every part of the therapy process for me. She told me what she wanted to accomplish in our sessions (find the root of the problems that had brought me to her office), how she would accomplish it (let me write on my whiteboard, with no pressure to talk next time or the time after that), and what her greatest hope was (for me to get to a place where I could choose to return to her office if I needed her instead of forcing myself to see her). It seemed so easy when she explained it that way.

My parents thought she was a genius. They had liked the fifth doctor, mostly because he included them, but they loved Sheryl. Every time Sheryl poked her head out of her office to say hello before escorting me out, my mother would tell me, *I feel like she's the one.*

She could have been the one, I think, but we all know she wasn't. She couldn't be.

When she said she was leaving, I asked if it was for a bad reason. She said it was.

I asked her if she was coming back. She said she didn't know.

I said I was sorry. She said she was too.

I hate to come back to the exes analogy, but you know how people say they sent a drunk text to their ex or stalked their old friends' social media or looked up their names online? I do that with Sheryl. Is that bad? Is that creepy? Maybe, but it's like an addiction. I was left with so few answers, I had to seek my own.

I haven't found any, though. Using a search engine only brings up her old website and credentials. The things I already know.

Hey, Dr. Tsui. Are you going to leave me like the others? If you do, just know I'll internet-stalk you too. Doesn't that make you feel better?

CHAPTER FOURTEEN

THE HOSPITAL HALLWAY is deathly quiet.

I didn't know what to expect when Benzaiten met me at her shrine and told me to come with her, but I definitely didn't think we would wind up at a hospital.

I've never had to visit a hospital before. My grandparents were relatively healthy until they passed away, and my parents have only been to the ER once or twice, never long enough for me to stop by.

But I don't need first-hand experience to know how unnerving hospitals can be.

Maybe, I think as Benzaiten checks the room numbers in the hallway, she wants to remind me of how lucky I am. After two and a half weeks of dragging me around to different cities with only a daruma plushie and a couple of stamped admissions tickets to show for it, she's given up on trying to change my mind by convincing me the human world is beautiful and wonderful. Her plan now is to make me realize I don't have a reason to want to be a robot vacuum cleaner when my family and I are healthy.

That won't work, though. I'm fortunate in a lot of ways, but recognizing my privilege doesn't invalidate the hurt still growing in my chest like a deep-rooted weed.

Around the corner, in the nearest room, someone sniffles. Benzaiten peeks in. I try to pull her back by the flowing sleeve, but she shakes me off, and soon, after a quick glance over my shoulder, I join her.

"Shh," a man says. He sits on a chair beside the bed. His hands fold around a woman's small palm. She lies on the bed, her eyes fixed on the ceiling. Tears leak onto her pillow, spreading across the white cotton fabric. Wave after wave of indescribable sorrow seeps out from the couple. It hurts to even look at them.

Benzaiten steps back. Keeping her voice low, she says, "He must have split off somewhere."

Who?

She grabs my hand and pulls me forward, her fingertips nearly pinching mine, but I slip out of her grasp. Taking a step back, I give her a look. I don't know if she's talking about Daikokuten or a child spirit, but regardless, she should have told me. I was prepared for an excursion around town or even a visit to an art supplies store, the way she suggested at the museum, but not a hospital visit.

She lets out a breath and does a little dip of frustration, the hem of her dress hovering an inch above the hospital floor. "I hear a spirit, Machi. He's somewhere around here. We have to find him."

Everything in me is saying *No. Stop. I don't want this.*

But I let her grab my hand and pull me along the corridor. It feels like I'm with Angel again, getting hauled along on outings I never explicitly agreed to. And, just as I did during that final adventure, I have a bad feeling I can't shake.

I keep waiting for a nurse or doctor to stop us and demand to know where we're going, but no one even glances at us. Everyone is too busy rushing to the next patient, hoping to save a life. I guess in a way, Benzaiten is doing the same thing.

"Where?" she whispers. Then she answers her own question, her eyes hooking onto something behind me. "There."

Outside a hospital room, a couple leans against a giant teddy bear, talking to someone in the room. The bear's rump is planted on the floor, undoubtedly picking up germs. Something glints near the plush toy's right leg, but even as Benzaiten dashes over and crouches to get a closer look, I can't make it out. Her hands, eager and greedy, wrap around it. The glinting thing moves, taking shape in her arms. She steals a glance back at the couple with the bear, then grabs my hand and flashes us out.

I don't know if it's because she's doing it too often or because her energy is so frenetic, but when we appear at the shrine, I collapse onto the offering box, my heart pounding.

"You're safe now," Benzaiten says.

The words aren't for me.

I look up, squinting in the fading sunlight. Her sleeves obscure most of whatever is in her arms, but until I manage to stand, my knees wobbly, I don't understand what it is.

"I'm naming him Kenji," Benzaiten says.

Loosely clutching the white fabric of her sleeve is a tiny baby.

I stumble back, nearly losing my footing. I take out my whiteboard and write, *What are you doing? What's going on?*

She hardly bothers to read it. "Stop freaking out. He's a new spirit, but his energy is powerful. Can you believe I could sense such a tiny thing?"

The baby lets out a small noise, more like a dog's whimper than anything I've heard from a human. His eyes roll as he works to orient himself in a stranger's arms. He lifts an impossibly small fist, the fingers like those of a doll.

"Shh-shh. It's all right." Her smile is warm. She takes his hand and kisses it, her lips the color of a dusty rose. "I have you now."

Are you going to help him cross over?

I have to tap her shoulder four times before she reads my message, and when she does, she only shrugs. "I need to make sure he's safe first. He's so small. Look at how small he is. Did you hear I named him Kenji? Isn't it perfect?"

Unease drips into my stomach. I don't like the way she's looking at him.

Is it okay for you to do this?

She rolls her eyes. "Machi. I'm a goddess. I can do what I want."

The drip gets faster. I imagine it's slowly poisoning me, the toxin so diluted, it'll take days for me to feel it.

How are you going to help him?

"Machi, can you quit it?" She takes a hand and pushes my whiteboard back to me. The tail of the speech balloon shape jams into my ribs. "I heard him. He needed me. Weren't you the one who kept nagging me to help the other spirits?"

I look away, wiping the board clean.

Stupid. So stupid. I don't know why I even tried to say anything. She's just like Angel. Once she sets her mind to something, she's never giving up.

But Benzaiten cried for you, a little voice in my head says. *She knows what happened with Angel and Sunny. She would never do anything like that to you.*

I swallow hard, searching the shrine for something familiar. Sheryl was the one to teach me that, little ways of ensuring I stay in the moment, but Dr. Tsui gave me a recent reminder. After telling him about Benzaiten—which I still can't believe I had to do—he said if I ever started to feel overwhelmed, the way I did at the club with Angel and Sunny, I should find something to keep me grounded.

I mean, it's kind of hard to stay grounded when affiliating with a goddess, but I get the point.

Benzaiten's golden eyes rise to my face. "I'm sorry. That was too much. I didn't mean to say that." In her arms, the baby squirms, uncertain and restless. She moves to her altar, leans against it, and, in a single, fluid motion, rips the bottom of her dress.

I stand, too surprised to move, as she swaddles the baby with the torn piece of fabric. She does it like it comes naturally, like she's done it a thousand times before. As I watch her, I think of what she said about the other child spirits, the ones she couldn't keep.

"There." She brings him to her face and kisses his forehead. "Is that better?"

The baby gurgles. He's gotten used to her, his eyes latching onto hers again and again.

"Don't look so worried," she says, and though her words are for me, she can't take her eyes off him. "Everything is fine."

What are we going to do now? I start to write.

But as her ripped dress waves in the sudden breeze, she and the child disappear.

I don't remember how to walk for the next few seconds. When I turn, I catch a glimpse of silver, then a pair of dark blue eyes.

If Daikokuten wants to say something, I wish he would just come out and say it.

But I don't exactly have a right to get upset with someone for not talking.

It takes a moment, but he emerges from the shadows, bits and pieces of darkness pulling together to form his broad shoulders. I'm almost too busy staring into his eyes to notice the hammer. Which is quite a feat. I mean, it's a *hammer*.

I tense as he draws closer. The color of his eyes changes like a desktop screensaver, shifting from ocean blue to navy to black.

"You know it, don't you?" he says.

I hesitate, then shake my head.

"You're afraid of losing her." He narrows his eyes. "But you're even more afraid you already have."

I suppress a shiver. The very air around him is cold, like we've been plunged into the sea.

"You shouldn't have ever met her," he says.

I want to look away, but his eyes are so captivating. A rat skitters along the ground beneath his heavy boots, then sits right beside his heel.

"She'll make you regret it," he says. He leans in. He smells like steamed rice, earth, and money. "She'll make you regret everything."

I close my eyes and flinch back, crouching the way I did in that stupid souvenir shop. Pulling my hands over my head, I wait for him to do something. Say something. At least bop me with his hammer and put me out of my misery.

It's quiet.

I look up.

He's gone.

WHEN MY PHONE buzzes, it startles me so badly, I nearly fall out of my chair. I've been jumpy ever since my one-sided conversation with Daikokuten, and the silence of the house doesn't help.

Picking up my phone, I glance at my mother's message: Call?

I plug in my earbuds and respond with a thumbs-up. My phone goes crazy, shaking and vibrating like an overeager golden retriever until I tap the screen.

"Hi," she says. "I was thinking of you. Have you gone to the store yet? Your dad's not here, but you can text me. I don't mind switching between apps."

I check my phone like I think I might be on a call with the

wrong mother. She never gave in to total despair after her parents' death, but she seems strangely bubbly. Either she found money stuffed in my grandparents' closet or she's lonely.

I'm going to the store after this.

"That sounds like a plan," she says.

I haven't heard those words since I was little, when she would offer up two seemingly fair options just to give me the illusion of choice. *Do you want to buy artichoke hearts or asparagus spears? Which one is calling your name this week?* Then, after waiting for my response, she would reply, *That sounds like a plan.*

"Did I say your father is away?"

You did. I pause. Are you all right?

"Oh, yeah." I can hear her chewing on her thumbnail. "I'm fine. How about you? Are you doing okay? We've been away for, what, two and a half weeks now?"

I start to correct her, but when I open my calendar app, I freeze. It really has been that long. Two and a half weeks since I met Benzaiten, which means there aren't even three weeks left before the deadline she set for my prayer.

"Machi? Is something wrong?"

Sorry. No.

"Okay."

She goes silent. I can hear her hair shifting on her pillow. I've heard it so many times, her head beside mine when she would curl up next to me on my bed. I think back to the sleepy little girl. The woman on the hospital bed. The man's hands on hers.

Mom? Why did you call?

"I can't call you?"

You can. I mean, you do. Something's wrong, though. Right?

"No. Yes?" She exhales. "I don't know. Do you remember when we used to hang out on your bed and talk about things?"

I press lightly, as if I don't want to hurt the keyboard. I was just thinking about that.

"Really?" I can hear her every breath. "Do you miss that?"

I don't know. Did we ever stop? Like for sure?

She doesn't quite laugh. Wonder, an unspoken question, twists through the threads of her voice. "I guess we didn't."

Why are you thinking about that?

"I don't know." Inhale. Exhale. Inhale. "Do you know your grandma used to do that with me when I was little?"

I sit on the edge of my bed. She did?

"It's hard to imagine, isn't it?" She does that same not-laugh and ends up coughing. It makes her seem older somehow.

I don't have many memories of either of my grandparents aside from those Christmas visits, which always involved the discussion of moving back to my mother's home state. My grandmother wasn't afraid to play dirty, quick to guilt-trip my mother or take her down memory lane, only to say, at the end, *Wasn't that nice? Don't you want to remember?* As if she could ever really forget.

"She did her best," my mother says. "Most mothers do."

I don't want to think of the woman in the hospital room, her face hollow and sharp in the shadows. She didn't even get a chance to try with her baby.

I wonder what she's doing now. If she's eating. If she's sleeping. If she wakes up with tear streaks on her face.

I've been thinking a lot about funerals and crossing over to the next world, but what happens to the people left behind? Who takes care of them?

"We would talk about all kinds of things. I won't say I told her everything, but—" My mother's voice breaks. "I miss her. I miss both of them."

I start typing but delete it all twice.

"I didn't even say goodbye."

I fix my left earbud. I want to listen harder. Tell her I'm sorry.

"Everyone says it's hard to be a parent. It's hard to know what you're doing. Are you a guardian? A friend? When a child misbehaves, do you yell? Do you laugh? How do your parents' actions impact what you do to your child? 'It's hard to be a parent,' people say." Her breath is a wisp in my ear. "But sometimes, it's hard to be a child too."

I can't take care of the woman who lost her child. But I can take care of the woman who lost her parents.

I know, I type back. I'm here.

The moment she reads my message, my mother sucks in a breath, lets out a choked sound, and starts to cry.

CHAPTER FIFTEEN

"IS THIS ALL for today?"

I can't even bring myself to look up. Angel may have been the one to love fruit snacks and multicolored yogurt tubes, at least until she got tired of them, but I'm the real child here. I'm the one who had a breakdown next to a bunch of Toridachi merchandise that night at the club and, now, the one who ran to some hipster café called The Bean Jive to buy cake pops because she couldn't stop thinking about someone who probably never thinks about her.

I know I should move on. I've finally started connecting to Dr. Tsui. I even told him about Benzaiten. Inadvertently, sure, but that's still something.

I lift my head to nod at the cashier—but at the sight of him, my heart falters. I squeeze my hand around my wrist until I think I might shatter my own bones.

I gawk at him. Will. The lost hiker from that sixth-grade camping trip. He has the same caramel hair, but it's shorter now, only partially hiding the small metal stud in his left earlobe. I wonder when he got it. If it hurt.

He hasn't changed much. I didn't know him well before and could never face him after. He didn't seem to hold it against me—none of them did—but I'm sure he blames me in some capacity. After all, I'm the reason he was the top candidate for cannibalization.

"Um," he says. "Is this . . . all? For today?"

I nod. I think. I can't be sure. Even as he rings me up and hands back my change, I can't stop looking at him.

Noticing my staring, he gives me a tight-lipped smile. He must think I'm checking him out. Or trying to vaporize him with my eyes.

Then he tilts his head. "Wait. Do I know you?"

For a second, everything goes dark, as if I've been plunged back into that claustrophobic tunnel.

I grab the cake pops and take off running, the way I should have the moment I realized he and the others were gone.

The sound of my boots on the pavement reminds me of the pulse of the bass at the club. Of the thump of my mother's phone on the floor when her neighbors, the ones who made her life a living hell, called to say her parents had died. Of my heartbeat in my ears when I left the house, armed with my tippy-tappy device and a corroded nickel.

I fully intend on running all the way to Benzaiten's shrine, but I haven't had a PE class since my freshman year, and even then, I always got lapped by the track girls. By the time I reach the fading torii, I have to take a few minutes to catch my breath.

Not that it matters. Benzaiten doesn't appear.

Once I've managed to stop gasping like a fish out of water, I dig into my pocket and pull out my change from the cake pops.

Before I can fling a nickel into the box, Benzaiten materializes, her ponytail unwinding like a scroll. The baby's mouth opens wide as he reaches for a piece of her hair.

I don't know whether to tell her about Will or not. I feel like I should. Or maybe I just want to. Maybe I want to hear what she thinks. Maybe I want her to calm me down and say it wasn't as awkward as I feel like it was.

But I'm afraid if I tell her, she'll immediately assume I have feelings for him. She's the goddess of love, after all.

Everyone thinks finding a boyfriend is the answer, but it's not. I don't want my happiness to be based around one person. Not even two people. I've learned my lesson.

"What do you want, Machi?"

Something pulls in my chest.

I watch Benzaiten, waiting for her to look at me, but she hardly lifts her eyes from Kenji. Her gaze flicks from my hands to my face. "What is this?"

I turn the wrappers to let her see the paper labels, but her expression doesn't change.

"Cake pops?"

We stand, blinking at each other.

She runs a hand through the baby's downy hair. "Why are you showing these to me?"

You take me places to try new things, so I thought I would bring something to you. I spread the cake pops like a hand of cards. The little sign next to the display said chocolate and funfetti were the most popular flavors, so I bought two of each.

Benzaiten's eyes skim over my words. "Oh. That's nice of you. Can you unwrap one for me? I don't want to put him down when he looks so peaceful."

Kenji always looks peaceful. It's freaky. My exposure to babies essentially ended when I was no longer a baby myself, but even I can see he's unnaturally good-natured. I keep expecting Benzaiten to turn him over to reveal a battery pack.

I unwrap the chocolate cake pop first, handing her one and keeping the other. I let her take a bite. Then I nibble on the top of mine. The cake is spongy, but the outer shell keeps it from being too squishy. I can imagine Sheryl saying, *That's the beautiful thing about cake pops, Machi: they may have a hard outer coating, but they're sweet and soft inside.*

I look to Benzaiten. She breaks off a piece and places it in Kenji's gaping mouth. She glances at me, then does a double take when she realizes I'm staring. Narrowing her eyes, she says, "What? He's a spirit. He can eat mortal food."

I point at the cake pop, but she doesn't say anything. I sit on the offering box and write, *What do you think of the chocolate cake pop?*

She doesn't even look at the board.

I finish my cake pop, twist the wrapper around the stick, and drop it into my bag. Benzaiten rocks Kenji, the swaying motion hypnotizing.

What are we doing today?

"I thought we could take it easy." She slides the rest of the cake pop into her mouth and chews, the chocolate outside crunching between her teeth. As she swallows, I take the stick. "Thanks. You know, just while Kenji is getting adjusted to me."

I study the baby. His eyes are the color of molasses. His eyelashes are thin and delicate, and his eyebrows are sparse. His cupid's bow dips low. He has shallow dimples that only appear when Benzaiten laughs or leans in close and hums in his ear. He's cute, I suppose, but I don't see why she's so obsessed with him.

I turn my head, disgusted with myself. She's lost spirits before. Of course she would be happy to have a child again.

And he's a *baby*. He never even got to leave the hospital. If he had lived, maybe he would have grown up to be as sweet and thoughtful as the boy who fell in love with the fish at Kingyo Sukui. As graceful and talented as the ballerina who pushed herself to jump higher, dance harder, be better. As innocent and warm as the sleepy girl who just wanted to curl up with her kitty toy and dream of fairies and princesses.

Or maybe he would have ended up like me, bitter and lost and alone.

As if reading my mind, Benzaiten shakes her head and says, "He had so little time. His memories have this beautiful, lacy quality to them. Here."

Before I can pull away, she brings my hand to the soft crown of the baby's head, my fingertips grazing the swirl of his hair.

I tumble into cotton.

IT'S THE VOICE he has heard in his dreams. In all the times before, the voice was sweet, the words curling around him, forming the strings of his heart. The voice is different now, rising and falling in cacophonic, orchestral pain.

He floats. Something tells him it's time to leave, but he clings to the warmth around him, his fingers stretching. He thinks, *Just a little more time*, but no one is listening. He is pulled out into a cold white world of sights and sounds, and he doesn't like it. He opens his mouth and wails, voicing his displeasure.

Then he's warm again. A sense of security sweeps over him. He closes his eyes. If he tries hard enough, he can almost believe he's back where he was. He sighs.

Noises. They shake him awake. They put something in his mouth. He's choking, but they're in too much of a rush to care. He squints, his hands waving, seeking warmth. There are voices everywhere, but none is the one he wants. Where are the dulcet tones? How does he get them back?

Everything hurts. He screams, the way he did before, and waits for the warmth to fix everything, note by note. But it doesn't come, and it hurts. It hurts it hurts it hurts it hurts it—

I YANK MY hand away, snipping myself free from the memories I never wanted. I take a step back, but I'm unused to my own body. I fall, my palms biting into the stone path. My skin smarts but doesn't break.

She doesn't take her eyes off the baby. "Are you okay?"

I didn't ask to see that. He didn't understand what was happening. The memories did have a laciness to them, like each one was filtered through a thin doily. But there was nothing beautiful about them.

I remain on the ground. I can't stop thinking about his parents, so hidden in their grief. I have to swallow to keep myself from crying.

"Oh, oh, oh." Benzaiten brushes a thumb along the child's forehead. "Machi, I'm going to get something to sit on. I can't hold him like this."

I don't even try to respond, my fingers running along the cracks in the path as she and the baby vanish. I study my palms, tracing the places where the stones have pressed themselves into my skin. The longer I examine my hands, the more I feel like someone is here.

I turn. Sitting at the edge of the torii is a silver rat. We watch each other, engaging in an unexpected staring match.

I lose.

I crawl closer. My fingers are inches away when he shows up, his boots appearing behind the rat's sleek body. His mallet taps against the pavement. I get to my feet and move a few paces back, avoiding his night-sky eyes.

"You okay?"

It's strange. His voice is gruffer than I remembered, but beneath the barbs is genuine concern. He seems more worried than Benzaiten.

Yes, he tore apart their found family. Sure, he can't leave her alone, even when she's doing the right thing. Yeah, he has a hammer.

But no matter how much she ignores him, no matter how angry she gets, he keeps hoping. He *stays*.

I've never known anyone like that.

"You ever think maybe there's another side to the story?"

My eyes meet his, but before I can consider taking out my whiteboard, the rat skitters up to his shoulder, and he dissipates.

"Here we go."

I look back to the altar. Benzaiten stands in the center of the stone path, setting down the daruma doll she won from Japantown. She tests it, sinking her hands into the plush, then sits in its center. It envelops her like a beanbag chair.

She lifts her head. "What are you doing over there?"

I return to her side, sitting on the offering box. The baby clutches the ends of her ponytail. When his hand buzzes, her hair falls back onto her shoulder. He raises an arm, his eyes focusing on his wavering fist, and coos, the sound rising at the end like a question.

"Yes, that's you." She kisses his forehead. "Mommy loves you, Kenji."

I pull at my sleeves. I will not think of the parents in the hospital room.

It's not as if Benzaiten stole the baby. If not for her, the child would have become a wandering spirit. If anything, she did them a favor.

"No wonder no one visits this shrine." She glances around the shrine grounds, keeping her head close to the baby so he can play with her hair. "There's, like, nothing here. Just an offering box and an altar nobody has dusted for years."

I pull out my whiteboard, taking my time as I write out my message. I make each letter prettier than it needs to be. *What if we fix it up?*

She raises an eyebrow. The baby giggles. She smiles at him and does it again, finding pleasure in performativity. She beams as his laughter pops up like bright wildflowers.

I tap my hand on my whiteboard.

Annoyed, she looks up. "What are you talking about?"

We could fix the shrine together. Repaint the torii. Start watering the plants. Add some stalls or something. People might start praying here again.

I realize, as she lazily turns her head to read my message, I might not want that. This is where she and I hang out. The whole reason why I snuck over to this shrine was because I was hoping it would be abandoned. I mean, what if someone makes a Yelp page for it? What will I do then?

She waves a hand. "There's no point in that. Kenji and I are okay with this daruma doll. Aren't we, Kenji?"

The baby babbles, his vowels wide and long. I can't be sure, but I think his eyes flash gold, matching Benzaiten's perfectly.

I stand. Unsettled energy jolts through my legs. I look down, half-expecting my jeans to buzz in and out of sight.

When she took me to Japantown, I imagined I was an ice sculpture moments away from shattering into pieces. I didn't realize then how Benzaiten would thaw me, melting my heart a little more every time she dragged me somewhere or looked at me with her amber eyes. But even as I edge onto the stone path, I feel myself stagnating, stuck in an unfinished state.

The worst part is knowing I was heading somewhere. I had snagged on thorn after thorn, sagging lower each time, but just when I thought I was on my way up again, it all stuttered to a stop, hope just out of reach.

Talk to me, I want to say. But I stay silent, placing my whiteboard in my bag. It clunks against something.

The funfetti cake pops.

My steps are slow. I don't take my eyes off her. I wait for her to notice my retreat, drop her lips into a frown, and ask, *Where do you think you're going? What about the other cake pops? Come back, silly mortal. I still haven't granted your wish yet, remember?*

I remember. I'm just not sure *she* does.

I reach the torii. She remains on the path, cozy in the center of the daruma plush, her divine arms never tiring of holding the baby. Even when he flickers, disappearing for one terrifying second, she maintains that same placid expression, certain he'll come back.

I walk home, my heart sinking. Every time I turn a corner, I swear I see a silver rat, its dark eyes never leaving me.

AS SOON AS Andrew opens the door, he takes a breath and says, "I'm sorry."

I peel my eyes off the PULL sticker and tip my head to the side.

He shuffles his feet. "I didn't mean to make you feel uncomfortable the last time you were here."

Right. He mentioned having a daughter my age, and I flipped out like he had insulted my mother's cooking.

Well, okay. Bad example. He has every right to insult my mother's cooking.

I wasn't upset at him, though. I never was. I just couldn't take it anymore, surrounded by the ghosts of the ballerina and Angel and Sunny and everyone I've ever connected with, afraid Andrew would be the next to leave.

"I was afraid you weren't going to come back," he says.

I shake my head, frustrated with myself. I don't know how to apologize when I can't even explain what made me run in the first place.

"I'm sorry," he says again, unwittingly shoveling another pound of guilt over my head. "I'm glad to see you again."

I smile, and his relief is instant, his shoulders relaxing and his eyes softening. Opening the door wider, he says, "Come in."

One of the dogs I gingerly patted on the head the other day has been adopted, he tells me as I make my way through the store, but they got more rats. He takes his seat at the counter, and I roam around, my boots clicking against the hard floor.

The ginger cat makes a tight, tense circle in the crate. I kneel beside the rat enclosure.

Only to find Daikokuten's rats staring at me.

I lose my balance, tipping to one side and catching myself with a scrabbling hand. The two new rats are familiar, silver and well-groomed. They watch me with a freakishly human level of concentration, their eyes beady but observant.

"Whoa," Andrew says, standing from his stool. "Are you all right?"

I nod, trying to slow my heart rate. He frowns as I turn back to the rat enclosure. The two silver rats have disappeared, replaced by a brown and white pair.

I stand, still wobbly from shock, and meet Andrew at the counter. I don't even know exactly what I'm doing until I reach him, but the second I spot the lingering uncertainty on his face, I take out my wallet. It's not really much of an apology, especially since I can't tell him he did absolutely nothing wrong, but if I throw money at the problem, maybe it'll go away.

Or maybe I've been spending too much time around two of the Seven Gods of Fortune.

I extract two twenty-dollar bills from my wallet and hold them out to Andrew, but he shakes his head.

"You don't have to do that," he says. "My family and I didn't go into the shelter business—if you can even call it a business—for the money. We make do, though. We had money before, and we have money now."

I try again, waving my forty dollars in his face, but he gently pushes my hand away. Defeated, I slide the money back into my wallet.

As I return my wallet to my bag, my hand brushes against something. When I pull out a funfetti cake pop, I present it to him like that had been my plan all along.

He looks up and grins. "For me?"

I nod.

"Thank you. I haven't had a cake pop in forever. Do you have one too?"

I root around in my bag for a moment and take out the other one. He gives me a thumbs-up and sets the calculator off to the side.

"Cheers," he says, knocking his cake pop against mine.

The plastic wrappers crinkle, laughing.

MACHI?

Once I send a thumbs-up, my phone starts buzzing. I fix my earbuds and tap my screen. Beneath me, the mattress sculpts itself around the curve of my spine.

"Your mother's out shopping," my father says. "Angry-shopping."

He can't see me, but I make a face. When my family fights and my mother can't stand to be in the same house as the rest of us, she storms out, locks herself in her car, and speeds away to the closest mall. Most of the time, she doesn't buy much. She just blows off steam, power-walking through the stores like she's ready to rip off a mannequin's head.

"Now that we're almost done cleaning the house, I said we should talk about what to do with it. Right?" My father pauses like he expects validation. "I said I would start looking for real estate agents or ways to list the house online, but she went, 'Are you crazy?'"

I set my phone on my bed, roll onto my side, and curl my knees to my chest. My wall is blank. I close my eyes.

"She got all snappy and said she wants to keep it."

I don't know what we would do with the house. Maybe it's a good idea to let it sit under her name, just so we can spare blissfully ignorant house buyers from having to live in that town.

"She even said she's thinking of having us move here. As if it's only *her* decision."

My eyelids snap open. I sit up. Move there? All of us? To that town? The one where she had to campaign to get *out* of AP math because the administration was convinced she would be bored in any other class? She insisted on taking a placement test, even though the dean said the decision had already been made. Once the test results came in, she was quietly moved to the normal track.

"It would be cheaper. That's what she told me. And she says she feels an emotional connection to this place."

A connection she willingly severed for years.

"It was a whole thing." My father blows out his breath. "Anyway, she's out shopping now. I don't know when she'll come back. I thought I would let you know."

I've been lucky. Racism hasn't personally affected me as much as it affects so many others. The worst I've gotten here is the constant mispronunciation of my first or last name and a few slightly insensitive questions about my language or culture. I don't want to move to a town that has hated my family since my grandparents were little.

"That's all," my father says. "I'm going to take an angry nap now. Love you."

He hangs up. I remove my earbuds and wrap my arms around my pillow. My first instinct is to ask Benzaiten to help somehow, but I know that's not happening. Not when she's busy giving Kenji the love she used to give me. So I close my eyes and join my father in dreamland.

Prompt #5:
What is your best friend like?

Oh, Dr. Tsui. What a loaded question.

I'm sure it's sad to still think of Angel and Sunny as my best friends. But they were my *last* best friends, and I, despite writing about them in almost everything I've shown you, still don't think you have a clear picture of what they're like. I've focused on what our friendship looked like at the beginning, how it changed when Sunny joined us, and why it went up in flames, but I've left air holes. I thought it was to let the story breathe, keep it from blowing up in the kiln, but I'm realizing it's because I was afraid they would pull me back in. Make me miss them. So let me start filling in the painful gaps.

In a way, I was closer to Sunny than I ever was to Angel. Of the two, my heart was more similar to hers. I may have wished I could be more like Sunny sometimes, admiring her intelligence and unending kindness, but there were a lot of things for which I could never envy her. Before Angel and I came along, she didn't have any close friends. She told me, one day, she had never slept over at another girl's house. Not even when she was little. All the sleepovers were on weekends, and her life was a never-ending flood of Things to Do. If she wasn't in school, she was at a lesson or tutoring a classmate or helping around the house or working on orchestral arrangements with her instructor. It seemed like every one of our hangouts had to be scheduled at least a month in advance.

But she had an entire life plan. She could list the colleges with music scholarships faster than I could list the schools I had already attended. She knew she would be double-majoring in music and communications and, upon graduating, would test out a career in music while working for a corporation with a decent amount of paid vacation.

How do you do it? I asked her once as we sat together, our eyes on the horizon.

Do what? What am I doing?

How do you keep it all together?

She was quiet for a minute. I didn't look at her. We didn't have an explicit rule against eye contact, but we liked watching what was in front of us instead.

Everything is decided for me, she said. *I have a say, but not much. It's like I'm watching my life get built up, brick by brick, and maybe it's something I want, but maybe it's not. By the time I figure it out, maybe it'll be too late to say, "No, this isn't right." And then what?*

I don't know, Dr. Tsui. Then what?

That's another reason why I understood her on that last day. Her actions hardly ever came from an ugly place. She left me there, struck silent, not because she wanted me to hurt but because she wanted to save herself from hurting. She was given a choice for once, and she chose Angel. Of course she chose Angel. If she wanted to get away from the predictable, the planned, she couldn't run to anyone *but* Angel.

That's another reason why I understood. I would have chosen Angel too. I *did* choose Angel. Again and again. Until she didn't choose me back.

Angel had a way of finding the most eclectic songs. She would create entire playlists and give them esoteric names like *Sunday Morning (9:14 a.m.) Vibes* and *Lo-Fi Chillhop Jazz with Sprinkles of Rock.* She would send me links and write, *Doesn't this song make you feel like you're at a prom, and the lights are a deep violet, and your dress is red but looks maroon in the light, and someone asks you to dance, and in the shadows, he looks like your neighbor, but he's actually some guy named John?*

Yes. That's exactly how that song made me feel.

I wouldn't like the songs at first. They always sounded like clashing noises and the occasional death-metal scream. She was a fan of synthesizers and vocoders, and when I would play those songs through my computer speakers in my room, alone, they seemed creepy. I would tell her she had weird taste in music.

Then we would lie on the floor, and she would play the song again. And with her, my eyes closed and my heart open, the entire sound would change. The pain in the singer's voice would dribble out like last words. The layers of noise would peel back, back, back, until I could detect every purposeful note, every thematic chord. The things I thought were creepy made so much sense and carried so much meaning when she was there, and from that moment on, I understood.

Angel likes talking on the phone. She's one of the few people I know who does. When she called me the first couple of times, I couldn't understand the appeal. All the awkward pauses and static made me want to squish myself into a ball and retreat from human society. But one night, when I texted her about some dumb thing I can't remember now, she called me.

What are you doing? I asked in lieu of a greeting.

Choo-choo. All aboard the Late Night Train. Next stop: Sleepytown.

What are you talking about?

Some people sound different over the phone, but she didn't. If I ignored the ambient noises, the slight crackle, I could believe she was in my room, picking through my clothes or hiding under the bed to grab my ankle and scare me half to death.

You said you can't sleep, right? Her voice got raspy when she was tired. *Then talk to me until one of us nods off.*

But if you drift off first, won't I still be awake?

Yeah, but you'll get so bored of my snoring, you'll fall asleep. You see?

No?

Just talk, she said, and with that, she launched into a halfintelligible rant about her English teacher. She hated him because he was obsessed with those long-winded authors who used scatological humor to break up long paragraphs about the nature of the universe.

You want to find the meaning of life? she said, presumably using me as proxy for her teacher. *Me too, but I know I'm not going to find it between a description of a burnt forest that's supposedly an analogy for the destruction of the planet and a "cute" little story about an elf that can't find a toilet in time.*

I was quiet for a while.

Machi? Are you asleep?

No. How am I supposed to get tired when you're so amusing?

She scoffed. *What am I, your court jester?*

I don't know who fell asleep first. She swore she did, but I couldn't recall hanging up on her. I like to think we dozed off at the exact same time.

But our friendship wasn't perfect.

I mean, yeah. Clearly.

Even before that summer, though, we had our issues.

Angel once had this major crush on a guy. She would never stop talking about him. She asked me, over and over, how hot I thought he was. I don't know what she wanted me to say. Wouldn't it be weird for me to agree and go, *Yeah, I wish I could date him* if she also wanted him? But it didn't matter because I didn't see the appeal. I tried to provide lukewarm responses, but I guess I didn't act well enough. One day, while we were waiting for a bus, she rolled her eyes, stood up, and left me there.

There was also the time we were sitting on the admin building steps. She was telling me about negative bias. I'm sure you know what that is, being a therapist and all, but just as a little refresher: We remember the bad things more than the good. It's actually rather sad. Our brains can be hardwired into accepting negativity as the norm. We think, *Another bad thing happened.*

No surprise there. If something good happens, we write it off as a fluke or forget it entirely, and when something bad happens again, we think, *Ah, here we go. Back to normal.*

Angel is smart. I always told her she should take more psych classes, maybe even become a psychologist, but she just leaned forward and said, *Hey, have you ever heard of this thing called "SYSM"?*

No, I said. *What is that?*

It stands for "Shut Your Stupid Mouth."

She didn't like talking about school.

I don't think that was much of a fight, but I could feel the anger spinning off her skin. The next time she told me about a psychological discovery, I kept my stupid mouth shut.

Then there was the day she said she wanted me to meet her cousin, some up-and-coming entrepreneur with hundreds of thousands of dollars to his name. She was convinced we were meant to be. She was practically planning the wedding, dreaming of the day we could be a real family, even if it was just through marriage.

I told her I wasn't that interested. He was older, and I had never met him. Besides, I didn't think love was supposed to work like that.

She kept pushing. She said he was going to be on the cover of magazines someday. *And as, like, a businessman in a suit, not the subject of an exposé on child predators, which is what my other cousin is probably going to be known for.*

Her words.

She wouldn't let go of the idea, so I said, *I really appreciate it, but I think you may be going a little overboard.*

And I think YOU may be going a little UNDERboard.

We were lying on the floor in an empty classroom, as usual, but I could feel her energy pulsating. Her enthusiasm was like someone extending a hand and inviting you to jump into a game of double Dutch. All you wanted to do was hop in and feel that zeal, the glow that comes with being recognized.

Isn't he already an adult? Like a real adult? The ceiling was cracking at the corner. *What if we don't like each other?*

You will. She said it so easily, like once the words left her lips, they were law. *He's going to do great things. He can make you into someone.*

I sat up. *What does that mean?*

She got to her feet and ran a hand through her hair. *You know what I mean. We should go to class.*

I got my bag and met her at the door. *I'm someone all on my own.*

Really? She snagged a passing classmate by the backpack strap and spun him around to face us. *Do you know who she is?*

He followed her finger to me. *No?*

Thanks, she said, and she released him. Then she grabbed someone else. *Do you know who this girl is?*

Angel, I said, flames of humiliation licking my chest. *Stop.*

No? she said, analyzing the person's blank expression. *Okay, thanks.* She looked at me. *So when do you want to meet my cousin?*

I've always known, deep down, if I told someone the worst of what she had done, I would attract every type of why. A confused why, an irritated why, an accusatory *how could you put up with this?* why. But that's why I wasn't surprised when, on that last day, Sunny said nothing. That's why I knew, as soon as Angel turned on me, Sunny was going to stay silent. At the end of the day, we all just want to feel special.

You know, I was mulling over something the other day. In some ways, what happened with Angel and Sunny is like the story of drug addiction. If you were to reread my entries, assuming everything is metaphorical, it would seem almost coherent. Angel and I met when I was young, but I didn't really know her until a few years had passed. Everything was different with her, and soon, I needed her. When Sunny entered the picture, she created a direct conflict. There was friction. She was the part of me that knew something was wrong. But then Angel won her over too. Then it was only a matter of time before it all blew up in my face.

It's not a metaphor. Everything I've told you is real. Even the things about Benzaiten.

But it's funny how it kind of works, isn't it? How it could all be in my head? Wouldn't that be a wild twist?

Dr. Tsui, I haven't been sleeping well.

CHAPTER SIXTEEN

"I HAVE AN idea."

I pull my blanket up to my chin. That sounds like something Benzaiten would have said, pre-baby. I know I should go back and see if she has any more ideas about granting my prayer, but even if I go, she won't be thinking about me. She's all about Kenji now.

Guilt swims through my chest. I place a hand to my heart like I think I can suck it out with one palm. I know Kenji deserves a happy ending. We all do. I just wish it didn't feel like Benzaiten's prioritizing everyone but me, the only person desperate enough to pray to her in the first place.

Adjusting my earbuds so I can hear my mother better, I send a text to my father.

"She typed a question mark," he says to my mother, stress fraying the edges of his words.

"What do you think about moving here?" my mother asks.

My legs fold up to my arms, making me into a human pretzel. It's summer, but I'm freezing. Why?

"Because," my mother says when my father reads my one-word message, "I don't know. It's not so bad."

My father manages to swallow his mirthless laughter.

Last night, he told me about their trip to the market. As he and my mother collected ingredients for spaghetti, a man stopped and complimented them on their willingness to try new things. My father, hoping he was reading too much into the stranger's words, asked what he meant, to which the man said it was good for Asians to eat foods other than just rice and fish.

But yeah. It's not so bad.

Moving is certainly an idea that exists, I type. My stoic father reads the text in a flat voice, flawlessly conveying the tone of my message.

"There's no need to be snippy," my mother says. I'm not sure which one of us she means. Probably both. "Seriously. Think about it."

Why are you even considering it?

"Well, the local population is aging, so there have been a lot of retirements. It wouldn't be hard for any of us to find a job, if that's what you want to do when you graduate. And you do your school stuff online, so it wouldn't be a big adjustment."

She tries to keep her tone airy, but insecurities poke through her words. I imagine myself exploring every gap, pointing out the illogicalities of her thought processes until she smacks me away like a bug.

She's not wrong, though. I *do* go to school online, and I *should* worry about finding a job after graduation. I don't have a lot of options, and Benzaiten won't let me become a robot vacuum cleaner.

Or, at least, that's how she felt when I first met her. I'm not sure she even cares anymore.

Those are things you consider when moving, I type to my parents. Not reasons FOR moving.

"Machi," my mother says once my father has read my text aloud. "This is just an *idea*."

Is it? It sounds a lot more like a plan.

She's silent for a few seconds. When she speaks, her first

couple of words are too forceful, shooting out like a firecracker crammed into a box.

"I thought you would be excited. It's not as if you like living there."

I frown, pressing my cheek into my pillow. When did I say that?

"You didn't *have to* say it. You don't ever act like you're happy there. And plus, you hate everyone in town."

A silence covers us like frost. My mother seems to hold her breath, hoping I let this slide. My father has become nothing more than a text-to-speech reader. I hope I'm misunderstanding the implications of her words, but I don't think I am.

What does that mean?

"You know," she says, edging around the question. "You get it, don't you?"

I don't type a response.

"I mean, how long have I known you? Your entire life." She's scrabbling now, reaching for something safe. "You didn't get close to anyone in elementary school. The most memorable interaction you had was with that girl who invited you to her birthday sleepover, right?"

I don't even remember any birthday sleepovers.

"And in middle school too. You didn't seem to like anyone there. I mean, there was that girl who wanted to talk to you, right? But she dropped out?"

She got expelled, actually, but that doesn't help my case.

My mother goes quiet. She has realized only high school remains, and we all know what happened then. I want to her to say it. Give me her best. Remember my worst.

"I simply mean," she says, backing off, "you don't have many happy memories there. Why not make new ones?"

"Here?" my father asks.

"Wh—no. No, honey. I'm thinking our daughter could

make some happy memories in ancient Rome." She huffs. "The two of you get on my last nerve sometimes. This is where I grew up, you know. You should treat it with some respect."

I pull the blanket closer, feeling the worn fabric between the pads of my fingers.

"I'm going out. Talk later."

Beep, beep, beep.

I roll over, about to unplug my earbuds and pretend none of this happened. My fingers wrap around the cord, but before I pull, my phone buzzes. I pick up.

"She's gone," my father says.

Is she mad?

White noise hisses in my ear. He puts his phone back to his face. "I guess so." He takes a breath. "That didn't go very well."

Maybe I misread everything. Maybe every time her parents took a jab at our town, she wanted to nod along. Every time they told her to move home already and she turned to us to roll her eyes, she was putting on a show just to make us happy. Every time she swore she would never go back, she was denying the call of her heart.

When I was little and unused to my grandparents' cutting remarks, I would lie on my parents' bed—since my room doubled as the guest room—and imagine every biting comment was another plume of smoke I had to inhale. With every breath, my lung and heart would blacken. At night, when they thought I was asleep, my mother would lean on my father's shoulder and say her parents simply didn't *get* our town the way they did. Her parents were stuck in their own ways, too stubborn to move here, and while she and my father had to respect their choices, they were allowed to complain about it.

Was that all a lie? Did she sense the fumes in the room and create smoke screens with her words, easing us all forward just to stop every Christmas from going up in flames? *We're on the same side*, she seemed to say, but not because she meant it. She softened the smoke, lightened it, until instead of poisoning us, it lulled us to sleep. Then she lay in bed, close enough to reach both my father and me, and felt the hopeful flame still burning inside her, hidden away.

I don't get it, I type at last.

"I don't either," my father says. "But grief can do funny things. And no matter how old you get, losing the people you love doesn't get easier."

We hang up. I lift a hand to the ceiling and pretend, when I drop my arm back onto the bed, I have batted away every last wisp of smoke.

IT'S CLOUDY TODAY, rare in the heat of summer, but at least I get to the torii without sweating through my clothes.

I remove my shoes and take a seat on the offering box.

She doesn't show up.

I wait a little longer. Maybe another divine being trapped her in a conversation. Maybe she's taking the baby to the spirit world. I know it will be difficult no matter what, but if she brings him there herself and watches over him as he is assigned to a place where he can be fully rehabilitated, it might hurt less.

At the edge of the torii, a silver rat sniffs the air.

I stand and approach it. It stays still. I expect Daikokuten to show up and tell me to stop bothering his rat, but if he's around, I can't see him. I reach for the creature, but my fingers freeze just before I make contact. I can't tell if Daikokuten has stopped me through divine intervention or if I'm just afraid to touch it.

I withdraw, tucking my hands in the pockets of my jeans. A few minutes pass. I find my wallet, take out a nickel, and toss it into the box with a little too much gusto. It slams the wooden bottom, its *plonk* echoing.

It's quiet. Then she appears, nestled in the daruma doll plush. Even after all this time, I don't know how she gets here. My eyes sink to the baby, who is almost entirely hidden by the goddess's sleeves. All I can see is his little cap, crocheted with a scarlet heart.

She tosses the coin to me. I slap my hand to my chest, catching the nickel against my heart.

"I said you don't have to give me offerings."

I pocket the nickel and take out my whiteboard. *You didn't show up.*

Again.

"Oh, yes. I was going to put Kenji in the carrier, but he was being so cute. I had to find a new dress too. I mean, it looks exactly the same, but remember how I tore my old one to swaddle him? I don't like keeping him strapped to me because it's hard to see his face." Her eyes shine as the baby sticks his fist in the ends of her ponytail. When his hand disappears, he lets out a baffled gurgle. She giggles. "Don't worry. Your hand will come back, child."

I loved Angel, and I loved an in-love Angel, but sometimes, I couldn't stand being around her when she had a significant other. Between all the *babe*s and *I love YOU more*s and dirty inside jokes I didn't get, I felt my heart growing colder.

I look away.

"Did you see Kenji's hat? Isn't it adorable? He likes soft fabrics, but it seems he isn't used to wearing things on his head. If he fusses too much, I take it off, but I'm hoping he adjusts." She gives me a look as she rocks the baby. "What's up with you?"

I write the words slowly, hoping it will sink in if I make the letters pretty enough. *For one, my mother is thinking of moving us back to her hometown.*

The *o* in *mother* has a flick at the top like a devil's horn. I erase it with my thumb.

Benzaiten kisses the baby's head and reads the whiteboard. "Is that so bad? It could be a new beginning for you. Maybe that's what you need."

Irritation flickers in my chest like a small flame from a lighter. *You make it seem simple, but it's not. I don't like that place, and until a few weeks ago, my mother didn't either. There has to be something else going on.*

I hold up my board, but Benzaiten can't stop smiling at the baby. She pulls his hat up an inch and kisses his forehead, ignoring the subsequent buzz along his scalp.

I erase my words, write a new message, and move to her side, kneeling beside the daruma doll. The baby's hand nearly bangs my cheek, but I don't flinch. It would likely go through me. Even if it didn't, it wouldn't be the most painful thing to happen here today.

"'When are you giving the baby to the spirit world?'" Benzaiten reads. She narrows her eyes, flecks of gold peeking between her lashes. "When he's ready."

When will that be?

"I don't *know*, Machi."

I recoil. She sounds like Angel at her most exasperated.

Don't you think he should be sent away soon? I tense every muscle in my hand to keep it from trembling. *You didn't spend this much time with the other child spirits.*

"They were older. Kenji is a baby."

It's only going to get harder.

"Wow, thanks for that brand-new information." She sets her fingers on the edge of my whiteboard and pushes it back toward me. "I guess you're not a mortal after all. You're the goddess of painfully obvious statements."

I ignore the sting. I've heard worse. *But if yo—*

"*Enough*," she snaps. A pale blur streaks across my vision. Something knocks into my hand, not fast or hard enough to be painful but shocking nonetheless. I look down at my fingers and find a black mark running across my knuckles. My whiteboard pen has skittered across the shrine grounds, landing beside the offering box. As I stare at it, Benzaiten says it again: "Enough."

I whip around to face her, tensing the muscles in my neck and shoulders like I might punch her.

"Don't look at me like that," she says, but I just keep staring. "I *said* to stop *looking* at me like that. You're upsetting Kenji."

Stop talking about Kenji for one minute, I want to write.

"You don't get it, do you?" Her voice drops to a near-whisper. "You will never, ever, *ever* get it."

Get what? I ask in my mind.

"You're a mortal. You can go to college or find a job you chose yourself. You can start a family. You can live out your life and die happy." She clutches Kenji to her body like she wants to keep him warm, but she gives off no heat. "Machi, I can't have that."

I'm sorry, I want to say. But I also don't. Sorry for what? Being mortal? Having a definite end to my existence in this world? I didn't choose this life. I certainly didn't choose to end up here, wordlessly arguing with a goddess over ghosts and moving to a racist town I have been taught to hate.

"Do you know how much I wish I could be you?"

Do you know how much I wish I could be anyone but myself?

I can't take it anymore. I reach for my pen, but as soon as my fingers brush it, she kicks it away.

"Stop. Just *stop*. You will never understand." She holds the baby tight enough to make his edges blur. He squeaks. "You act like you know what's best for him, but you don't. You're just making everything worse."

As always.

She doesn't say it, but I hear it.

My fingers stretch toward the whiteboard marker, but she blocks my way with one ballet flat. "Stop already. Stop, Machi. Just get out."

I tell myself I'm ensnared in a nightmare. Any second now, I'll wake up. It will be the early morning, and I can restart. I can wake up again, better this time.

My fingers slide forward without my permission, hopelessly reaching, reaching.

"I cannot believe," she says, emotion pouring out of her voice like ichor, "you were just going to throw your life away."

I freeze.

"Don't play dumb," Benzaiten says. "I'm a *goddess*, Machi. I heard you that night. Not just what you wished when you first tossed that nickel into the offering box. All of it."

A shiver hisses up my spine. I feel as if she's stripped me bare, my clothes, my skin, my everything torn away, floating above us like phantoms.

"You didn't want to be a robot vacuum," she says quietly. "You didn't want to be *anything*. And do you know how awful that is to hear? Do you know how badly it hurt to know you were down here, the entire world at your fingertips, and all you wanted was to leave it all behind?"

Stop, I think. *Please, please, please stop.*

"I couldn't stand by and let you give up," Benzaiten says. "That's why I returned to the mortal world, the way I promised I never would. Do you know how difficult it was for me? To see you and all those children in pain? But I helped you, I helped them, I'm helping Kenji, because that's what I was made to do. So instead of getting all pouty because I don't take you out on fun adventures every day, maybe you should take some time to think about how lucky you are. Because you are, Machi. You're *lucky*, and you don't even know it."

I close my eyes. She sounds so much like Angel. Like my mother. Like that voice in my head that's constantly screaming at me to just *talk* already. Just *get over it* and *talk* like a *normal* person, the way everyone knows I can.

I can't, though. If I do, it's all over. If I speak and she still doesn't care, that means it really *is* over. I really *am* boring, really *am* beyond help. Because no matter how many times she "fixes" my wish, no matter how many ways she tries to reach me, through festivals and parties and saving people who are already gone, I am still unchanged. I am still unaltered.

"I can't even look at you," Benzaiten says. "Just go already."

But I can't move. I'm too busy falling victim to the ironic process, thinking about my beaten-up schoolbag and my smashed-up clay piece and how Angel looked in the club, the closest thing I had seen to a goddess before Benzaiten, and how Sunny didn't even glance back at me before leaving me behind, the way I never thought she would. I'm thinking about disappointed parents and dead grandparents and an entire football team's worth of doctors who say it's all in my head and how I never wanted any of this, never asked to have a goddess swoop in and rescue me, because all I really needed was for everything to stop. Forever.

"Get out," Benzaiten says, and before I can even remember how to breathe, she's screaming it. "Get out, get out, GET OUT!"

"NO!"

I slap my hand over my mouth.

In Benzaiten's arms, Kenji wails, his eyes squinching as he reaches for her ponytail. His image shakes, his energy levels spiking. She shushes him, pressing his forehead to her chest. I don't think anything beats there. She rocks him. Kisses him. Gives him a tense smile. Nothing works. He won't stop.

"Look what you did," she says. "Just leave, Machi."

I rise. I get all the way to the torii, then turn.

"That was my first word since Angel and Sunny," I say, "and you didn't even notice."

She looks at me, her eyes wide from the belated realization. For four full seconds, she's stunned into silence. Her gold eyes swim with every feeling in existence. Her lips part. I think she might tell me to come back. She's proud of me. She's so happy to hear my voice.

"Oh," she says, her words hardly audible above the baby's cries. "So your prayer is answered. I guess now you have everything you could ever want."

I swallow.

Say something.

It's the same thought I've had every day since Angel and Sunny, but my throat burns like I've eaten four ghost peppers in a row.

I take a step back. Another step. Then I pivot, grab my shoes, and run, my socks hitting the pavement. Behind me, Benzaiten is silent, and the baby keeps crying.

Tears prick my eyes, but I don't let them fall until I reach the bus stop near the apartment. I slow to a stop, drop my shoes on the ground, and sit on the bench. My chest heaves, my heart thundering and my vision flashing like I'm about to faint. I touch my throat, almost expecting to find my fingers aflame.

I look over at the apartment. At the bottom of the stairs, a silver rat watches me with unfeeling eyes.

CHAPTER SEVENTEEN

ONE WOULD THINK, after speaking for the first time in a year, I would be a whole new person, sauntering through the streets and calling out HELLO to every passerby. Everyone got their wish for me. I spoke. My parents and Dr. Tsui will be happy, I'm sure. And Benzaiten got her wish for me, too. I saw the beauty in humanity, albeit fleetingly and only ever when we were together. Only when we actually mattered to each other.

It's easy to think life is beautiful when you're with someone you know cares about you. It's when you realize they've *stopped* caring that it all comes crashing down.

Again.

I lie in bed and feel sorry for myself for a while. Maybe even sorrier than I did the first time. I tell myself to do something productive, but every time I try to read another chapter from my online textbook, my vision starts blurring, and I have to wipe my eyes to check if I'm crying. As if I haven't cried enough.

By noon, I've done nothing but skim through a bunch of long-form articles about tortoiseshell cats, which, like my brief infatuation with Yelp, isn't exactly the kind of thing I can brag about on job applications.

Not that anyone would hire me anyway. Verbal or nonverbal, I'm not enough for anyone.

Every time I expose even a tiny bit of myself—to Angel,

to Sunny, to Sheryl and Dr. Tsui and Benzaiten—I wind up getting burned.

My parents text, but I decline their requests to call. My mother must assume I'm bent out of shape about the idea of moving. My father gives me space.

I decide I will head to the Yip Yap Shelter at one. Andrew doesn't ever pressure me to talk, and I need to get out of the house. I can smell myself decomposing, a useless lump in a bed.

One o'clock comes and goes. I don't move.

She didn't even care.

I can't pretend to know what it's like to be a deity. I see her for a few hours every couple of days. I don't know what she does when I'm not around. And she has existed for thousands of years, if not millions. She must want a mortal life sometimes. I could see, every time we encountered children, the way she ached for them. Her arms opened for them. Her eyes grew wet for them. I understood. Or I tried to.

What if I had told her about Dr. Tsui? What if I had said, *Oh, by the way, I accidentally mentioned you to my therapist, and knowing him, he's going to look you up and realize I was talking about interacting with a deity like it's no big deal, and he's going to wonder if I've lost it, which I most definitely have?*

I roll over in bed.

I bet she would've been happy.

Wonderful, I can hear her saying now. *Now I have another devotee. Let's just hope he's more interesting than you.*

It's better this way. She has her baby, and I had a couple of fun weeks. Now we can both move on.

I just wish I knew how.

I eat plain toast for dinner.

DR. TSUI OPENS his office door. The blinds have been slanted, letting in some light. I wonder if he could sense my doom and gloom through the waiting room wall or if he always has the blinds open at this time. We weren't supposed to have a session today, but I emailed yesterday to see if he could slot me in.

It's not an emergency, I made sure to add. I think a part of me hoped he wouldn't see my message, or wouldn't consider it important, so I could at least say I had tried.

But no. Of course my parents chose a compassionate doctor willing to make time for his clients. Because I am, as Benzaiten said, *lucky.*

I sit in the same chair as always, my eyes landing on the triplet figurines. The perfect trio.

He pushes the door closed, takes his clipboard from his desk, and drops into the empty chair. "Good morning, Machi."

"Good morning."

He blinks. Blinks again. His mouth opens and closes like the metal jaw of a rusty robot. "Did you say something?"

I nod. I can't help but take some pleasure in his surprise.

"Machi." His voice verges on cheery, which is exhausting. "Could you tell me what happened?"

I shift, scooting to the left and setting one hand on the armrest. I open my mouth, intending to say something witty.

Then I burst into tears.

It's mortifying, sobbing in a doctor's office, even though it's not the first time. It happened with the first doctor because I was so unsure of what to do at an appointment when I couldn't and didn't want to talk. It didn't happen with most of the others, though the fourth one was stiff and hesitant enough to make me kind of want to cry. I almost let a tear or two slip down my cheek when I was with the fifth doctor, but that was because my mother was weeping, telling the teddy-bear man she didn't know what to do with me. I got teary with Sheryl a few times, but it was easy to regain control when I wrote my responses and wasn't expected to speak.

Dr. Tsui reaches for his box of tissues, a pastel cube perched on his desk beside the figurines. He holds it out. When I shake my head, he places it on the coffee table and studies me. I wish he would do it like Sunny and I did, listening but not looking.

"Machi," he says. "How can I help you today?"

I concentrate on breathing, not wanting to trigger those uncontrollable crying hiccups. Once the threat has passed, I swallow a few times, still getting used to the idea of speaking again. "You know how I mentioned someone named Benzaiten?"

He hesitates. "Yes, I do."

I feel the rasp of air as my throat opens and closes. In between reading articles about animals and searching *How to talk to therapist about things you know he won't believe*, I looked in the little compact mirror on my dresser and practiced speaking to myself. A year is a long time.

It didn't fix anything, though. Sure, I can say how I feel, but what's the point?

"Machi?" Dr. Tsui says.

"I wanted to talk about her." I suck in my cheeks. "Benzaiten."

He nods. "Okay. I'm listening."

"But first," I say, "could you face the wall?"

He doesn't miss a beat, pivoting to the wall, his pen still in his hand.

I speak slowly, stopping every so often to gather my thoughts. I don't tell him everything, obviously, but I say I met someone at a shrine. Someone who heard my prayer to become a robot vacuum cleaner. Someone who wanted to help me find the goodness in life again because she's always found humanity so beautiful.

"But it doesn't matter," I say, watching the seconds tick toward the end of our session. "It's over now."

Dr. Tsui, who has been scribbling furiously this entire time, looks up from his notes. "What do you mean? What's over?"

I look back at the figurines. "Everything."

DR. TSUI ISN'T Sheryl. But maybe that's okay.

I still miss Sheryl's patience and gentle optimism, but Dr. Tsui has helped me too. I must have known it for a while now, deep down, but I wasn't sure until today.

After I told him about the fallout with Benzaiten, he said he was proud of me for making an appointment with him and letting him hear my voice for the first time.

I understand if you feel like avoiding new connections for a while, he said as he escorted me to the door, *but I really want you to keep reaching out. To me, of course, but to others too. Take your time, but don't give up on seeking those human connections, okay?*

I nodded, too tired to speak. And though he told me I didn't have to do it right then, I wound up taking the bus to The Bean Jive, if only to keep myself from wasting another day wallowing in my misery.

So here I am. Seeking.

I stand on the corner, my arms crossed and my tongue caught between my teeth. Will sways behind the counter like an idle animation. The metal stud in his left earlobe has been changed to a jet-black circle ringed with gold. Boredom is spelled across his face, his eyes glassy. But the second he spots me, he perks up and gives me his best customer-service smile.

"Hey. What can I do for you today? We have a special going on now: buy one cinnamon-flavored item and get the second half-off."

I take a breath, then another. I'm a human puffer fish, inhaling more and more air until I'm floating. I tell myself to speak before I make it more awkward than it has to be, but the only sound coming from my vocal cords is the chirp of crickets.

"Hey, you okay?" He frowns. "Do you need some water?"

I shake my head.

"Are you sure? It's free."

I shake my head again.

He blinks. "Wait. Aren't you the girl from before?"

"S-s-sixth grade," I blurt out.

"Huh?" He wears his every emotion on his sleeve, as much a part of him as his eyebrows, which, I notice now, are slightly too thick at the inner corners. "What was that?"

"Sixth grade."

It would be good if I explained what I meant, but my lips stick together. I clasp my hands, making a mess of my fingers.

"That's what you want?" He raises an eyebrow. "I don't think we have that here."

"The hiking trip."

One would think, after spending almost an entire hour talking to Dr. Tsui earlier today, I would do better. But my throat is already hurting, and every time I speak, a little voice in my head screams to shut up.

Will tilts his head. "Wait, what?"

"I'm, um, ah, wait." I reach into my bag, only to realize I left my whiteboard at home. I was overconfident. I should have known talking again wouldn't be as easy as I thought.

I slide a napkin out of the nearest holder and make a writing motion.

"Oh." He nods, spins in a complete circle, and recenters himself, realizing the pen has been in front of him the whole time. He hands it to me. "Here. Sorry."

"Th-th—" I stop. Oh, God. I sound like an angry cat. I run my thumb along the pen's barrel. *We went to middle school together.*

Impatient, he reads upside down. "Oh, we did? That's cool. Sorry, I don't remember a lot of people, except some guys I played baseball with. You know the Tsukadas?"

He talks so quickly. I'm trying to tell my own story, but I also feel obligated to ask about baseball. This is too hard.

I shake my head.

"Oh. Well, they're super nice."

Okay, I'm sure they are, but they're not why I'm here.

Do you remember the hike in sixth grade? I write. My hand is shaking.

"Oh, yeah. It was super crazy. All the helicopters came and stuff, but I guess the vegetation was too thick for them to see us. We probably should have gone out in the open and waved our hands in the air when we heard the choppers, but we were dumb."

I chew my lip. *I was the one who lost you. I'm so sorry.*

He examines the napkin, taking longer than usual. The bushy stems of his brows draw together, but he doesn't speak. He just watches me like he's not sure what to make of me.

Join the club.

I step back. The bus stop isn't that far. I can sprint there and hide until the bus arrives and takes me far, far away.

"Wait," he says. "What does this even mean?"

"I was there," I half-shout.

A few people give me curious looks but return to their meals.

My face heats up. "Sorry."

"It's fine. They stare all the time. But what do you mean?" He taps his finger over the word *lost*, then lifts his hand to check for an ink stain. "How did you lose me?"

"The—I—" I stop and return to the napkin. *I was in front of you in line. I was the reason you all got lost.*

He laughs. Not the reaction I was expecting. "What are you

talking about? We got lost because we got tired and thought we could catch up later."

But I was supposed to be watching you.

"You weren't our mother."

I recoil. I don't know why. It's not like that's a revelation.

His voice softens. "I mean, you don't have to think you're the reason we got lost. It was our own fault for not paying attention."

"But still," I say. "I should have noticed."

"Why?"

I clutch the pen, my fingers squeezing the grip until I feel I might crush it or shatter my fingernails. I release. "I don't know."

"I swear it's not your fault. It's ours. And also that camp leader's because who trusts a bunch of sixth graders to watch over each other? We didn't even *like* most of our classmates. Or I didn't." He shrugs. "Besides, it made for the best story I could tell for years, until, like, last year, maybe? That's when I almost fell off a cliff."

"Sounds like you don't have the best luck with the outdoors," I say. Then my hand flies to my mouth. "Oh, God. Sorry."

His laugh is infectious. A woman sitting at the closest table smiles. He leans on the display case. "Guess I don't." The amusement drains from his face. He looks at me, his eyes scanning mine. "Have you felt guilty about that this whole time? I mean, that was, like, five years ago."

I don't reply.

"You shouldn't. Really. None of us held it against you." He drums his fingers on the glass. "We were too busy deciding I was the best human sacrifice to play the blame game."

I can't speak, so I nod and write, *Thank you.*

"Yeah. No problem." He takes a cookie from the basket beside the counter and places it in my hands. "On the house."

"I should be the one paying for you," I say, trying to give it back.

"Nah. I had a good laugh today. Good memories." He pushes the cookie toward me and smiles. "I don't think I ever knew your name."

"Machi."

"Will," he says. His fingers stretch for the pen, but he stops like he thinks I need it. "Come back sometime, okay?"

I hold the cookie, feeling the edges with my fingertips. "Okay." I step back, swiping the napkin with all my scribbles and returning the pen. "Thank you. N-next time, I'll buy you something."

"We'll see."

I cling onto the napkin and the cookie. "O-one more thing? Is there a cinnamon special because the store has too much cinnamon?"

"It expires in two weeks," he says, lifting a hand as I leave.

I SHOW UP to the Yip Yap Shelter with a mission.

And by *mission*, I mean *pipe dream*.

Andrew opens the door to the shelter, blinking sleep out of his eyes. "We brought in a stray cat, and the resident grump isn't too happy about it."

Something about his greeting, or the lack thereof, reminds me of my parents. The way we used to be. We rarely bothered with *Good morning*s or *Welcome home*s. My mother had a habit of dropping her purse, casting off her jacket, and launching into a rant about something stupid her coworker had done before the door could even close behind her.

I crouch beside the feline newcomer. Without taking my eyes off the cat's splotched fur, I say, "A tortoiseshell."

Andrew almost misses the stool behind the counter but manages to right himself, glancing at me. For a while, neither of us speaks. Maybe he's wondering if he imagined it.

I lift a hand to the crate. The new cat sniffs it, the way a dog would, but loses interest and sits near the ginger cat, who staunchly ignores it.

I run my hand down the tortoiseshell. It's likely female, as I've learned most tortoiseshells are. It turns its fluffy head, staring as I move my hand along its spine. After a few more pats, it decides I'm not so bad and returns to observing the other cat.

"Right?" I ask.

"R-right," Andrew says. "That's a tortoiseshell."

Nodding, I scoot over to the rats. They're sleepy this morning, cuddling together. One has fallen asleep in the center of the spinning wheel. There's no sign of any eerily silver rats. I wonder why Daikokuten won't stop following Benzaiten. What he wants. He didn't seem evil. Just intimidating. And now I'm starting to think he was right. Maybe I *do* regret ever meeting her.

"Hey," Andrew says.

I swivel toward the counter.

"Could you always talk?"

I look back at the rats. "It's complicated."

He thinks for a second. "All right."

In the corner, the one remaining dog sleeps on his back. He chases something in his dreams, his little paws batting the air.

"Hey," Andrew says. "I know I introduced myself a while ago, but I'm not sure you ever told me your name."

"M-Machi," I say.

"It's nice to know your name after all this time." He sets his elbows on the counter. "Thanks for visiting us."

"Thank you for letting me." I bite my lower lip, struggling to muster up the courage to do what I came to do. Say what I came to say. "I, um, wanted to—I was just wondering if you ever needed help, maybe. Here."

He tilts his head, his expression pensive.

"I understand if not," I say quickly. "I didn't—I'm not—I don't know a lot about animals. But if you needed help, I would be happy to volunteer."

Happy.

Yeah. I would be happy.

Andrew blinks. "Really?"

"If—if you wanted me." My face flushes. "I mean, help. If you wanted help."

His expression softens. "Yes. Of course we do. It's just, you know, we're a family shelter."

And I'm not family.

"So," he continues, "we haven't gotten around to making volunteer applications or anything. We should, and I've been meaning to, but it just keeps slipping my mind. But would you be willing to give me an email address for now? I'm sure we can figure something out."

I hang back, still chewing my lip. When I see a rat doing the same thing, I stop.

"We would love to see more of you," Andrew says.

He holds out a piece of paper and a pen. Two things I've come to know well.

My fingers curl around the pen. Writing carefully, as if I think he'll judge my ability to care for the animals based solely on my penmanship, I form the letters of my email address.

"Perfect," he says once I return his pen and paper. "I'll be in touch. And if you don't hear from me, feel free to come back and give me a hard time for letting it slip my mind. Really. Give me your worst."

I nod. My hands have begun to shake.

He studies my email address, his eyes tracing every letter. "I'm really happy you came today."

I swallow. "I am too."

Then, slowly, I smile.

CHAPTER EIGHTEEN

I'M DREAMING OF hand-feeding an orange to a chicken when a voice cuts through the haze, severing the orange in half.

"Machi. Machi, Machi, Machi, please wake up."

I open my eyes. "Orange chicken?"

"What?"

Benzaiten is standing above my bed, her hair rushing around her face. Her eyes are the troubled gold of sickly autumn leaves.

Almost sure I'm still dreaming, I reach for my phone and check the screen: WEDNESDAY, JUNE 26, 4:44

I roll over.

"Don't you dare go back to sleep. And before you ask, I knocked at your door politely, but you didn't answer."

It's not even five in the morning, I want to point out. But I haven't decided if I'm speaking. Aside from the orange chicken thing, I mean.

"Machi, please. I need you."

I open my eyes and stare at the wall. "Why would a goddess need me?"

She sighs. "Don't be like this."

I don't know why she's acting so indignant. She said it herself. She said a lot of things. And I did too. I spoke for the first time in a *year*, and all she did was throw my one accomplishment back in my face.

"*Machi*," she snaps. "Get out of bed."

Hearing the words *get out* again feels like a slap.

I turn, pressing my face into my pillow. If that's how it's going to be, I'm not getting up.

"Machi, please." Her voice unravels, the threads tangling. "Kenji is *missing*."

I sit up, my heart pounding. "What?"

She exhales through her nose. "That's, like, the seventh time I've said that. Though I guess you were asleep for the first six. Do *all* mortals sleep as deeply as you?"

I run a hand across my eyes and step out of bed. "It's *four in the morning*."

"Don't exaggerate. It's *much* closer to five." She shadows me as I head to the bathroom and splash my face with water. "He wouldn't calm down, so I spent days doing everything I could. *Days*, Machi."

I turn off the faucet and bury my face in a towel.

"He cried so much," she continues. "He kept losing spiritual energy, even when I fed him and made sure he was comfortable. I tried every toy I had, and when that didn't help, I bought new toys. But nothing worked. He wouldn't stop."

I lower the towel and hang it back on the rack. "Why are you here?"

Benzaiten rolls her eyes. "I *told* you—"

"He's missing," I finish for her. "I know. But why are you *here*? Why are you asking for *my* help?"

I wait for her to huff and say she doesn't have time for this. She needs me because I was one of the last people to see him. Maybe I can pick up his scent like a bloodhound. Mortals can do that, right?

"Because I don't have anyone else," she says softly. Like a child.

I look at her. I wonder if, when she first saw me at her shrine, I seemed as scared as she does now, her face pale and her eyes teary.

Taking a deep breath, I return to my room and crimp my fingers around the hem of my shirt. When she doesn't look away, I clear my throat. "I'm changing."

"And?" She rolls her eyes. "Mortals and their sense of modesty."

I grit my teeth as I change into jeans, a shirt, and a jacket, dropping about seven hangers in the process. My downstairs neighbors must hate me.

She crosses her arms as I set the hangers back in my closet. "Does this mean you'll help?"

I pull my closet door closed as quietly as possible. "You're not really giving me much of a choice."

She sniffs. "You were much easier to boss around when you didn't talk."

I give her a look.

"But," she adds, "it's nice to hear your voice. It's not nearly as squeaky as I thought it would be."

Sighing, I grab my bag and pack my whiteboard and marker. I wish I could say I didn't need them, but my ability to speak is still flimsier than a cheap café napkin.

When I turn, she's still standing by my bed, her dress grazing the blanket I tossed over the edge. I can tell she wants to say something but doesn't know how to voice it.

I know the feeling.

I take a breath, then hold out my hand. "Come on. Let's find Kenji."

I THINK WE both know he won't be anywhere Benzaiten suggests, but we try anyway.

Japantown isn't awake yet. The neon lights are dim in the

early light, weaker than a faint blush on already-ruddy cheeks. I stare at the lanterns, my stomach sinking.

The museum's doors are locked. The deep-brown wood is stark against the gray sky. The owl in the logo surveils us from above, waiting for us to accept what we don't want to admit.

The hospital is hauntingly quiet. With every *tock*, *tock* of a clock in the hallway, we're pushed closer to the truth.

Benzaiten flashes us back to her shrine and kneels at her own altar, trembling.

"Machi," she says. "Do you smell a rat?"

I don't have time to answer. She grabs my hand, and I close my eyes as the wind swirls around us. I stumble forward from the momentum, and when my vision clears, I find myself centimeters away from a giant statue of a rat.

I scoot back toward Benzaiten, barely managing to avoid squeaking like a rodent myself.

"DAIKOKUTEN," Benzaiten shouts. She stomps her ballet flat. "Get out here."

I glance around the shrine. It's larger than Benzaiten's, but that's to be expected. I think the checkout area at Let's Grow Already is bigger than that shrine.

Statues line the path, most depicting Daikokuten as a round, smiley god sitting on or holding rice bags, a mallet over his shoulder. Some make him look more like a warrior, occasionally with a peculiar mustache and goatee. He had that same roundness and facial hair in some of my online searches, but he certainly doesn't resemble any of those statues now. Rat figurines are sprinkled throughout, sometimes appearing beside him and sometimes big enough to stand on their own.

Benzaiten marches up the steps toward the altar, dragging me behind her like a rag doll. I imagine myself bumping up the stairs, cartoon-style.

When we reach the top, the air shifts. It's freezing. I pull my jacket tighter.

"I know you're here," Benzaiten says.

The back of the shrine is dark. I clutch her sleeve like she's my mother. The second I touch her, a chill races down my spine. Her divine fury pulses out of her like invisible earthquakes, shaking me to my core.

"Come out and talk to us, you coward," she yells, her anger leaving me cold.

"The name-calling is unwarranted."

Dim lights flick on above us, casting a firefly's glow onto the floor. Daikokuten stands in the center, not even five feet away.

She wastes no time, grabbing him by the collar of his dark dress shirt and yanking him toward her. They're so close, their eyelashes brush together.

"Where?" she hisses.

I take a step, but he extends an arm. His mallet materializes in his hand. I inhale, afraid I'm about to witness a battle of the gods, but he only pushes her away with the handle, his eyes icy. "Let's do this civilly, please."

I'd forgotten how gravelly his voice is. How chilling his carefully impassive tone can be. But if I were to dig deeper, I know I would find something beneath all that.

"*Where?*" Benzaiten repeats.

I search his eyes for malevolence. I've hardly interacted with him; all I know is he did it once. Took away her family. He can do it again, and this time, he doesn't have to worry about ruining his relationship with her. That ship sank long ago.

Her lips tremble. Even in the dusky light, she glows, bits of incandescence settling on her loose hair. Shadows dust her cheekbones, her eyes chaotic galaxies. "Answer me."

"Let go," he whispers. He lowers his mallet and brings one hand to the fingers still grasping his collar.

I expect her to shake the answers out of him like he's a Magic 8 Ball, but she takes a hiccupping breath and nods. Releasing him, she crosses her arms. "Tell me. What did you do?"

He reaches out and uncurls her fingers, such a natural, tender gesture.

I squirm. It's like I'm watching something I shouldn't, an unsanctioned fly on the wall.

"Don't do that," he tells her.

"I'll do what I want." Benzaiten shakes him off. "Just as you did what you wanted."

"Never wanted to do it."

She scoffs. "Yeah, right. 'I never wanted to destroy our family, send those innocent child spirits to a council who couldn't care less about them, and break your heart.'" Her eyes gleam. "'I never wanted to take your new baby just to hurt you and spite you and break your heart all over again.'"

He watches her. His love for her buffets me, a gust over a grain field. "That's what you think?"

"I don't *know* what to think," she says, "but I know it's you." Her eyes fill with tears. "It's always you."

His pupils bleed darkness, turning his blue eyes black. He looks away, but she takes his face in her hands and forces him to meet her eyes.

"I was taking care of him. I was holding him, and I just left him for a"—her voice fractures—"a minute. I needed to think. I needed one minute to think."

"He was suffering."

"No." The anger in her voice turns to anguish. "I was *saving* him from suffering."

"There's a reason why we can't keep them." He says it so patiently, almost like he's talking to a child, but that only infuriates her further. He catches her flying fist with his palm and wraps his fingers around her knuckles. "You know I did the right thing."

Jerking back, she pulls her hand to her chest and steps away. "I will never, *ever* think you did the right thing. Not for our children. Not for Kenji. Not for anyone."

Kenichi.

Kenji.

History repeats itself. Sometimes in a person's lifetime, but certainly in a god's. The pain may be familiar, rooted in the same circumstances and involving the same deities, but that doesn't make it any better. In fact, the hurt only compounds.

The echoes of the first time reverberate through her, bringing her to her knees.

"Bring him back," she mumbles. "You can bring him back. Please. I'll do anything. I'll do better. I promise. I *promise*."

He can't look at her. "It's done."

"No."

"Benzaiten."

"*No*."

She rises and puts a hand to his chest, right where his heart should be. He goes still. Her fingers curl into a fist. I take a step, ready to keep her from socking him in the shoulder.

"He had parents," Daikokuten says, his voice freezing her in place. "All of them did."

She shakes her head. "Stop."

"You weren't their mother. They weren't meant to stay with us. They were in pain."

Plink. Her tears hit the ground, falling too fast to dissipate before impact. *Plink.*

"Stop," she whispers.

"Don't act like I wanted to do this."

Plink. Plink. Plink. Plink. So much silver falls, shining drops of rain dripping from the petals of wilting flowers. She covers her face.

His hand rises but falters, uncertain. He turns his blue eyes to me.

I move to her and, slowly enough to give her a chance to push me away, wrap my hand around hers. She doesn't stop me.

"What am I supposed to do now?" she asks.

"Go home," he whispers.

I wait for her to argue. Say there must be something more she can do. Tell him this isn't over.

But she wipes her cheeks with the back of her free hand, turns, and flashes us out of his shrine. His blue eyes are the last things I see.

When the colors filter back in, forming the dusty shrine, she releases me and falls, her knees hitting the ground. I sit beside her, my leg touching hers.

"I'm sorry," she says. "I failed."

I don't think she's talking to me, but I keep my hand on hers anyway.

"I hate myself." She laughs, but there's no music running beneath her voice. "I do. I ruined everything."

"No," I say.

"Yes." She tilts her head to the early morning light. "I answer prayers about creativity and love: 'I want to meet someone who will inspire me.' 'I want my hand to stop shaking so I can finish this piece.' 'I want to write the perfect song, but I just need an idea.' 'I want to see my art in a museum someday.'

"And love." She drops her gaze to our hands. "What do I know about that? It didn't work with Daikokuten. He was the only one I ever . . ." She closes her eyes.

"I'm sorry," I say quietly.

"I should have stayed in the other world. I shouldn't have come back." She pulls her hand from mine. "What was I doing? Playing house? Pretending I was their savior?"

I inhale, air scraping up my chest. "You thought you were doing the right thing."

"Did I?" She draws her knees to her chest. "You told me I wasn't."

I say nothing.

"You should go," she breathes.

"I don't want to."

"Well, I want you to." She sets her head on her knees, turning away. "Go away."

"I don't want—"

"GET *OUT*," she screams.

History repeats itself.

CHAPTER NINETEEN

I TALK TO myself.

I don't have any new thoughts of my own, so I open my notebook and reread my entries aloud to practice speaking—only to stop after a few paragraphs. It's like I'm reviving my ghosts. Besides, I've almost readjusted to hearing my own voice again. It's figuring out what to say that feels unreachable: A sun high above a stage. A sleeping kitty on a top shelf. A comforting warmth a lifetime away.

In the corner of my room is a little pile of everything I will learn to hate. There's the ticket from the museum. The spare scraps of paper from my letter to Dr. Tsui, the margins chopped off to fit into the notebook he gave me. A sticker from the cake pop I ate with Andrew. The napkin from my talk with Will. Some of the nickels I tried to offer to Benzaiten so she would appear and take me on another adventure. I even printed my grandparents' obituaries, two stories in one article, linked in life and death.

I first started my collection, comprised of things most people probably would have just thrown away, because I thought I could tape everything onto my walls. Make my room look a little less like a prison cell.

But I don't want to touch those things again, all the good memories turned bad. So they'll stay there in the corner, my own shrine of self-pity.

Maybe it's better to go back to silence. It's not too late. Dr. Tsui is paid to work on my issues, so regression would be a good thing for his wallet, if nothing else. Since my parents never knew I spoke, it wouldn't be hard to crawl back onto the bandwagon and pretend nothing ever happened. Why not? Even when I do speak, it doesn't change a thing.

ANDREW SENT ME an email promising he would create and forward an application form soon, but he hasn't said anything since. Sure, it's only been a couple of days, but that's probably enough of an answer.

He doesn't want me either.

I stare at my boots, scrutinizing the way they press into the pavement outside the shelter. I can't even lift my head and peer through the glass door to see if he's there.

Just as I turn on my heel, fully prepared to take off running, the door clacks open.

"Hey. It's kind of early, but we have AC in here. Did you want to come in?"

My stomach drops.

That's not Andrew's voice. It's distinctly female and just the slightest bit sharp at the edges, like the speaker is just as wary of me as I am of her.

I count to three. "N-no, it's okay." I look over my shoulder, preparing to provide an excuse, but all my words disappear.

"Are you sure? We got new rats, which isn't exciting to most people, but I think they're kind of cute."

I open my mouth. "S-Serena."

She looks softer now. That's what I think first. Most people grow harder when they age, but she didn't. She wears a sweep of mascara and some light eyeliner. Her hair is cut shorter, ending just below her chin, but I know it's her. Serena, the girl who was expelled in the seventh grade, not long after telling me we should be friends.

She doesn't recognize me the way I recognize her, but something in her eyes shifts. I can't tell if her guard comes up or goes down. "Do I know you?"

Andrew said this is a family shelter.

Serena is Andrew's daughter. The one who stuck the PULL sticker on the door.

I take a step back and turn, my head spinning.

"Wait," she says.

I watch from the corner of my eye as she scans her surroundings. She grabs a jar of dog treats and sticks it in the doorway. Her boots tap against the sidewalk as she steps over the jar and moves closer.

"You don't need to leave."

I can't decide if nodding or shaking my head would be better. That wasn't really a yes or no question. I have my whiteboard, but it feels wrong to use it with her. She was always so honest with me. It would feel wrong not to be just as honest with her.

"Here." She reaches for me, but I flinch back. Her eyebrows drop. "Sorry. I didn't mean to freak you out. Come in, okay?"

I hesitate, my teeth clenched. I shouldn't. But frankly, if Serena really *is* Andrew's daughter, I'm going to need an explanation.

Now that I'm looking at her again, though, I can see the faintest echo of his softness in her face. A softness I spotted in the girls' bathroom that day in middle school and never managed to forget.

"Come," Serena says.

Like a puppy, I follow her inside. She yanks the treats out of the doorway and sets the jar back on the table. Weaving around the counter, she pulls up a second stool. I can't make my legs move, so I stoop beside the ginger cat, wondering how I got to be so awkward.

"S-sorry," I say, my cheeks burning.

"No problem. Personally, I'd hang out near the puppy, but I get it. No hard feelings." She looks at me with familiar eyes. "I'm not that good with names, but I'm okay with faces. And I think I remember yours."

The ginger cat still hasn't warmed up to the tortoiseshell, it seems, but the tortoiseshell persists, watching the grump with flicking ears.

"Middle school," I say finally.

"Oh." She takes her phone from her pocket and sets it on the counter. She brushes her hair behind her ear. "Is that why you ran?"

It takes me too long to respond. "Ran?"

"You know." She rests her chin in her hands. "You saw me, figured out who I was, went, 'Oh, there's the girl who got expelled,' and decided even cute animals aren't worth the hassle?"

"Oh." I waddle in a semi-circle until I face her, my hands clamped over my knees. "No. Th-that's not it."

"Okay," she says, obviously not believing me.

"It's not." I stand. She pats the extra stool, and after a few seconds, I sit. "I'm not so good at socializing. But I talk to your dad."

A photograph has been taped to the counter, hidden behind the register. I immediately identify Serena, her hair shorter but her smile just as bright, and Andrew. On Serena's other side is her mother. I didn't know much about her when Serena and I were in middle school, other than her apparent fame.

"This is your family's shelter?" I ask.

Serena nods, tipping back on her stool. "It's just us here."

"I thought—" My sentence splits. Maybe I'm remembering wrong. "I thought she was a fashion designer."

"Oh, she was." She puts a pointer finger on her phone and swirls it around the counter. "That changed after I was expelled."

This is the second time she's mentioning her expulsion, but I still wince.

"After that, or even before that, I guess, I was in a bad place. My mom thought it was the industry. You know, it's glamorous and all, but even on a small scale, it can get toxic. She had so many connections, so *I* had so many connections. And when you're twelve, you're not supposed to have connections. Not like that. So my mom 'retired' and tried to start fresh.

"She got into all this spiritual and natural philosophy. Animal rights, human rights, saving the planet. Hippie-dippie stuff. She decided to open up a shelter, and my dad and I kind of got dragged into it."

"Is that bad?" I ask.

Andrew—I should call him Mr. Yip; it's a little weird to be on a first-name basis with Serena's father—seems happy, but that could be nothing more than a good customer-service mask.

Serena squints at the rat enclosure. "It was cool to have a mom everyone seemed to want, but we're all happier now. Besides, some of her old coworkers and fans show up here and make huge donations. That probably paid for all the therapy. And rehab. And organic food, when she was super into that."

I look at her, the way her hair curls at the ends, reaching for her chin.

There were so many rumors. *She got a nosebleed in science because she was snorting drugs in the bathroom. She showed up drunk to English and fell asleep in the middle of the discussion.* For the first few weeks after her disappearance, the entire student body was obsessed. But if I could have asked her a question then, it wouldn't have been what drugs she was doing or what it was like to get expelled; it would have been *Did you mean it? What you said about being friends?*

But instead of saying any of that, I ask, "Is it hard to work with your parents?"

"It was at first." She holds up one of her hands, examining her light-pink nails. "I was so angry all the time, so furious and embarrassed. Schools treated me like a liability. Rehabs treated me like a chronic. My parents didn't know what to do."

I glance at her, scanning her face for some sign of an impending vulnerability hangover. But all I see is Serena. Serena sharing everything with me when all of five minutes ago, I was gearing up to make a mad dash back to my house and never return to the shelter again.

She seems happy. And not just happy but honest and sincere and so impossibly Serena.

"But we started opening up," she continues. "Me, mostly, but my parents too. If I was feeling bad, I flat-out told my parents, and they would coach me through it. They would let me cry or give me some time with the animals or play a board game until one of us fell asleep. Instead of condemning me, they comforted me, and that made all the difference."

A knock at the door startles me enough to almost knock me off the stool.

Serena sighs. "Man. I forgot one of my mom's old friends was coming in to look at the puppy. He made an appointment and everything. Some people are all about schedules."

"Oh." We stand. I push the stool closer to the counter. "Okay, I should go."

"Yeah, I can't turn him away." She leads me around the counter. "But hey, are you free tomorrow? We can catch up over lunch or something."

I watch as the tortoiseshell approaches the ginger cat. "Okay."

We exchange numbers. I haven't given my contact information to anyone except doctors for what feels like years.

She escorts me to the door, where a man in a neon-purple suit waits, a leash hanging between his fingers. As her fingers brush the door, she checks her phone, reading over my contact information. Her eyes rise to me. "Machi. I remember you now."

I tighten my grasp on my phone. The edges dig into my fingertips. "You do?"

"Yeah. From the bathroom." She raises her eyebrows. "Well, now I'm definitely looking forward to tomorrow."

My throat tightens, then releases the exact words I want to say: "Me too."

When she closes the door, the man in the purple suit racing over to the puppy, she lingers in the doorway and lifts her hand, waving until I turn away.

CALL?

I barely have time to plug in my earbuds before my phone starts buzzing.

"Hi, Machi," my mother says in my ear.

"Hi."

A long silence. My mother seems to pull the phone away from her cheek, static bursting through the line. My father asks, "What's happening?" in the background, but she doesn't answer.

"Machi?" My mother's voice is loud in my ear. "Did you say something?"

"She said something?"

"Hi," I say again, feeling like a child saying her first words.

"Oh my God," my mother says. "Machi, what happened? Are you talking now? Will you really speak to us?"

My father stammers, unable to form a coherent sentence. "Machi? What did you say? Can I hear?"

I frown. "Hi?"

"Oh, Machi. Thank God. What changed?"

"I don't know." I take out one earbud as they wrestle for the phone. "I can't explain it."

"Was it the doctor?" My mother sounds like she's about to send him a thousand grocery store gift cards. "How did he do it?"

I lie on my bed, spreading my arms. "Did you want to talk about something?"

"If it wasn't the doctor," my mother continues, "does he know you're talking?"

I suppress a sigh. "Yes."

"I can't believe he didn't tell me." Now I imagine my mother canceling the grocery store gift cards. "He has my number."

"What about patient confidentiality?" my father asks.

"I'm her *mother*."

I tap my contacts app. Serena Yip. I knew her last name but never connected the dots.

"Why did you call?" I ask, dropping my phone and dragging my laptop onto my bed.

"I can't call just to talk to you?" my mother asks.

I try not to roll my eyes. I'm sure she was only calling because she wanted to discuss the move. It's not like she could sense the change in me with her patented Mother's Intuition™.

I used to believe in it, though. Mother's intuition. My mother always seemed to know what to do. When I was a baby, she was the one to realize I was allergic to something in my favorite cereal, searching all the grocery stores in the area for a new cereal I could eat instead. When she found out all my classmates had backpacks and I didn't, she took me shopping—God, I hate shopping—and didn't let me leave until I told her which one I liked. Even then, after crying in the car, I couldn't admit how badly I wanted one.

I couldn't bring myself to admit I liked the one with the little yellow bird because it looked so happy, but she knew anyway, and for four years, until it fell apart, I treasured that Toridachi backpack.

"It's good to hear your voice," my father says.

"Thank you?" I say, because there's no good response to that.

"Don't you need to meet that bank guy?" my mother asks my father. "It's almost three."

He lets out an exaggerated groan. "Can't I stay? Our daughter just spoke. Who cares about escrow or whatever fancy bank guys talk about?"

She doesn't respond.

"Okay. I'm going." He makes his dad grunt as he gets to his feet. "All right. Bye, Machi. Can you say bye to me?"

I open a drafted essay. "I'm not a child."

"You're *our* child," he says. "Bye."

I sigh. "Goodbye."

My mother is quiet for a minute. My father closes the door with a soft *thunk*. She waits another couple of seconds before speaking.

"It's okay if you don't feel ready to talk about—well, talking." She takes a breath. "I don't understand why, but I've given up on trying to know everything. Even if it's just everything about you."

I hit the return key. "Thank you."

White noise.

"Can I talk, then?" my mother asks.

I chew on my lip. "That sounds like a plan."

She's quiet for a few seconds. "Do you remember when I used to say that?"

"Of course. That's why I said it."

"Right." She exhales. "When I was four or five, there was this awful storm here. The rain was pounding the windows,

and the wind was strong enough to blow down entire buildings. Or maybe it only felt that way.

"At first, I was so excited. A big storm meant school was
canceled. My parents stayed with me. No one wanted to risk
getting in a car that day."

My mother has the voice of a storyteller. It rises and falls
in a way that could so easily feel contrived but instead pulls
in every listener. If her story is a song, her voice is the metronome, keeping a certain order while maintaining the flow.

"Your grandfather"—she stops, a heartbeat, a rest—"went
over to the neighbors' house. Your grandmother and I called
him crazy, but he said he wanted to check on them. He was a
very handy man. A very kind one too, when he wanted to be."

I set my head on my hand. I never thought my grandfather
was a bad person, but he said so little. Most of what snuck out
of his mouth was either a scathing review of something new
he and my grandmother had come to hate about our city or
a plea for us to move to their town. If we had given up and
moved, would he have shown me his softer side?

"He hustled over to the neighbors' house in a poncho made
from plastic bags. My mother and I watched from the window, even though he had told us not to stay near the glass. We
stood, our hands inches apart, while my father knocked on the
door. I could see his mouth moving. He must have been asking
if they were okay, if they needed anything.

"They never opened the door. But I was at the window. I
could see them peeking through their curtains, waiting for
him to leave. The parents. The children. Everyone looked, and
no one answered."

My mouth twists. I can't say I'm surprised, and it's not like
my opinion of the neighbors can drop much lower anyway.

"While we waited out the storm, my mother lay with me
on the floor, away from the windows, and told me stories. I

fell asleep to the sound of her voice, and when I woke up, the storm had passed, and the sun was shining through every window."

I think of how my mother would lie beside me. When she first said her own mother did that with her, a part of me felt betrayed, like what I thought was ours was really only an imitation. But the other part knew it was the way she showed love, a family tradition.

"That's a nice story," I say softly.

"Isn't it?"

I picture my grandfather younger, the way he is in the old pictures my mother keeps in a dust-covered photo album. There he is, running headfirst to a house full of people who hate him for no good reason. An entire family of individuals who fall into the same mental traps, a disdain passed down from one generation to the next. Those children in the window grew up to be the ones who would find my grandparents.

"Mom," I say.

"Child," she says, copying my tone.

"Those stories your mother told you." I run my finger over my laptop keys. "Could you tell them to me?"

"Oh, I don't know if I remember."

"Oh."

She brings the phone closer. "Or, well. Maybe one."

CHAPTER TWENTY

SERENA NARROWS HER eyes. "Step off."

"No," I say.

We stare each other down, her gaze unexpectedly intense. She whirls around and slams her credit card on the counter. "Charge it."

The café cashier, a pink-haired woman with a blank expression, takes Serena's card and slides it into the reader.

"Serena," I say. "I spend so much time at the shelter. I should pay for you."

"But I invited you." She takes her card back and slides it into her wallet. "Plus, I'm rich."

I blink. Well, when she puts it that way.

"I can cover it next time?" I say.

"No." Serena accepts her receipt, stuffs it into her pocket, and leads me to a booth. We sit across from each other, unwrapping our food. "It's kind of crazy. My dad mentioned a girl who showed up one day just to hang out and visit the animals, but I never thought it would be you."

I take my turkey and cheese sandwich and tear off part of the crust. "He's nice."

"Yeah." She sets one elbow on the table and leans on it. "He used to say he didn't think you could talk."

"I couldn't."

She lifts her chin from her hand. "What do you mean?"

I nibble at the oat-covered crust. "It's a long story."

"I have time," she says.

I shift in my seat. I don't know where to begin.

Tilting her head, she gives me a small smile. "That's okay. No pressure. If you ever want to talk, though, I'm here. And I'll never judge."

"I know," I say.

And I do.

"You know what else is weird?" Serena asks, sidestepping my self-imposed barrier and leading me back into the conversation. "Seeing everyone so grown up. Like, of course we're getting older, but finding classmates' pictures online or spotting them around town makes me feel ancient."

I let my eyes drift to her face. Beneath her dark lashes is a light dusting of freckles, invisible until she's only a foot away. When we stood at the bathroom mirror all those years ago, I don't think those were there. Or maybe I was too taken by her words to notice her face.

"I saw Will," I say suddenly. "At this other café."

"Will?" She squints, trying to think.

"If you remember the sixth-grade hike where some kids got lost," I say, running my thumb along my knuckles, "he was one of them."

Her eyes widen. "Oh, yeah. I'm, like, almost positive I had a crush on him."

I take a small bite of crust. "Oh?"

"But then again, I was high, so what did I know?"

I almost choke on my sandwich. She says it so casually.

"Anyway," she says. "What's he like?"

"He's nice," I say. Then, realizing I used the same word to describe her father, I add, "I mean, we didn't talk for long, but he's . . . nice."

Sigh.

"That's"—Serena gives me a wicked grin—"nice."

I stuff my sandwich in my mouth to stop myself from talking. I may have regained the ability to speak, but whether I should use it is an entirely different question.

"I don't know if you remember her," Serena says, "but I used to hang out with this girl named Liz." She twists the top off her pink lemonade and takes a swig. "She got a nose job last year, but ever since then, all she ever posts about is how much she hates it. Sometimes, I think no matter what she does, she'll always hate something about herself."

I watch her, unsure of what to say.

"We're not friends anymore," Serena says, "but I still wish her the best. I hope she can find happiness within herself someday."

I take another bite of the turkey sandwich, the lettuce poking my nose. I think I know which one Liz is. She might have been the one to pull Serena out of the bathroom.

"What about you?" She picks at the lemonade label. "What are your middle school friends up to?"

"What friends?" I ask, and though I mean it to be light-hearted, it doesn't come out that way.

She looks up. "You didn't have friends?"

"No." I rip some lettuce sticking out from beneath the bread. "I didn't."

She draws in the condensation on her bottle. "Middle school was hard. But you have friends now." Her eyes flick to me, an unvoiced question.

"I did." I take a napkin from the table dispenser. "I don't anymore."

We eat in heavy silence.

She's about a quarter through her sandwich when she says, "Maybe I'm reading into it, but it seems like you miss them."

I bite into the tomato. I don't like tomatoes.

Serena takes her lemonade bottle and swirls it, the pink drink licking the insides of the glass. "After the seventh grade, I cut myself off from a lot of my friends. You can't get better in the environment you were poisoned in, as they say. Not that my friends were the reason why I was like that. That was on me. But I had to get better before I could even think of involving others in my life."

I can't imagine Serena Yip by herself. She was constantly around people. Seeing her in the bathroom was likely the only time I saw her without her friends, and even then, it didn't take long for them to get to her.

"I had to face my demons before I could find my true friends again," she says. "And I'm not saying you have to do anything like that, but you could. Because I bet there's a friend you want to reconnect with, and the gap feels so impossible to bridge. That's because you're trying to build a bridge out of burning wood. You need to put out the fire first."

I think of Angel and Sunny. I don't know if I want to bridge that gap.

But I also don't think going back to it, even just in my mind, would burn nearly as badly as it once did.

"What if the friendship I really want to keep," I say, "has already been, um, extinguished? How do I rekindle it?"

"Well, I never said you wanted the fire." Serena sets down her lemonade bottle and places her hands on the top. "You want growth. Because friendship is like a plant you and everyone else share. You have to nurture it, right? So start with the worst of it. Identify that 'last straw' and decide what you could have done better. Then just work from there."

We munch on our sandwiches without speaking for a few minutes. This time, I'm the one to break the silence.

"You're really insightful."

"Don't sound so surprised."

I look up. "Did I?"

She sucks some aioli off her thumb. "Nah. I'm just giving you a hard time."

"Oh." I smile. "Okay. Good. But thank you. I'll try to start working on, um, fixing it."

Somehow.

She watches me. "It's really not that deep. Sometimes, a log is just a log, or whatever the saying is."

A cigar is just a cigar.

My mind wanders to the figurines in Dr. Tsui's office. For so long, I felt they were taunting me. A trio, just like Angel, Sunny, and me. I knew it was stupid, but I was lost and willing to look for signs in anything. Peer into a crowded church and think everyone will judge me. Spot a yellow bird in a market and see it as an omen. Find a set of figurines and believe they're a wordless curse. But Serena is right. Sometimes, decorations are just decorations.

"Just reach out," Serena says. "Your expression tells me something about this friendship means a lot to you. Don't give it up."

She tilts her head. Her roots are dark, as they were in the seventh grade, but the ends of her hair fade to a soft blonde.

"Hey, Machi," she says.

Thinking she's going to scold me for staring, I lower my head.

"Machi," she says again. "Let me ask you something: In the bathroom that day, what did I say to you?"

"Oh." I shouldn't have expected her to remember. It was years ago, and she probably wasn't in a great state of mind. "It was nothing."

"No, I know I said something. I remember your expression."

I lift a hand to my cheek like I think I can peel off my own face and study it. "What do you mean?"

"I was not sober," she says, a disclaimer, "but I remember looking at you and seeing so much at once. I saw loneliness. Frustration. Confusion." She draws a finger down the lemonade bottle, cutting a line through the condensation. "A lot of sadness."

I glance up at her. "You remember that?"

"I remember a lot of things." She tilts her head. "Of course, I also *don't* remember a lot of *other* things. But that? You? I remember."

My eyes begin to sting. I blink hard, praying I won't burst into tears and soak my poor sandwich.

"What did I say?" Serena asks.

I look away. "It's not important."

But she won't stop staring.

Caving, I tell her, "You said, 'You and me, we should be friends.'"

I wait for her to laugh in her easy way and say, *Well, I guess that's what happens when you show up to school high.*

But she lets go of the bottle and lifts her eyes to the ceiling.

"Sorry," she says, "for taking five years to make it happen."

I close my eyes. Somewhere in me, a tree tips, creating the beginnings of a new bridge.

THE SHRINE FEELS so empty now.

I stand at the torii and bow. When I raise my head, my eyes flick from the hollow offering box to the silent hanging bell. I leave my shoes outside and walk along the edge of the path. When I reach the offering box, I pull out my wallet.

I don't have any nickels.

I rummage around in my coin pouch. Nothing.

So I sit on the offering box and wait.

I don't know if I expect her to show up. No matter what happens, I'll find myself surprised. If she appears, I'll jump like she's the last person—or, I guess, deity—I was expecting. If she doesn't, I'll leave disappointed. Every path leads to the same question: How did it turn out this way?

I move to the altar. I don't remember how to do this anymore. She usually turns up before I get to this part.

"I don't know if you're listening." My voice is dangerously thin from my talk with Serena. I clear my throat, but it doesn't help. "Maybe you hear whatever is said at your shrines. I imagine that would be hard. A constant roar of prayers."

I remember the cord around Benzaiten's neck. All the pendants. I wonder if mine disappeared. I don't think it did. She said I got everything I could have wanted, but I didn't. I didn't want any of this.

"I'm sorry. I'm sorry I couldn't stop it. I'm sorry I didn't leave when you wanted me to leave. I'm sorry I didn't stay if you secretly wanted me to stay. I never know what to do."

A breeze whistles through my hair. I look up, hoping it's her, but there's no sign of her gold eyes or her flowing dress.

"I want to fix this." I wrap my arms around myself. "Do you?"
Silence.

This was dumb. I should have known she wouldn't show up. I left her on the ground. Why would she come back?

As I leave the shrine and slide on my shoes, I feel the hair on my arms rise like willowy zombies.

I turn. Standing on its hind legs is a silver rat.

I slide my bag off my shoulder and search for a pen and paper. All I can find is a gum wrapper, but I decide that will have to do. I just hope it doesn't get swallowed.

Once I finish writing, I fold the wrapper in two. The rat watches me with dark eyes. I crouch beside it and extend a hand. It sniffs the wrapper, its nose wriggling as the scents of mint and ballpoint pen combine, then bites the wrapper with its tiny mouth and skitters away.

Not even a minute later, a voice rises from behind me. "Bit sacrilegious."

I turn and do my best not to wince at the sight of Daikokuten's hammer. "What is?"

He takes his mallet and rests it on his shoulder. "Asking to meet right outside her shrine."

"Oh." I glance at the shrine. With the darkening sky, it seems even sadder. "I didn't know where else we could go."

"To my shrine." He puts a hand on my shoulder. "That okay?"

I stare at his fingers and nod, closing my eyes. The wind whips my hair across my face. I'm still combing it back in place when I open my eyes. We stand in the same dim room, the inner part of his shrine.

He removes his hand and wraps it around the mallet's handle and eases himself down, sitting cross-legged.

Following his lead, I drop to the floor and hit my knee on the ground.

He frowns. "You okay?"

I hope the poor lighting hides the flush of my cheeks. "Uh-huh."

He watches me, his eyes a deep blue. After a few seconds, he says, "You could have poisoned the rat with that cheap foil wrapper."

As if on cue, a silver rat scrabbles over his leg, disappearing into the darkness.

"S-sorry."

We go silent again until he clears his throat. "You said you wanted to talk?"

I nod. I do want to talk.

I stare at my hands, tracing the feathered lines across my palms. *Talk.* I'm the one who called him here. This was supposed to be the first step in repairing my friendship with Benzaiten. *Talk.*

"When it was just you and me," he says, his voice low, "you remember what I said?"

"Which time?" I ask. It comes out sharper than I'd intended. Though in my defense, the guy tends to just drop in, say a couple of ominous things, and leave, so if anyone's to blame here, it's him.

His mouth twitches. "I said maybe there's not just one side to a story."

That's right. I remember now.

"Looks like you understand what I meant."

Every time I think of her face, the way she cooed at the baby and refused to read my whiteboard, I shrivel, hearing it again: *Boring, boring, boring, boring.* Of course I wanted Benzaiten to be happy. Of course I wish Daikokuten could be the common enemy. But it's not that simple.

"I loved her," he says.

"I know," I say.

We tumble back into a brief silence.

"She was always intrigued by the mortal world." He takes his mallet, spins it once, and sets it on his lap like it's as light as a drumstick. "No deity visited your world more than she did."

She said she stayed away for a long time. It must have been after Daikokuten. She was hurting for years, and I was the one to bring her back. Then I watched her fall in love with the mortal world and get hurt by it, all over again.

History repeats itself, and so on.

"She spent time with mortal children. Helped artists create." Another rat, or the same one, clambers over his knee. "Some called her foolish. I thought she was passionate. Stubborn. Whatever she did, she did with her entire heart."

"That's why you love her," I whisper.

He says nothing.

At the edge of the dimness, a rat stands on its back legs. It observes us with cool eyes, off-puttingly humanoid. I stretch out a hand, but its gaze is fixed on Daikokuten. I think I prefer the silly ones at the Yip Yap Shelter. The ones that tumble over each other, wrestling and play-fighting and falling asleep side by side. They reminded me of Angel and me, in a way, before she realized I wasn't the best friend she wanted; I was just the bridge to better places. And once she was done walking, she left me behind to rot.

"Don't know what she saw in me," Daikokuten says. "I was too afraid to ask."

I meet his eyes. An entire night sky spreads across each of his irises. In all honesty, I have to wonder the same thing.

Then it hits me.

"Yin and yang," I breathe, picturing the symbol on my journal.

He narrows his eyes. "What?"

"Nothing."

Benzaiten fell for him because she needed someone to pull her back. After traipsing along the mortal world, creating chaotic joy everywhere she went, she wanted someone to lead her home. Calm her down. Put a hand to her face and remind her to take a moment and simply be. She wanted someone like me.

But Daikokuten didn't bore her; he betrayed her, at least in her eyes.

Maybe I betrayed Angel too. By not being the person she wanted me to be.

"It was only a few young spirits." Daikokuten takes a breath. "At first."

That's how it starts. If I hadn't asked about the first spirit, we could have left. None of this would have happened. I wouldn't have met Daikokuten, and he wouldn't have sent his rats to track us with their button eyes.

"She said she did it. Before." He runs a hand down his

face, his fingers making a *shuuk* sound as they rub against his stubble. "But she would get in trouble. Spirits aren't meant to remain in this world, even with a deity.

"But she thought if there were two 'parents,' it would be better." He makes a sound too pained to be a laugh. "Must be why she stayed."

I study him. It has to hurt, thinking she only kept him around because she hoped he would guard the child spirits with her, as if he was her tool, her way of finding a loophole. He hides the sorrow well, but doubt turns his eyes to pitch-black pools.

"I didn't stop her. Thought she was doing the right thing." He looks up. The sudden eye contact throws me. I study my hands as he adds, "Like you."

He means I thought she was doing the right thing, just like he did, but for a split second, I can almost believe he sees it too. The similarities between us. We have both been the yin: responsible, quiet. Boring. We want to follow the rules, but there's a part of us that can't live without that fire. It's too bright. Too beautiful. We would rather burn fast than live in the cold.

"But you saw what happens," he says. "The longer the spirits stay, the more unsettled they get. They were suffering more every day." His voice shakes. He takes a second to compose himself. "Wasn't so much about caring for them. It was more about her wanting to feel like their mother."

It's all she wanted. That's why she could never understand me. She would have done anything to have the chances she thought I had. To become the person, the mother, she wants to be. The desire consumes her like a selfish inferno.

"Every day, I ask myself if I did the right thing. If I should have let her argue with me until one day, she would give up and let me take them. And every day, I know she never would've let those children go."

I can't look at him. "So you went behind her back."

"Knowing it would break her heart." He raises the mallet, spins it once, and returns it to his lap. "Yeah."

But he didn't break just her heart. He must have known she would hate him forever, and though he doesn't say it, I can see how much he cared about the child spirits. When he talks about them, his face softens, his mouth slanting like he's afraid their names will shatter in his mouth.

"You understand?" he asks, his voice in pieces.

"No," I say.

"Yes, you do," he says, and something about his tone makes me want to trust him.

I keep my head turned and pull my knees up to my chest. "Are they okay? The baby and all the others."

"They're safe."

I exhale. Somewhere in the spirit world, the ballerina, the girl afraid to close her eyes, and the baby are finally healing.

"She's mad at me," I say.

"Nah. Just hurt."

"How do I fix it?"

"You're asking the wrong god." He shapes his mouth into a smirk, but his eyes remain sunless.

I trace a line down my jeans, feeling the denim stitches. When I asked to meet him, I must have had a plan. But somehow, a part of me knew it would end up like this. The two of us, alone, floating in bittersweet understanding.

"Always thought if I could do anything to fix it," he says, his words loud in the stillness, "it would have to be something that reflected her passion. Dug into the depths of her emotions. Made her feel . . ." He searches for a word, then shakes his head. "Made her feel."

I look back at the rat. It hasn't moved. "Are you going to fix it?"

"Don't know how. Don't know if I'm ready. Don't think she is." I can feel his eyes on me. "But I think you're ready."

I stand. "Is that your way of asking me to leave?"

"No." He gets to his feet. "That your way of telling me you want to leave?"

"No."

We stare.

"You're a lot kinder than you let others think," I say.

He puts a hand on my shoulder and flashes us back to Benzaiten's shrine. He doesn't let any emotion show on his face. "Bye."

"Bye," I say, but at the last second, I snag his hand. "Wait." When I release him, he peers down at his fingers like I've tainted them with my mortality. "Just for the record, I don't think she stayed with you just to use you."

Small fireworks of hope explode at the edges of his irises.

He turns. "Maybe."

Then he disappears.

I'VE COLLECTED SEVEN, but I don't think that's enough. After going through the entire couch and pulling out enough hair to make a wig, I decide to appeal to a higher power.

Mom, I write, do we have any coins?

This is Dad. Mom is out and left her phone behind. Call?

I squint. We both know this doesn't require a call, but I pick up my phone anyway.

"Hi," my father says when I call. "Can you say hello?"

I run my nails along the hem of my shirt. I know he's still getting used to hearing my voice, but I'm not a parrot.

"That's okay," he says after a moment. "Sorry. Is everything okay?"

"The coins," I say quietly.

"Oh. Money drawer."

I move to my parents' bedroom and open the bottom drawer. Sure enough, a coin jar sits on the far-right side. It almost looks like it's hiding. "Thank you. I'll pay you back later."

"You don't have to do that. You're our daughter."

"No," I say. "I want to."

"Well, all right." He exhales. "Your mom is having a hard time. She's out angry-shopping again."

"Oh." I pull out the coin jar and place it on my lap. "What happened?"

"We ran into the neighbors." He clears his throat. "I shouldn't talk about this. You have your own things to worry about."

"No, please," I say. "Can you tell me?"

He hesitates. "Well, we ran into the neighbors." He takes a breath. "Your mother thanked them and said she was sorry she hadn't been there."

I pick through the coin jar. "And?"

"And they basically ignored her."

I open my mouth, preparing to say, *It's not like that's surprising.*

But for the first time, I wonder if it was.

Maybe her old neighbors' snub *did* surprise her. Maybe all this time, ever since they told her about her parents, she's been building something in her mind, thinking they were finally meeting her halfway. Maybe now, she's mourning in every way possible: mourning the parents she lost, the parents she could have had, and the life she could have lived if only their town had accepted her for the person she was.

I lift my head. The smoke begins to dissipate.

"This has been really hard for her," I say quietly, lining coins up on my bare leg.

He breathes out. "Yeah. It has been. We had a talk, and I'm sure we can discuss it in more detail later. But that whole moving thing, it's not about the house or the cost of living. It's not about any of that. It's just her way of—I don't know. Trying to process all of this. So just give her some time. We're all working through our own stuff."

I nod, though he can't see me. "Okay. Thank you."

"I love you, Machi."

I catch one of the coins just before it falls. "I love you too."

Hi, Mom,

I heard you're angry-shopping again. I hope you bought something fun. Remember that time one of your coworkers permanently deleted one of your files—"by accident," she claimed—so you didn't come home until seven, and when you did, you dropped all your findings on the ground and announced, "I'm done with Christmas shopping"? I think it was, like, August.

Maybe it's a cop-out, writing this email to you instead of saying it. I'm still relearning how to speak up, though, and you know I've always been more of a literary person.

I'm sorry I haven't been there for you. Most of the time, you told me I don't have to be the one to support you. You're the parent. But you're also your parents' child, and I don't think support should flow only from mother to daughter.

You've told me some stories about your parents, like how your mother used to lie with you and talk about anything and everything and how your father ran out in the middle of a storm just to check on the neighbors.

That doesn't change the fact that they wanted you to move back to a place that almost wrecked you, but now I see there were other parts of them. Better parts.

So tell me more of those good things. Tell Dad too. Tell everyone who will listen. Write them down somewhere so you won't forget.

I know it's not my place, but Mom? I think you should see a doctor. A psychologist, like Sheryl or Dr. Tsui. There are a lot of good therapists out there, Mom. And not just good thera-pists. Good people. I know that now.

It will be okay. I promise it isn't your fault. I know it's easy to brush off my promise, even if I'm not the first person to make it, but a doctor can help you start to believe it.

I'll talk to you soon. Okay?

Love,

Machi

I press send. Slowly, slowly, the smoke clears.
I breathe in.

CHAPTER TWENTY-ONE

THE CLOSEST ART supplies store has a website that looks older than I am, the background a blinding ice blue and the text all in Comic Sans, so I'm not expecting much. When I step inside and start browsing the aisles, though, it seems like a relatively normal store. A man with a parrot on each shoulder and a paint-splattered apron crouches beside a display of Styrofoam balls, but that's normal artist stuff.

"Welcome to Art with a—Machi?"

I look over my shoulder. Will stands with his hands in his apron pockets, his chin sticking out as he analyzes my face. I draw back. "You work here too?"

"Yeah. Second job." He steps closer. "Honestly, I like this place a lot more. Less coffee-grinding. More eccentric people."

Near the Styrofoam, one of the parrots squawks, stepping all over the man's shoulders. I twitch, imagining the bird's claws on my own skin. "That's one word for them."

He grins. "What are you doing here?"

"I want to make something." I glance at the closest item. Puff paint. I don't even know what that is. "But I'm not artistic, so I have no idea what to do."

He nods, stroking a nonexistent beard. "Well, what did you want to make?"

"I don't know."

His mouth wiggles. "That makes it a little difficult."

"Yeah." I turn in a circle like I think something will jump out at me and scream, *Buy me.* "How do you know what you're good at?"

"Like in life?"

"Like in art." Though I wouldn't mind knowing what I'm good at in life either. "How do you know whether you're good at painting or drawing or"—I think of the art teacher's fist on the clay cat—"other things?"

"You try everything."

I blink a few times. "What if I don't have the time or money for that?"

"Then I guess you choose whatever medium speaks to you."

I give him a blank stare.

"Or," he says, "I can suggest something?"

"Yes, please."

As I follow him through the aisle, a little voice tells me he's going to leave me behind, the way I left him and the others during that hiking trip.

I shush the voice.

Will slows and picks up a kit. "This is a beginner's watercolor set. It comes with good paper and basic brushes."

I study his hands. "You paint?"

"Not well." He shrugs. "I think it's fun. And the cool thing about watercolor is it's hard to get really precise lines or details, but it's really expressive. There's something beautiful in the mess, you know?"

I loved the mess. The mess of Angel. Of Benzaiten. There was always something to fix. Maybe that's why I wanted to be a robot vacuum cleaner. I'm not good at much, but I know how to draw lines, how to pick up on the little things, how to take a mess and make it into something more manageable. At least until everything bleeds out again.

"I know." I accept the kit, running a thumb along the plastic edges. "Thank you."

"Yeah, for sure." Will scratches his ear. "Did you need help with anything else?"

I take a breath. "I was wondering when you would be available for that cookie I promised you."

He frowns, but only for a second. "Oh, you mean from The Bean Jive? That was nothing."

"Then it's not a big deal if I repay you."

He shakes his head and smiles. "Fine. I give up. Actually, I should be free in ten minutes. Would that work?" He waits for my nod. "Then I'll meet you outside."

We part ways. He approaches the man with the parrots, and I move to the checkout line, watching the watercolor kit as it rolls along the conveyor belt.

"Is that all for you today?" the cashier asks.

I open my mouth, but scores of yellow dots pull my focus away. When I turn to the left, I find erasers shaped like little yellow birds lined up in a cardboard display box.

"God, don't you love Toridachi?" the cashier asks.

No, I want to say as I pick one up to study its tiny beak. *It's stupid and childish, and I don't need it. I don't need anything.*

I hand the eraser to the cashier. "I do."

Beep.

Will meets me outside, his apron gone. His mouth relaxes when he spots me. He must have half-expected me to flee.

"Hey," he says. "There's a good café around here."

We don't talk on the way there. I can tell he wants to, his mouth opening and closing, but he can't seem to choose a subject. I enjoy the silence. I've gotten better at talking, but it still feels strange, like I'm breaking a rule.

The café is a pop-up booth with only a counter, a hanging menu, and some ready-made meals and desserts. In front, a few tables and chairs have been scattered like birdseed. Will checks the menu, his hands in his pants pockets.

I fold my arms. "I feel like I've been to more cafés in the past couple of weeks than in the entire rest of the year."

He pivots, his eyes on me. "Is that bad?"

"No." I read the menu. "Are you sick of cinnamon stuff?"

"Oh, definitely. People at The Bean Jive are suckers for BOGO deals."

After a minute of squinting at the menu, he decides on a blueberry bagel with strawberry cream cheese. I get another cookie.

"Thanks," he says as we sit at one of the tables. He has to drag a chair from the middle of the pathway, but he doesn't complain. I guess after almost getting eaten in the middle of a hike and nearly falling off a cliff, moving a chair isn't all that bad.

I study him for a moment. "Thank you too."

He mashes the strawberry cream cheese packet, warming it with the palm of his hand. "It's sort of weird, seeing you again. I lost touch with so many people after middle school."

"You didn't really remember me," I point out.

"Well." He gives me a sheepish look. "No one remembers much about middle school."

I do, but I don't tell him that. "Do you remember Serena?"

He opens the packet and starts spreading the cream cheese along his bagel. "The one who got expelled?"

"She's a lot better now," I say, defensiveness creeping into my tone.

He raises his eyes to me. "I wasn't judging her. I was always kind of curious about what happened to her. There were so many rumors. I'm glad she's doing okay."

I start to say something, but someone interrupts me.

"Machi?"

For a brief moment, I can't place the voice. Panic rises in me, but I don't fully understand why until I turn.

Angel faces the other way, her arms crossed. Sunny watches me, her eyes occasionally flicking to Will. Her mascara, as meticulously applied as her pencil against a notebook or her bow across strings, makes her eyes look huge. I look back at Angel, but she still won't even glance at us.

"It *is* you," Sunny says.

I stay silent. Again and again, I see the way Angel's face twisted as she told me I was boring. I think of the next morning, when I woke up and instinctively checked my phone. How jarring it was, seeing an empty screen. I was close to texting them when I remembered.

I tell myself not to think of Dr. Tsui's figurines, but I can't help it. One girl sets down her instrument and tells another to leave. And then there were two.

The least you can do, I want to say to Angel, *is look at me*.

"Machi," Will says, his voice steady. "Do you know them?"

I nod.

No one speaks.

"Let's go," Angel says, taking Sunny's arm.

I stare at the table, but I can still see her expression in the periphery. Sunny watches me as Angel pulls her away.

I keep my head down long after they're gone.

Will picks up his bagel, takes a bite, and chews. I can hear every sound like my ear is pressed against his cheek.

"Friends of yours?" he asks.

"Not really." I close my eyes for a second. "But I wish them the best."

"Cool. Then I wish them the best too." He holds out his napkin. "Want some bagel?"

GOOD NEWS, SERENA'S text says. I send back a question mark, but it takes a minute for her to respond. What are you doing now? Can you come to the shelter?

I think I've had enough socialization for today. For the entire weekend. Possibly the entire rest of the month. I don't think I can. I'm sorry.

That's okay. Then can I call?

I hesitate. I haven't called anyone but my parents and my doctors for a year. Okay.

She wastes no time. My phone buzzes, and as soon as I accept the call, she says, "Good news. Or maybe not. I guess it depends on how you feel and what you say."

I sit on my bed. "What?"

"I was talking to my parents about you."

"Oh." I don't know what she could have told them. "Is that bad?"

"No. No, my dad said you were interested in volunteering, right?"

I hesitate. "Right."

"Well, they talked it over and wanted to offer you a job at the shelter. Like an actual job. You could work with us." She waits a beat. "If you want."

I inhale too much air and start coughing. Plugging in my earbuds, I stand and try to walk it off. "Sorry. What?"

"Are you okay? Were you dying for a minute there?"

I cough again. "Yeah."

She laughs. "What do you think? Are you interested? Like at all?"

"I-I don't know anything about actually caring for animals. And I've never had a job before." If this is an interview, I'm bombing it.

"That's okay. We're not hiring you because you're an expert."

"Oh."

"No, I mean, like, we want you to work with us because we like you, and you care about the animals." I can almost see her waving a hand, shooing out the bad vibes. "We can work out all the details later. And I'm a really good teacher. Probably."

"Are you sure? About the job, I mean."

"Are you kidding? I've been wanting them to hire someone else for ages, and if it's you, that's a major bonus."

From somewhere in the background, a female voice shouts, "You're just trying to get her to cover your shifts."

"Am not," Serena yells back. "Though if she wanted to do me a favor every once in a while, I wouldn't say no."

"You're despicable," the woman declares.

"It's genetic." Serena's voice returns to its normal volume. "Anyway, you don't have to give us an answer now. My dad said he'll see you soon enough, and if not, you know where we work. And you have my number."

"Okay." I'm still not quite sure what's happening. "Th-thank you. Tell your parents thank you too."

She takes a breath. "She sa—"

"Not now," I hiss. "And don't shout it."

Serena sighs. "So bossy. You know, if you end up working with us, I'm going to be your superior. You can't mouth off to me like that."

"I guess I can't work with you," I say.

When she laughs, she lets out a little snort.

"Hey," she says. "I was thinking about how my dad said he didn't think you could talk and how you said for a while, you kind of couldn't."

I nod like I think she can see me.

"I don't know what that's about, and I don't want to force you to tell me, but like I said before, if you want to talk about it, I'm here."

She is. She *is* here. And so am I.

I think I'll take her up on the offer sometime. I might even tell her everything—what happened with Angel and Sunny, my robot vacuum cleaner wish, how lost I felt, and how, even before we really met, I was still holding onto the hope she had given me, praying someday I could feel it again.

For now, though, I only tell her I want to take the job. And my first order of business will be ensuring that grumpy ginger cat finally finds a home. Maybe I'll ask my neighbor if she would be interested in getting her current cat and her robot vacuum cleaner a new companion. Because even robot vacuum cleaners need friends.

I'VE JUST OPENED the watercolor kit when my phone buzzes with a text from my father. Time for a call? he asks.

I plug in my earbuds, preparing myself, and mash my thumb on the screen. "Hello?"

"Hi." He breathes out. "Your mom is sleeping."

"Oh." I swallow. "Did she see my email?"

"She did. It was a very nice message, Machi. She cried reading it. Then she passed out. I'm sure she'll answer you soon, but I think she's sleeping it all off."

"Okay," I say, because I don't know how else to reply.

"It probably doesn't help that we saw the neighbors again. She tried to say something, but they wouldn't even look at her."

I think of Angel. How she kept her back turned the entire time. And how it didn't hurt as much as I thought it would.

My father sighs. "I told her to give it up, but you know her."

When I unlock my phone, my text conversation with Serena pops up. Thinking of her bridges metaphor, I say, "Maybe some things are meant to be burned."

"Machi." My father's voice is laced with concern. "What do you mean?"

"Not literally." I dip a brush in my cup of water. I don't even know how to start. "I was talking about bridges. Mom keeps trying to build bridges that everyone else cuts down and burns.

She can't overwork herself like that. Sometimes, it's better to just let the bridge stay unfinished. The other people can see what she did. If they want to build with her from the other side, that's great. But if not, that's okay too."

My father is quiet. I think I've lost him.

"Hello?" I say after a minute, raising my brush like it can help me get a better signal.

"I was thinking," he says. "You're so different."

I blink. Am I? I mean, other than the talking thing, *am* I so different? I had so many thoughts, even when I was quiet. I just didn't express them.

But I suppose the very nature of my thoughts has changed. Instead of dwelling on the past, all the upsetting things that have happened, I've been swept into the present. All the impossibly strange things that are still happening.

"What happened while we were away?" he asks. "Did that doctor really help you that much?"

I think for a moment.

The last time Dr. Tsui and I met, I told him about seeing Angel and Sunny and how, in the moment, I really thought I was going to die. Then I told him about Will and how he may not have fixed me, but he helped me fix something, and that made all the difference. I told him about Serena and my potential job at the Yip Yap Shelter and how I'm starting to feel like I'm a part of their family. And I told him about how I'm learning how to be a better part of my own family. How I want to listen to my parents, hear their stories, because someday, hopefully a long time from now, they'll leave, the way my grandparents did. That's how it has to be. We all leave, in the end. But if we're lucky, we don't leave alone. We don't leave sad. We leave feeling lucky to have been there at all.

Then, once I had finished spilling my guts, I looked up at

Dr. Tsui and said, *Sorry. I feel like every time I come in, I wind up dropping, like, seven bombs on you.*

That's how life is sometimes, Dr. Tsui replied. His eyes sparkled behind his glasses, light refracting off the metal frame. *Isn't it beautiful?*

I traced the light from his glasses back to his wall. My eyes fell to the triplet figurines, their expressions so serene, as if they knew no matter what happened around them, no matter how bad things got, they would keep playing. Together.

Yeah, I said. *I guess it is.*

"Machi?" my father says. "Hello?"

"Hi," I say, jumping in before he thinks I've taken a second vow of silence. "Sorry. Yeah. I think Dr. Tsui's part of it."

"But not all of it?" I can almost hear my father's frown. "What, then? Did you have a spiritual awakening?"

"Something like that."

"Hmm." Static whispers along the line. I have the feeling he's stroking his chin like a wise old man. "Is that why parents never seem to be there in coming-of-age stories?"

I wrinkle my nose. "What would you know about coming-of-age stories?"

"Hey, I used to be a teenager too." He exhales nostalgia. "Back when dinosaurs roamed the planet. My best friend was a T-rex named Squid."

"Dad, why are you like this?"

He laughs. "I kid. Though my childhood best friend's nickname *was* actually Squid."

"You've never talked about that," I say.

"Well, he's out there in the world somewhere. Probably not going by the name 'Squid' anymore, though I've heard stranger terms of endearment."

"No, I mean your childhood." I take the paintbrush and

draw it across the paper. It makes a squiggly, unsteady line. "Your parents."

Now it's my father's turn to go quiet. I wish I could see his face. Hug him if he needs it. He might not want to remember.

"Dad," I say. "What about your parents?"

In his silence, I work on the painting. I thought I knew what I would make, but with every passing second, it changes. With every brushstroke, it evolves. It won't stay still, will never be the same.

"I don't know where to begin," my father says softly.

I think of the therapy notebook from Dr. Tsui.

"Start with your happiest memory of them," I say.

Somewhere in the background, a bird warbles, notes poking through the stillness. I imagine it's returning to its nest, happy to be home.

"Well, I guess there was this one time," my father says.

I lift my brush, and together, we paint pictures.

CHAPTER TWENTY-TWO

PLONK.

I wait a few seconds.

Plonk.

A few more.

Plonk.

I dip my hand into the jar. I was going to carry the coins in my wallet but wound up finding enough to fill an entire mayonnaise container. I got more than a few looks as I carried it through the streets. Too bad I wasn't around the art store. I would have blended right in with the parrot man and this one lady who, as I waited for Will the other day, painted her face with clown makeup before entering the shop.

Hey, I'm not going to judge. Will doesn't. Neither does Serena, or her father, or even Dr. Tsui.

Plonk.

"I can do this all day," I say.

"Please don't."

I turn. Benzaiten wraps her arms around herself, her sleeves dripping pure white. Her hair is tied back, and her eyes have faded to a sickly amber.

"You can keep the nickels," I tell her, setting the jar on the offering box. "I don't really want to carry that home."

"I'm not a coin drop-off, Machi."

I cross my arms. "I know."

We stand, my heel touching the offering box and her ballet flats resting on the center of the stone path. My eyes travel along her face. She emanates such a heavy sadness. It's hard to look at her.

"Why are you here?" she asks. "I told you to leave."

"Twice." I ignore the pang in my side. "But I came back."

She lowers her head. "You shouldn't have."

I twist my fingers behind my back. "But I did."

When she walks, the movements are stiff. She hesitates with each step. When she reaches her altar, she sits. Her dress flows down to the tops of her ballet flats.

"I have all this baby stuff now," she says. "It's not like I can return it. It's not like I *would* return it. But I can't look at those things anymore."

"You can donate them," I say.

She could play Santa Claus and hold Christmas in July, just as the ballerina spirit's dance studio put on *The Nutcracker* in the early heat of summer.

"Yeah." She bows her head. "There's one thing I can thank Daikokuten for: He left the little heart hat on Kenji."

I swallow as another wave of grief crashes over her and laps at me.

"So when Kenji is given to a home for rehabilitation and some other spirits are assigned to take care of him, they'll see how adorable he is. They won't be able to help themselves. They'll definitely"—she shudders, her body flickering— "definitely take good care of him."

Daikokuten said they'll be okay. And I believe him.

"Benzaiten," I say. She flinches at the sound of her name. "Do you know where Kenji's parents are now?"

She looks up, her eyes flashing gold. "I'm not a mortal tracking app." They fade back to a bleached copper. "But I do check on them."

I sit on the offering box, pushing the jar of coins to the side. "And?"

"And what?" Her voice is flat, no emotions rolling off her tongue. "They're devastated. How else could they feel?"

We sit a foot apart, our eyes tracing the crevices between the stones beneath our feet. Every so often, I look at her. She never looks back.

"I sit with them sometimes." She stretches her legs over the edge of the altar. "They don't see me, but I like to think they can feel me." She waves one leg, then the other. "I cry with them. Their hearts are so broken. And I don't know how to help.

"I still think of the child spirits I lost. Kenji, of course, but the others too. When I'm alone, I run through their names, and once in a while, I momentarily forget one. And it hurts. I have to rack my brain for the one I can't remember. Then I start listing them all over again.

"When you lose a child, you think nothing will ever fix you. No book or quote or amount of sympathy will ease the pain. I know you think I'm just some child-stealer, but I loved every single one like my own."

"I know," I whisper.

"Even the ones who live on. Like you remember the boy from Japantown? He takes such good care of his fish." Her eyes gleam. "He named them Tic, Tac, and Toe."

I smile.

"I shouldn't have kept those spirits. They weren't mine." She covers her eyes. Silver begins to leak between her fingers. "I just wish they were."

I move from the box and stand beside her at the altar. "I'm sorry. No one ever wanted to hurt you."

She doesn't say anything.

"I have something for you," I say, reaching into my bag.

"Is it more nickels?"

I pull out two pieces of cardboard. "I think you have enough of those for now."

"Cardboard?" She sniffles, her tears evaporating. "Wow. It's what I always wanted."

"Can you wait a minute?" I check the watercolor page sandwiched between the cardboard, my heart pounding. "Before I show it to you, please remember I'm not an artist. In fact, I haven't done more than doodle since elementary school."

"You made art?" She reaches for it. "Let me see."

"And," I go on, dodging her, "it's not good, and it didn't turn out the way I planned."

"Such is life." Her eyes sparkle. "Gimme."

I let her take the painting. Putting the cardboard away, I monitor her expression. "You said love and creativity are two of your domains, so—"

"Machi," she breathes.

I move to see my own work, even though I've analyzed it enough to burn it into my memory. The background is a light gray, the brushstrokes streaky. I can see little holes where air bubbles have pressed themselves into the page. In the center is a scarlet heart riddled with hairline fractures. Out of each crack oozes not blood or darkness but golden, radiant light, and in each beam of light is a little symbol: a plastic bag of fish, a pair of pink ballet shoes, a sleeping kitten toy, a heart cap, and a robot vacuum cleaner.

"Machi," Benzaiten says again. She takes my hand. "It's beautiful."

"I mean, not really." I edge closer. "But I tried."

She squeezes my fingers. "Machi, I—I'm sorry."

"Me too."

"No, I mean it. I'm sorry. When we were at the shrine, I said some truly horrible things." She blinks hard. "I shouldn't have."

"You didn't say anything that wasn't true."

"You needed someone. And I wanted so badly to be there for you. I couldn't just let you go." She laughs a little. "But now you probably wish I had."

"I don't," I say. And I mean it.

She takes a fluttery breath. "I just . . . I'm glad. I'm glad you're still here."

"Thank you." I hesitate. "I am too."

We're quiet for a minute.

Benzaiten's hand trembles, the paper jittering between her fingers. "So is this a goodbye present?" She releases me and touches her necklace, the pendants clinking like bottle caps. "Your prayer disappeared last week. I guess you felt it had been answered."

Last week. That was when I met with Daikokuten and finally understood him. When I emailed my mother and finally understood her. Went to the art store and found Will. Ran into Angel and Sunny and learned to wish them the best. Got a call from Serena and was offered a job at a place I've grown to love. Tried art for the first time in forever and listened as my father told me some of his story.

I pray I will realize the beauty of being human and rediscover my voice.

Exactly four weeks have passed since I made that prayer.

"It was answered," I say.

"With almost a week to spare."

"I'm a little disappointed." I squint at the fading torii. "I really wanted to be a robot vacuum cleaner."

"I know." She sighs. "You were never boring, you know."

I look away.

She shrinks. "So this is goodbye?"

"It could be."

I run my fingers up and down my bag straps. It could be.

There's no logical reason for me to return. She talks too much, or sometimes not enough, and she doesn't always make the best decisions. And she's a goddess. She doesn't need a mortal to visit her. She has other things to do, other people who would fall over themselves just to get one good look at her. No one would blame us if we let this bridge burn.

But even as I think through it, I know we're going to meet again. All the branches, all the possible paths, somehow lead to the two of us together. Or if they don't, I choose to follow the ones that do. And if we split, we can grow separately, then find our way back.

"It could be," I say, "but we made a lot of memories, didn't we?"

Her eyes spark. "We did."

"Happy ones."

She watches me, her expression guarded. Her fingers kiss my painting, touching the heart, then the robot vacuum cleaner. "So what happens now?"

"I don't know." I raise my head to the clearing skies. "But you know, the watercolor paint set wasn't the only thing I bought from the art supplies store."

She gives me a look. "Should I be concerned?"

I slide my bag off my arm and onto the ground and pull out a can of red paint.

Her eyes drop to the can. "You carried that *and* all those coins?"

Raising an arm, I flex my biceps. "I guess my arms aren't that small after all."

Her eyelashes flutter. Then, laughing, she says, "I guess not."

"I was thinking we could repaint your torii," I say. "This may never be your most popular place of worship, but even the most neglected shrine deserves some care and attention, don't you agree?"

She watches me, tears glittering in her eyes. "I do. I really do."

I take her hand, and I hold on.

ACKNOWLEDGMENTS

I WARNED EVERYONE this was going to be long.

I want to start by thanking the state of Hawai'i and all the people who make it a wonderful place to live, including bus drivers (especially Uncle Rex); educators like Sherry Rose; museum curators; and everyone working to keep Hawai'i a community, as well as the many people working to keep Japanese culture alive.

I'm eternally grateful to booksellers, librarians, reviewers, and all the bookish people who support readers. I especially wanted to thank Jan Kamiya and the McCully-Mō'ili'ili Library, but honestly, everyone who works with books is a hero in my eyes.

Thank you to Koan; the UH Mānoa Hawaiian & Pacific Collections; and the old team at the Dean's Office of the College of Arts and Humanities, especially Reid. I would also like to thank Dr. Todd Sammons, Esha Neogy, and the Children's Literature Hawai'i Steering Committee.

Thank you to all my teachers and professors, including but not limited to Dr. Cynthia Franklin (whose support throughout the years has meant so much), Dr. Gary Pak, Professor Laurel Flores Fantauzzo, Dr. James Caron, and Dr. Vernadette Gonzalez, Mrs. Kobayashi, Mrs. Robles, Mrs. Chong, Mrs. Nelson, Mrs. Oshiro, Mrs. Lee, Mr. Vierra, Mr. Arakawa, Mr. Casano, Ms. Goto, Dr. Kathryn Reiss, Dr. Bula Maddison, Dr. Vivian Chin, and Professor Rodney Morales.

I need to take a moment to thank all the authors who wrote back to me when I sent them letters gushing about how much I loved their work. I think the first author I ever wrote to was Sharon M. Draper, back when I was maybe twelve years old, but from there, I went on to write to everyone who ever wrote something that touched me—which means there are a *lot* of authors who had to put up with my rambling, including George Saunders, Zack Smedley, Jennifer Marie Thorne, and Mindy McGinnis.

To the *Ka Wai Ola* editors, my grammy's Honolulu Chapter of the National Writers Association, and Jayme Scally and the *Horizons* team at UH Mānoa: Thank you for publishing my work when it was, quite frankly, nothing but a mess of emotions.

Thank you to the publishing professionals who believed in me from the start: Rebecca Podos, Jennifer Laughran, Rebecca Kuss, and Lauren Knowles. I wouldn't be the author I am now without your support and guidance.

Thank you to The Nerd Daily for hosting *Benzaiten*'s cover reveal and for making proud book nerds of us all.

Thank you to Robin Reul, Susan Azim Boyer, Lisabeth Posthuma, Sarah Suk, Zack Smedley, Jodi Lynn Anderson, Jeff Bishop, Brianna Bourne, and every other author who gave *Benzaiten* a chance and provied such kind and heartwarming blurbs.

Savannah Brooks, thank you for pulling me out of the slush pile and sticking with me through every up and down. Your patience, support, and friendship both professionally and personally has meant everything. I am so proud to call you my agent and my friend.

Eight million thank-yous to the Soho team, including publisher Bronwen Hruska, art director Janine Agro, cover artist Yuta Onoda, copy editor Erin Della Mattia and proofreader

Joy Hoppenot, managing editor Rachel Kowal, publicist Erica Loberg, Rudy Martinez and Emma Levy from the marketing team, and intern Roman Parker. Alexa Wejko, thank you for seeing something in Machi and her story and deciding to take a chance on me. I could spend my allotted acknowledgment pages on just you alone. From the moment I e-met you, I could feel your warmth and passion, both for my book and for books in general. It has been an honor working with you. You said Will was the real angel, but honestly, I think it's you.

To the real Sheryl, who never left: You were such a source of light and happiness. You deserve a lot more than a reference in a book, but I hope you know how much you mean to me. Thank you for being there for me and for so many others.

Thank you, Iris, for supporting me before you read a single word, then for every word after. Adachitoka-sensei, Anna, Cady, Tori, Kenai, Rursu, Andaç, Eneri, Invie, Ro, Nanna, Deepthi, and the entire *Noragami* community, thank you for making me feel accepted, showing me how impactful stories can be, and giving me a home. I also want to thank Joey, Kekoa, Jeremy, Kyle, Karena, Kyra, Brandy, Jillian, and Lee; Aunty Debbie, Aunty Leila and Chaz, Rooke, Zoë, Samia, and Ka-Bang; and everyone who commented on my book announcement post in August 2023: Leif, Davis, Sunshine, Devin, Shane, Aunty Cay, Paige, Andrea, Joyce, Anna, Ellie, Sean, and Star.

Thank you to the friends who somehow managed to put up with me all throughout elementary, middle, and high school, including Kacey, who was so excited for me and did so much to make me into the person I am today; Allisen, my old literary soulmate who read all my bad stories and found the beauty in everything; Zara, who has cheered me on since we were little and has continued to do so even as I write these acknowledgments; and Jill, who endured my questions about romanization while I was also trying to say happy birthday *and* apologize for being such a nightmare when we were little.

Uncle Tom, Aunty Karen, and Kimi, you have been my neighbors in every sense of the word. It's an honor to know and love you. No matter where you go, you'll always be with me. That being said, please don't ever move.

To my mother's friends, of which there are a million: Your love for my family and me has meant the world. Special thanks to Paula and Maile; Nicole (my first follower on essentially everything), Aunty Rita, and Aunty Vivian; Aunty Rene, Hailey, and Danica; Uncle Harvey; and Deb and Cindy.

Thank you to Uncle John, Aunty Sandy, Jake, and Justin (go, Tsukadas); Uncle Stephen, Aunty Grace, and Jamie and Kacie, who gave me my first YA books; Aunty Michele and Melissa; Aunty Patty and Uncle Wally; Aunty Carol, uncle Donald, and Grant; and all my aunties, uncles, and cousins, especially Kyle.

Thank you to Aunty Jan, Uncle Jay, Tyler, and Brendan. Aunty Jan, every time I had any exciting news, you were one of the first people I wanted to tell. You and Uncle Jay have supported me all my life. Tyler and Brendan, thank you for being the brothers I never had—and for never annoying me as much as I'm sure actual brothers would have. I'm so proud of the people you've become.

Grandpa and Grandma, thank you for being so happy for me, both when I told you about the book deal and in all the years before. Grandpa, you've always been a reader. Thank you for texting me every day. I love you.

Grammy, you're the reason my mother and I are such bookworms. I remember how proud I was when *Kaka'ako As We Knew It* came out. I would like to thank you and Uncle Garron for being so supportive and for believing in me no matter what. I'm so lucky to call you family.

I couldn't dream of calling these acknowledgments complete without thanking my parents. Ma and Da, thank you for reading to me, telling me made-up stories late into the night, and praising my "books" when they were nothing but paper and crooked staples. You would have been proud of me even if I had never managed to publish anything, and that's the best story I'll ever be able to tell: the story of two people who believed in me even when I didn't believe in myself. I love you so much.

I don't think I could have done this without some serious divine intervention, so I want to thank God—for books, for publishing professionals, for everyone making a difference in this world, and for having a perfect plan for everyone. I'll admit I had times when I was afraid there *was* no plan, at least for me, but we're here now, and I'm so thankful.

Last, but certainly not least, I want to thank everyone else who has taken the time to read this book. I know it's cheesy, but when I was younger, I loved skimming the acknowledgments to see if the author ever addressed the reader. So, hi. I'm addressing you here to express my gratitude. Thank you for reading.

Sorry. This is probably one of the longest lists of acknowledgments ever. But I can't help but be grateful for that too. How lucky am I to have so many people to thank?

Okay. I think I'm done now. Thank you for being here, and I hope to talk to you again in the next book. ☺